I'LL BE NEXT TO VANISH

A PSYCHOLOGICAL THRILLER

MARK GILLESPIE

This is a work of fiction. All of the events and dialogue depicted within are a product of the author's overactive imagination. None of this stuff happened. Except maybe in a parallel universe.

www.markgillespieauthor.com

First Printing: July 2022

Cover designed by MiblArt

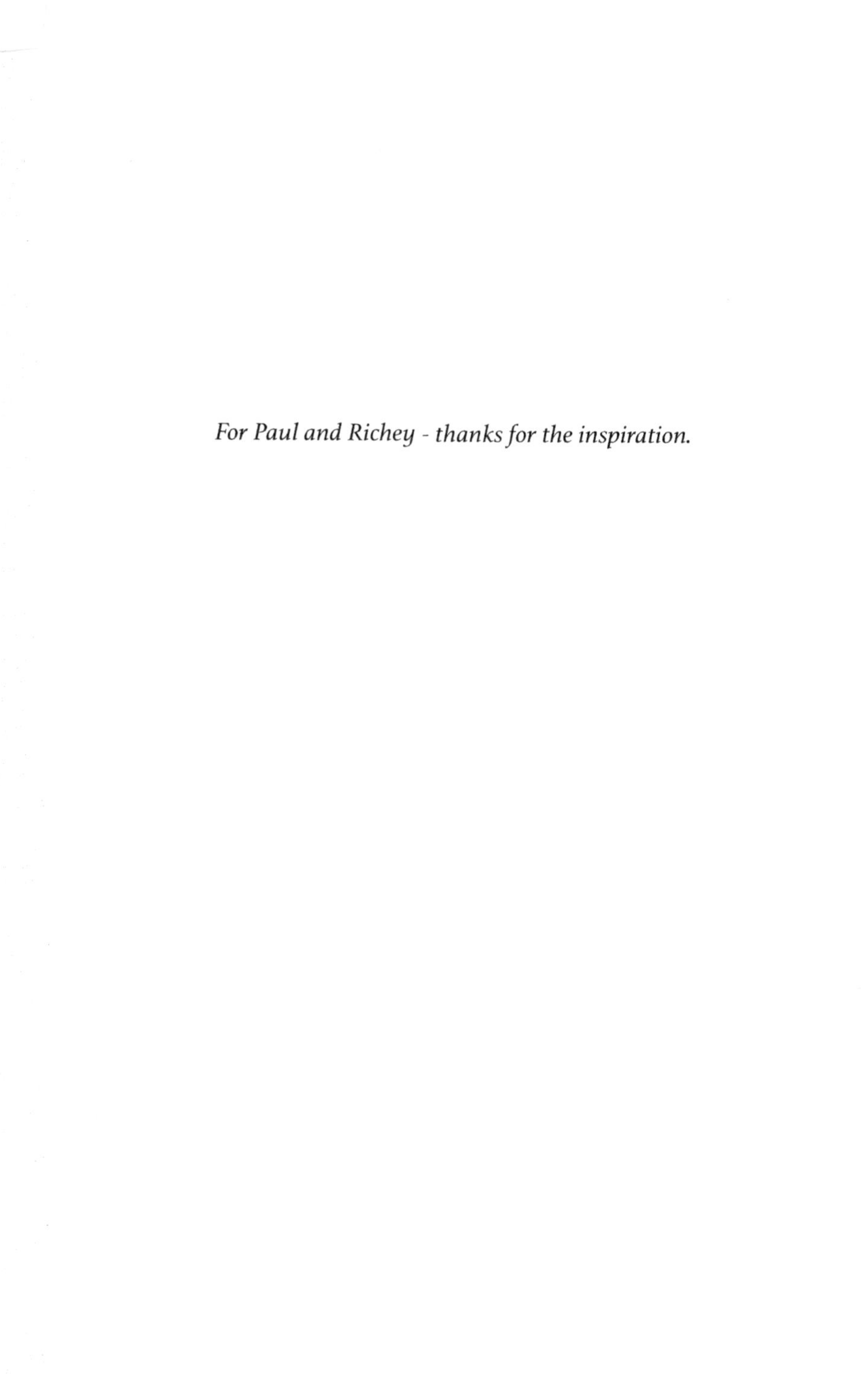

For Paul and Richey - thanks for the inspiration.

1

Charlie Lewis opened his eyes. He blinked hard, wondering where he was.

He was lying on a hard bed (like a rock!) and it was dark inside the room. What now? How much had he had to drink last night and why couldn't he feel the hangover yet? He lay there for a second on the rock, processing. No, that wasn't right – Charlie didn't drink anymore. Those were old thinking habits at work. Charlie was forty-nine, not twenty-seven. He didn't drink and he didn't smoke either. Didn't take drugs. Couldn't get more boring than old Charlie Lewis these days.

God, he missed the nineties. Everything except the hangovers.

His eyes were drawn to a cylinder of milky light spilling through a gap in the curtains. The light gave the room a soft, hazy glow. Dreamlike. Was it sunlight? Moonlight? Charlie had no idea what time of day it was. How could he be this out of it if he didn't drink or take drugs? He sat up on the bed and heard the headboard rattle against the wall. Cold air gusted through the bedroom and Charlie shivered.

With a groggy sigh, he reached over the side of the bed. His grasping fingers found a switch and he turned on the bedside lamp.

He blinked. Bright. It was too bright.

There was an old-fashioned digital alarm clock on the table. The LED display, a piercing retro red light, told Charlie it was 1.41am.

"Okay."

Now it was starting to come back. He wasn't at home in Glasgow. He was at the farmhouse in Kintyre, checking out for some quiet time.

And he'd been dreaming just before he woke up. Now that the fog was starting to clear, it was coming back to him. Not just any dream, but *that* one. The sticky, recurring dream that followed Charlie wherever he went, from country to country, continent to continent, and from the blaring lights of the big city to the isolation of his remote farmhouse getaway. He could go to Kintyre and escape the suits, the obligations, the fans and everything else that the music industry demanded of someone like him. This was his sacred time, away from the rampant egos that surrounded him in his day-to-day life. Away from the lack of privacy that permeated the industry he'd worked in for the past three decades.

But he couldn't outrun that dream.

Charlie's head returned to the pillow. He closed his eyes and saw the images, still playing in his mind like a private movie screening. Still fresh, still real. In the dream, Charlie was standing on a wide, brightly lit stage – a huge stage – playing in front of the biggest crowd he'd ever seen in his life. Thousands of bodies sprawled out across a muddy field that went on for miles and miles. A music festival? Was it Glastonbury or Reading? Wherever it was, this was a good place to be. Charlie saw all the smiling faces, all the hands in the air swaying from side to side like a field of barley in a soft wind. He heard a chorus of voices ringing out like a church bell, all of them chanting the name of Charlie's old band like it was a mantra. Sounded to Charlie like they were right there in Kintyre. Right there in the farmhouse with him.

"*Broken Gods! Broken Gods! Broken Gods!*"

Charlie's recurring dream was no less intense because he'd experienced it so many times before. In the dream, he was twenty-two, no creaky joints and no hint of a bald spot forming on the crown of his head. His skin was smooth, no longer creased with wrinkles. He was back on stage playing with the Gods, picking out the groove on his bass guitar and looking out over the sea of thousands that they'd hypnotised with music. They continued to wave their arms in the air, still chanting the band's name as if it was some ancient incantation to raise the dead. This was the power of The Broken Gods. This was what they'd been capable of back when they ruled the industry.

The Broken Gods.

Tommy Smith, the hard-hitting, barrel-shaped drummer with the gorilla arms. Little Bobby Reid, the slick and handsome lead guitarist, always hiding behind a pair of shades to conceal his chronic shyness. Bobby didn't say much. Neither did Tommy. Charlie was up front as always, singing and playing bass as he'd done since the band's inception as a crude garage outfit in the late eighties. They'd been four Glaswegian lads from the east end who could barely sing or play a note without making the neighbourhood cats howl in protest. As always in the dream, Charlie noted, there was a gaping void to his left. Someone else was supposed to be there and yet he never was. That man was missing. Ryker Marshall, singer and rhythm guitarist, was Charlie's songwriting partner. His best friend in the world. A man who'd vanished off the face of the earth in 1997.

Twenty-five years ago. Almost to the day.

"*Broken Gods! Broken Gods! Broken Gods*!"

Charlie opened his eyes and the dream disappeared. Something had made him sit bolt upright in bed.

Someone was knocking at the front door.

"What the...?"

He sat still, convinced that he'd imagined it.

But there it was again.

Three short knocks, *tap-tap-tap*. A patient, almost apologetic request for attention. That was definitely someone at the door, he thought. It wasn't the force of the wind and it wasn't the joints of the old building creaking in response to the pressure. At least, not this time.

There was someone out there.

"You're kidding me."

Charlie heard the fear in his voice. He glanced at the clock again, then grabbed his phone off the bedside table. Nope, the clock wasn't telling tales. It was 1.43am and somebody was out there, knocking on his door at that godforsaken time of day. Charlie wasn't expecting visitors out here, not even during socially acceptable hours. He didn't want visitors at any time, especially not here at the old farmhouse. He loved this place. This was his retreat from the world and to put it bluntly, visitors were not welcome. Charlie loved the isolation and end of the world remoteness of his farmhouse. His financial advisors had long ago suggested he invest in property, this was back when The Broken Gods had exploded into the stratosphere in the mid-nineties. Their popularity had skyrocketed and the band went on to establish themselves as the biggest rock and roll band on the planet. Invest in property, the suits had said. *You won't regret it Charlie.* And right enough, he hadn't. Charlie had always fancied the idea of having a house in the middle of nowhere. Somewhere beautiful, lonely and rugged. This desire to get away intensified as the novelty and thrill of fame wore off and instead, it turned into something intrusive. Charlie had visited Kintyre during childhood holidays with his dad and his younger brother, John. When it came to his initial foray into property investment, there was only one place he had in mind. With the help of his manager, Charlie found the old abandoned farmhouse that had been sitting vacant for a year and a half, bought it and left it at that for a while. It was only later that he started coming over and his girlfriend at the time, Leigh Taylor, had suggested he renovate it to make it more liveable. At first, Charlie was quite happy to leave it as it was – crumbling but functional. After much persuasion from Leigh however, he'd warmed to the idea of renovation. In the end, the project had been a welcome diversion from the rock and roll madness in the city.

The three-bedroom farmhouse was situated at the top of a steep hill, overlooking Machrihanish Bay to the west and close to a small loch. The property came with almost two hundred acres of land and had once been owned by a local farmer who'd retired to Campbeltown with his wife. It wasn't an easy place to get to, which made the late-night knock on the door even more troubling.

"Who is it?" Charlie said.

Stupid. He realised that whoever was knocking wasn't going to hear him from the other end of the hallway. Damn it, Charlie thought. *Damn, damn, damn.* He was trying to convince himself that he was angry when in fact, he was terrified. There was a sharp jolt of unease in his chest, as if he'd been impaled by something. What else could he do? He'd have to answer the door. He swung his legs over the bed, placing his feet down on the cold wooden floor. The wood felt smooth and unusually devoid of the crumbs that Charlie spilled due to his habit of eating snacks in bed whilst watching the old box TV – the only TV in the house. He might have given up drink and drugs but chocolate biscuits weren't going anywhere. Then again, he was going to have to consider it. Charlie had always been rake skinny but the onset of middle-aged spread around his abdomen hadn't gone unnoticed. Some of the more recent pictures of him on stage were a bit too 'ageing rocker' for Charlie's liking. The biscuits weren't going to help with that problem.

Knock-knock.

How could there be someone at the door?

There shouldn't have been another person around for miles.

Miles.

Charlie pushed himself off the bed, his heart racing. *Calm down for God's sake.* Who was out there? His imagination was starting to run away with itself and it was at times like these that he regretted watching so many true crime documentaries on Netflix. Shit, he thought. I always seem to imagine the worst. Charlie threw on a pair of tracksuit bottoms and a frayed olive sweatshirt. There was another series of knocks at the door. Patient. Stiff and robotic. Sounded like someone had programmed a machine to keep knocking until there was a response. Charlie couldn't make sense of it. Was this it? Was this where Charlie finally met his crazy, deranged fan with a gun in one hand and a copy of his latest album in the other? Someone who'd travelled hundreds of miles to meet him? Not just to meet him, but to...

Mr Lewis? What did you mean when you sang this? Were you thinking of me when you wrote it?

No, no, no.

It had to be one of the local farmers (although they were miles away) or perhaps it was someone from the Campbeltown police station reporting an accident on a nearby road, letting Charlie know that a potential noise disturbance or road closure was imminent.

Made sense.

Charlie walked down the hall, wincing as the floorboards creaked endlessly under his bare feet. The house sounded like it was alive and grumbling. This less than subtle approach was enough to give the game away, to let whoever was out there know (*the assassin!*) that Charlie was making his way towards the front door.

He stopped. Turned his head to the side, leaning his ear towards the door.

Was that a voice outside?

Charlie.

Another knock. Was that a little more urgency this time?

Charlie stopped about five metres away from the door. He cleared his throat. Looked at the giant coat hook shaped like a beckoning finger on the back of the door. He'd always intended to hang a weapon off that hook. A bat, a knife, something that would make intruders think twice about ever trampling over his privacy again.

He took a deep breath.

"Who is it?"

Silence. Okay, Charlie thought. He wasn't sure whether his late-night visitor had heard him or not. He'd whispered after all. It's good, he thought. It's okay. *You're safe*. At the same time, Charlie caught himself backing away from the door. Pure instinct taking over. But the creaking floor was a treacherous bastard that betrayed his presence in the hallway yet again. The old place had character, that was for sure. Character and a willingness to serve Charlie up for sacrifice.

They know you're there, Charlie thought. Whoever's out there. They *know* you're there.

Get a grip man, he thought. It's the police. It's a local with information about a closure or disturbance or something like that. Whatever it is, there's a perfectly logical explanation and if you ever grow a set of balls big enough that'll allow you to open the door Charlie boy, then you'll see that for yourself.

And still the underlying terror remained.

"Who's there?"

His voice was thick and groggy, still lost in sleep. But it was louder this time.

"Charlie? Is that you?"

"Who is it?"

"Charlie, it's me."

It was a man's voice.

"What do you want?" Charlie said. "Do you know what time it is?"

"Sort of."

"So what do you want?"

It was obvious what they wanted, wasn't it? It wasn't a local farmer and it wasn't the police either. This was definitely a crazed fan – someone who'd made the epic trek from God knows where to Campbeltown. And from Campbeltown, they'd driven as far as the road would let them. They'd abandoned the car, set out on foot across acres of wet empty fields to find Charlie's remote hideaway. It was no secret that Charlie had purchased a farmhouse in Kintyre but since he'd bought up a few of the surrounding farmhouses and since there were plenty of signs warning visitors about the consequences of trespassing, he'd never been bothered more than a few times over the years. The last incident was at least fifteen years ago when he'd escorted two hysterical women off his property after reluctantly signing autographs. That was back in the early 2000s. The locals didn't bother him. They treated Charlie like everyone else around here and that was how he'd always wanted it. They seemed fond of him. Some of the people he knew in Campbeltown had once sent reporters on a wild goose chase down to the Mull of Kintyre when they'd come asking for directions to Charlie's farmhouse. They looked out for him and he loved them for it.

"It's me," said the man at the door.

Me, Charlie thought. What sort of answer was that?

"Who are you?"

"It's...Ryker."

Charlie's jaw hit the floor and he staggered backwards down the hall. Cool it, he told himself. Now he knew for sure that he was still in bed. Still dreaming, none of this was real. Ryker at the door, was it? Sure it was. The answer was so ludicrous it was reassuring. After the initial shock, Charlie almost laughed out loud in the hallway as he stood there in his baggy lounging clothes peppered with holes and dry food stains. His hands weren't shaking anymore. So that's all it was – a continuation of the dream. He was in bed. Sleeping. Lucid dreaming, which meant if he really wanted, he could snap himself out of it.

"Charlie? Are you there?"

Are you sure it's a dream?

"I'm calling the police," Charlie barked. "This place is secure and I can assure you, it won't take them long to get here. Take my advice, *Ryker*. Turn around, get off my property and never come back."

"Charlie. It's me. It's really me. If you could just open the door..."

Screw it, Charlie thought. It's a dream so I might as well be bold. Fuelled by a surge of white-hot anger, he charged down the hallway and hit the switch for the exterior light. Another glance at that hook on the back of the door, longing for some kind of weapon to pull down and scare *Ryker* off. Send him sprinting back into the dark countryside never to return. A steel baseball bat would be nice. A big machete. Charlie had an axe back at his house in Glasgow that he'd bought for chopping firewood out here in Kintyre. Why didn't he bring it with him on this trip?

Idiot, he thought.

Relax, it's just a dream.

Charlie took another deep breath, then opened the door. He stepped outside, walking towards the visitor as if he intended to walk through him. It was an attempt to project confidence. As he marched out into the night, Charlie was talking, putting some real bite into his tone. "Did you hear what I said? I've called the police and don't let the remote location fool you buddy. Okay? We've got an arrangement, the Campbeltown station and me. They'll be here in minutes."

Impossible. But this guy didn't need to know that.

Maybe he already did.

Charlie couldn't see much of the man standing outside his farmhouse. In the pale light that hung over the doorway, he was half-human, half-silhouette. His face was more like a sketch than the real thing. He was smiling, slightly out of breath after the walk over the hills. He wore a long black raincoat that trailed down to his heels and reminded

Charlie of a vampire's cloak. His bluish-black hair was long, shoulder length. The matching beard was straggly and unwashed. Charlie's first thought was that there was something werewolf about the man's appearance.

"Charlie," the man said, taking a step forward. He stopped, ran his gaze over Charlie. "You look...*old*."

Without warning, he threw his arms around Charlie. Charlie flinched at the contact. Felt himself tensing up and yet not resisting. He could smell the outdoors on the man's clothes, on his skin. There was no alcohol. After all his experience in that field, Charlie would have caught the scent of drink in a split second.

He broke off the embrace. Pushed the intruder away, stabbing a finger at his chest.

"What the hell do you think you're doing mister? Showing up at my door at this time of night and pretending to be...to be..."

"It's me," the man said, his eyes unblinking and focused. His hands were up in surrender. "Charlie – it's really me. It's Ryker. I'm back from the dead man. Not literally, but you know what I mean. I'm *back*."

"You're not Ryker."

"Look at me," the man said. "Listen to my voice, old friend. Ah sure, I'm a little bit hairier than I was back in '97. Maybe my voice isn't exactly the same but is yours after twenty-five years? You don't sound the same to me, eh? You don't look the same either. Look at my eyes. You haven't forgotten me that easily, have you?"

Charlie shook his head.

"This isn't happening. It's a dream, isn't it?"

The visitor's smile remained intact. Slowly, he began to walk towards the house. Towards Charlie.

2

The Disappearance of Ryker Marshall
(Article taken from Rock Talk Magazine, issue 496)

Eddie Palmer reflects on the mysterious disappearance of The Broken Gods star twenty-five years ago.

Ryker Marshall vanished on April 23rd, 1997. His car was found parked near Erskine Bridge, a notorious suicide spot in west central Scotland. No trace of the man was ever found.

That's about all we know for sure.

We also know that Ryker's family are still reluctant to declare their son/brother/uncle as dead because his remains were never found. There's good reason for the Marshall family to hope. Since 1997, there have been numerous alleged sightings all over the world and it's these little nuggets that make it hard for Ryker's friends, family and followers to let him go, to believe that someone so talented, charismatic and vital is truly gone. He's been seen everywhere. If all the eyewitnesses out there are to be believed, Ryker's been in North and South America, Asia, Africa,

Australia and New Zealand. Sometimes he's been spotted in two different countries on opposite ends of the world on the same day. Put your finger on the map and wherever it lands, it won't land far from an alleged sighting of Ryker Marshall.

No one can tell the Marshall family to give up hope. What they think or believe in such a personal matter as this, is their business. But what about the rest of us? Are we, the fans, right to hold on to hope? Or is it time to let Ryker Marshall go?

The Broken Gods exploded onto the music scene in the summer of 1994, led by the seemingly unstoppable songwriting duo of Charlie Lewis and Ryker Marshall. Everyone knew it at the time – this band was something special. They were a breath of fresh air in a British rock and roll scene that had gone alarmingly stale between 1990-1993. But the Gods were something different. They were charismatic and talented. They were young philosophers and punks with electric guitars, crafting and performing unforgettable songs that were both blistering diatribes on western imperialism and great rock tunes destined for classic status. The lyrics stood as poetry and the music soared without words. The Gods had everything and thanks in particular to their two front men, Lewis and Marshall, they had charisma in bucketloads.

Ryker was always the more enigmatic of the two men. Without doubt, he was less polished for the cameras and there was a legitimate sense of danger and instability about the man that made you believe anything could happen in his presence. He was *real*, as the kids liked (and still like) to say. He was in fact, too real. He was raw and painful. His chopping left-handed rhythm guitar and vocals, on top of his brooding lyrics and songwriting, were exceptional and troubling. The man was an artist.

Charlie Lewis was no less talented than his best friend. With a ridiculous gift for melody, Charlie was also more assured on the PR front. During interviews, he knew how to give just enough of himself without giving too much. Look back at any peak-Gods interview and you'll see that it's Charlie who controls the room. Charlie was and still is the man. A terrific PR man, only slightly less inclined towards the self-destructive rock and roll lifestyle than his best friend. Although those wild days are long behind him now.

Between 1994 and 1997, Ryker Marshall stood as a symbol for the discarded and disenfranchised youth of Great Britain. He never let anyone get too close, often using his sharp, cutting sense of humour to deflect anyone who was trying to get too personal with their line of questioning. And of course, there was that one time he cut into his arm in the middle of a radio interview just to prove to the show's stunned host that he was no phony. Looking back almost thirty years later, how could we ever doubt that Ryker Marshall was anything but a deeply troubled young man? Not a god, but a boy crying out for help. In the end, severe depression took a hold of him. He drank staggering amounts of alcohol that would have killed lesser men. Took Prozac. There were spells in rehab for alcohol abuse and self-harm. It's alleged that he kept large bags of cash in his house because he didn't trust banks.

As the nineties pressed on, it looked like the writing was on the wall, both for the heyday of The Broken Gods and for Ryker himself.

Then, one day, he was gone. Ryker was last seen checking out of the Marriott Hotel on Glasgow's Argyle Street. He got into his car, drove off and since that sunny April afternoon, no one has ever found him.

Charlie Lewis was crushed by the loss of his friend. So

were the other two band members, Tommy Smith and Bobby Reid. The fans were hit hard too and some even took their lives, unable to cope with the loss of their shining light. But it was Ryker's long-term girlfriend, Sally Darbey, who was hit the hardest. Tragically, Sally would take her life five years to the day of Ryker's disappearance, jumping off the same Erskine Bridge where Ryker's car had been found abandoned in 1997.

Charlie lost his childhood friend. After Ryker went missing, there was never any doubt as to whether the band would continue. The Broken Gods disbanded. The dream was over. Without Ryker Marshall, there was no band. It was the right thing to do. Charlie dropped out of the music scene for two years but he eventually came back with his first solo album, *Elements of Style*, in 1999. The album was well-received critically and commercially and Charlie toured and released several more albums throughout the early 2000s, mostly to high praise. Eventually however, he got bored with being a solo artist. Two years ago, Charlie decided to form a band. Maybe he wanted to recover what he had with the Gods. Maybe he missed the camaraderie of being in a band. Whatever the reasoning, Charlie did it his way. He didn't hire other celebrity musicians or go with the best session players money could buy. The Dark Stars were formed when Charlie, searching for a rough and rootsy sound, decided to pluck two buskers, a guitarist and drummer, off the streets of London. So far, it's worked. The Dark Stars have released two successful albums, proving that there's still a lot of interest in Charlie Lewis and his music.

Still, as good as The Dark Stars are, they've never come close to matching the cultural influence of The Broken Gods.

But life moves on. And with that said – is it time for those of us holding on too tight to let Ryker go?

As mentioned, there have been many sightings over the years. For that reason alone, it's always going to be hard to say goodbye to someone who was such a big part of this writer's youth. One woman recently suggested that Ryker's been living in a kibbutz in Israel. He's also been spotted at an ashram near Rishikesh. None of these sightings have ever been confirmed and most sane and rational people believe he's dead and gone. Perhaps his remains have long since been consumed by wild animals on land or in the sea. Who really knows what happened? As time passes and no substantial evidence arises, it seems likely the truth about Ryker Marshall's disappearance will remain a mystery.

But we can dream.

Dream that wherever he is, he's happy.

In the UK, suicide remains the biggest killer of men under the age of forty-five. If you're struggling with your mental health, help is available at the LIVE WELL website via helpline, webchat and forum. Click the link for more info.

3

"I suppose this is where we spend all night staring at one another?" Charlie asked, turning on the lights in the living room. He covered the room slowly, walking like someone who was frightened of putting his foot in a steel trap. "We stare at one another while I try to work out if you really are who you say you are."

"It's me," said the wolf-like man who'd knocked on Charlie's door. His voice was hushed. "It's Ryker."

Charlie narrowed his eyes, the sharp focus of his concentration burrowing deep into the other man. It was still too dark to see it. To see Ryker in the stranger. He switched on the two lamps at the back end of the room, providing support to the main light. He removed the shades from the lamps. And yet still, the light wasn't as reassuring or conclusive as it should have been. Charlie didn't rush to a hasty conclusion about the man. It might have been his imagination but it seemed like the light was repelled by the wolf-man, who was now sitting down on the couch, glancing at some of the magazine and newspaper articles Charlie had shoved into his hand about Ryker's disappearance, almost as if to say, *look what you did.*

Silence surrounded the farmhouse. It was the witching hour, its absolute silence healing to some, maddening to others.

"There's a lot more where those came from," Charlie said, pointing at the clippings. "I've got a house in Glasgow, one in London, an apartment in New York and the farmhouse here in Kintyre. All those homes have drawers stuffed full of clippings about you. About...*Ryker.* It's kind of an obsession, I guess. Newspapers, magazines. I even print some of the better ones off the Internet. Makes for good reading, doesn't it?"

The man nodded but he didn't look up from the NME article (September 2002) he was reading about the vanishing.

Charlie unclenched a fist he didn't remember making.

It *is* Ryker, he thought. He was concentrating so hard he could feel the beginnings of a headache coming on. *It's him.* Older, haggard, a touch heavier. *It's Ryker, it's Ryker!* Sitting right there in the farmhouse. He'd come home like a stray cat, twenty-five years later. Charlie wanted nothing more than to silence the war between head and heart. To declare victory for both and believe for certain that underneath all that hair and dirt, it was Ryker Marshall sitting on his tattered couch. It was the sort of thing that Ryker would do – just turn up after twenty-five years and crack on with things as if it was no big deal.

But it was a big deal.

Sally had killed herself. So had many others in the aftermath, the fans who couldn't accept that he was gone.

It *was* a big deal.

No. Charlie was already rejecting the certainty, kicking it

back into the air as soon as it had landed. Why on earth would Ryker come back all of a sudden? And to Charlie's remote farmhouse of all places, and in the dead of night.

He stared at the man.

It wasn't a dream. He knew that much at least. With this much anger, he wouldn't have been able to stay asleep. Not like this. Charlie wanted to scream, pound the walls, to pull Ryker into a tight bearhug, then let go and punch him on the face and afterwards they'd cry together. Cry about all those lost years. About what happened to Sally. Did Ryker even know what happened to Sally in 2002? Sally Darbey, the love of his life who along with her younger brother, Fletcher, the band's original roadie, had been the first two people to believe in The Broken Gods. Back when they were a garage band. When they had barely an original song to their name. Back when no one else believed in them.

Sally was dead.

Charlie clenched both fists again. His arm were rigid at the sides.

"How did you get here?"

The man looked up from the newspaper clippings. He nodded, as if he'd been anticipating the question. "Wasn't easy. To tell you the truth, I saw a YouTube video where this guy filmed his epic trek to Charlie Lewis's remote farmhouse in Kintyre. It's got over two million views by the way. He started off in Campbeltown, rented a car, went as far as the roads allowed and then walked the rest of the way. Took him two hours to walk in broad daylight. Not easy to get out here, is it?"

He talked like Ryker, Charlie thought. Didn't mumble as much but the mumbling could have fizzled out with maturity.

"It's not meant to be easy," Charlie said. "I don't want people showing up on my doorstep every five minutes."

The man nodded.

"I had to come and see you, Charlie. You were always first on the list, you know? My oldest friend in the world. I saw the trespassing signs and I'm sorry that I had to walk through your private property and knock on your door at this time of night. Jeez, this is a scary place to be with only a torchlight to guide you."

Charlie held up a hand. "What's happening here?"

"What do you think's happening?"

"I don't know," Charlie said. He was pacing the room like a madman. His thoughts darted between the man who claimed to be Ryker and the fact that the floorboards in the living room were so quiet and not creaky at all. "I don't know what I'm supposed to say to you. Really, I don't. I mean, I know what I want to say. But..."

He took a deep breath and came to a stop. Now he was standing in front of the armchair, glaring at the stranger. *Ryker? Stranger? Wolfman?*

"Say what you want to say," the man said. "What you *have* to say."

"Honestly, I'm not sure that's for the best," Charlie said in a muted voice. "But do you really think you can just walk in here like this? That we're going to pick up where we left off twenty-five years ago and...?"

Charlie felt the words stick at the back of his throat.

The other man sighed, then turned back to the clippings on his lap. He looked through the bundle and placed them beside him on the couch. There was a look of something profound in his eyes and Charlie couldn't be sure whether it was guilt or something else. "I know. I've got a lot of apologies to make. And I've got a lot of explaining to do."

"You don't know the half of it," Charlie said.

An awkward silence lingered.

"Any chance of a drink?" the man asked. He stood up off the couch, scratching his beard as if there was a horde of fleas waking up in there. "That was a hell of a hike and I'm not as young as I used to be. What are we now, forty-nine? Fifty? Not much of a hiker, didn't bring enough supplies with me. Ran out of water an hour and a half ago."

Charlie stared at him for a long time. He couldn't stop staring, even though he knew how weird it must have looked.

"I don't have any beers or anything like that. I stopped drinking."

"Water's fine."

"Water? You serious?"

"Just water please."

Charlie nodded. Why was he so surprised? After all, he didn't drink anymore. There was every chance that Ryker had given up the booze too, especially thinking back to how much they'd put it away in their younger years. It wasn't 1995 anymore. They weren't young men in their twenties who thought they were invincible. The Broken Gods were history and the truth was that Charlie didn't know Ryker, *this* version of Ryker, even though they'd been as close as brothers once. Ryker could have been living as a monk for the last quarter of a century. It was as good an explanation as any other.

"Water," Charlie said, turning his back on the visitor. "Coming right up."

"Thanks mate. I appreciate it."

Charlie walked into the kitchen and poured a glass of water. The taps were usually sticky in the farmhouse, sluggish at best, and he was expecting a long wait. But the water gushed out as if the pipes had been given a new lease of life since his last visit. Charlie threw some of the cold water onto his face and dried off with a tea towel. Then he returned to the living room with Ryker's drink. He thrust the glass in Ryker's direction.

Ryker let slip a nervous laugh. He stepped forward, took the drink with a nod of thanks. All the while, he kept his eyes on Charlie.

"Thanks mate."

He was lifting the rim of the glass to his lips when Charlie attacked. Charlie charged forward, snarling like a wild animal. He grabbed a hold of the coat's collar with both hands and gripped tight. The collar (and the rest of the coat) was strangely dry for someone who'd just tramped through miles of damp fields. Cotton? Not the best fabric for walking around these parts, considering the unpredictable nature of the weather. But he didn't linger on that now. He let out a wild roar that wouldn't have been out of place in the heart of the jungle.

"You lying motherfucker!" he hissed. He pulled the man closer. Cocked back a fist and aimed his knuckles at the face.

The man's eyes bulged with terror. "What the hell are...?"

"Don't you fucking lie to me!" Charlie yelled. "I knew it was bullshit. I knew it."

"Mate, I don't know what you're talking about."

"Don't call me mate. I don't know who the hell you are."

Charlie pushed the man away with such force that he staggered backwards, then hit the floor with a bang, his body slamming against the unforgiving wood. He yelped in pain. The glass fell out of his hand and rolled across the floor, leaving a trail of freshly spilled water. Charlie threw himself on top of the man, throwing a barrage of angry punches that mostly hit the arms, although several landed flush on the face and ribs. The man howled in protest, begging Charlie to stop. He tried to sit up, to knock Charlie off balance. But Charlie used his weight to push him back down on the hard floor and keep him there. They struggled for about a minute like that. They were in the spilled water. Charlie pinned the terrified-looking man down and got his hands in between the neck. Now he was locked in. He squeezed down hard with his thumbs on the front of the throat. His face was on fire, distorted with rage.

How far was he willing to go here?

"Liar!"

The man gagged. His eyes ballooned to the point where it looked like they might pop out and fly across the room.

Charlie squeezed harder.

"S-s-s-stop! P-p-please."

"Who the fuck are you?" Charlie yelled. His voice was savage and unrecognisable. It was a strong voice, honed in the pubs, clubs, theatres and stadiums of the world. "Who are you? Why did you come knocking on my door in the middle of the night?"

Charlie had the power of life and death in his hands at that moment. And for a second, he thought about going all the way and teaching the bastard a lesson. His final lesson. Squeeze a little harder, wait it out and the deed was done. A little more. But despite the level of rage in his system, he couldn't do it. Something civilised retained control in his mind, ordered him to stop. Charlie let out a roar of frustration and released the grip.

It had been close. The man gasped for air. Said something that sounded like 'help' but the sound didn't carry far.

Charlie wasn't ready to kill the intruder, but he wasn't done yet. He was back to throwing punches to the face, shoulders, arms – anything he could hit. It still didn't quench the fire. The man on the floor refused to fight back but he did try to grab a hold of Charlie's arms in order to restrain him, with little success. Charlie swatted the flimsy attempt away and gave into another onslaught of emotion. He was so far gone in that moment that had someone asked Charlie his name, he wouldn't have been able to answer. He wasn't Charlie Lewis. He was something else.

The man stared up at Charlie, peering through the gaps in his fingers. "What are you doing? Why are you doing this? Charlie, it's me. It's *meeee...*"

Charlie stood up, moving backwards and almost tripping over his feet. He was out of breath, his arms building up with lactic acid. He stabbed a finger at the man. His vision was flooded with blinking white dots and he tried to blink them away.

"Ryker Marshall? Did you really think I was going to fall for it?"

The man looked around the room, confusion spilling out of his eyes. "Help," he cried out. "Enough, enough, enough."

Help?

"Ryker was left-handed," Charlie said, still stabbing a finger at the man's head. "You understand what I'm saying? I've known him since we were children. I had thousands of drinks with Ryker over the years – THOUSANDS. The man was my best friend, my brother, and I'm telling you he was left-handed. Not once did I ever see him lean over to the left with his right hand to pick up a drink. Left-fucking-handed!"

The man sat up. His eyes were swollen in fear and confusion. Charlie noticed a superficial cut had opened over his left eye and was running down the side of his face. The hair on his head looked strangely lopsided.

"That's why you attacked me?" he said. "Because I took the glass with my right hand? That's it?"

Charlie's upper lip curled into a snarl. "You think this is funny? Coming to my house in the middle of the night, knocking on the door and pretending to be my best friend? Who are you? What do you want from me?"

The man shook his head. His eyes darted around the living room again. "Alright, that's enough. Help!"

Charlie frowned. "What the hell are you doing?"

"Charlie," the man said. His hands were still up guarding his face, as if he anticipated more blows to come. "Take it easy, will you?" He eased his way back to his feet after the short but savage assault. His dazed eyes darted back and forth. He looked from corner to corner. At the window. At the living room door.

"Help!"

"Who else is here?" Charlie snapped.

"What?"

Charlie was about ready to start throwing punches again. "Were you trying to rob me? Is that what this is? Did someone else break in through the back while you were putting on this bullshit Ryker act?"

The mop of hair on the man's head was slipping further down his face. Yes, in some ways he did look like Ryker. Like an older, tired version of Ryker. But Charlie was beginning to see the differences and how they blatantly overwhelmed those faint similarities. It was obvious. He felt stupid for falling for it but he'd *wanted* to see Ryker so bad. And for a moment, he had.

Charlie felt like he was going to burst with anger. "Why do you keep looking around the room like that?"

"Like what?"

"Like you're expecting someone to come to the rescue. I asked you a question. Are you trying to rob me?"

The man's eyes settled on Charlie. His hands were up in the air again. "I'm sorry. I've failed. I didn't mean for you to find out like this."

Charlie flinched. He felt as if he'd woken up in the middle of a movie with no idea of what was going on. "Talk."

The man put a hand to the cut on his face and dabbed at the wound. "Sorry...it's all fake. All of this, it's fake."

Charlie stepped forward, his jaw hanging open. "What?"

"I'm sorry buddy," the man said. His arms flapped awkwardly at the sides as if he was a baby bird trying to figure out how his wings worked. "You're right. None of this is real. And I'm sure as hell not Ryker Marshall. I tried my best though."

Charlie's voice was a quiet hiss. "Who else is here? Who are you waiting for to come to the rescue?"

The stranger glanced back and forth around the brightly lit space. The light was harsh and it seemed to be coming into the living room from somewhere else now. Not from the ceiling, not from the lamps. What the hell was going on? The light clawed at Charlie's eyes. There wasn't this much light in the farmhouse, not by a long shot. He looked at the man standing beside the couch. There was only that look of dumb expectancy in his eyes. Like he was waiting for someone else.

And then Charlie heard it.

Footsteps.

They were approaching the living room.

4

Charlie was stunned to see lights going on everywhere.

Click-click-click. They shot down from the ceiling, the walls and there were even rows of scattered spotlights beneath him on the floor. *Click-click-click.* Charlie winced at the intrusion. He used his hand as a visor to shield his narrowing eyes from the ferocious glare. At that moment, he felt like an ant trapped inside the bulb of a torch. Light beams continued to pour through the windows and the mellow glow of moments earlier was obliterated.

"What the hell's going on?"

Charlie's voice was full of panic. He heard the footsteps coming fast. They were inside the house. *Someone else was inside the house.* And they were hurrying towards the living room with all the urgency of someone about to yell 'bomb!'

"Who's that? Who is that?"

Charlie was staring at the man who'd claimed to be Ryker Marshall. The imposter, still pawing at the piddly little cut under his eye. For a brief second, Charlie toyed with the idea of an alien invasion outside the farmhouse. Maybe it was the avalanche of bright light. Maybe it was the drugs of yesteryear still whispering sweet psychedelic nothings in his ear. The idea quickly lost traction. Charlie observed the way the imposter was shaking his head over and over, as if disappointed in himself, someone or something else. He stared at the living room door, waiting for the other person to arrive. Charlie glared at the man, demanding an explanation that, so far at least, wasn't forthcoming. The imposter's eyes were downcast. Apologetic. It was as if something tight had been loosened. A mask removed.

"Things went bad," he said. "Charlie, I'm really..."

The door swung open and a tall, balding man in a white shirt and grey waistcoat marched into the room carrying a clipboard and pen. His cheeks were flushed, the skin pockmarked around the nose and neck. His eyes were alert and firmly locked on Charlie. The reassuring smile on his face was at odds with his stiff, but purposeful gait.

"I'll take over here," the man said, nodding towards the imposter. "We'll get those cuts looked at shortly. Very sorry about that. Terrible business, eh?"

"Danger money," the imposter said, rubbing two fingers over his thumb in a 'money' sign. "I'll be asking for danger money. Just so you know."

Charlie gawped at them both. "Will someone please tell me what the fuck is going on here?"

By now, the light inside the room was unbearable. There was a searing heat in the air too and Charlie felt it clamping down on his skin. Too much of this and he'd pass out. "Why are you people in my – is this – is this even my house?"

"Charlie," the man with the clipboard said. He spoke in a soft, silky voice that reminded Charlie of the old guy who played Dudley Moore's butler in *Arthur*. The actor, what was his name? Olivier? Gielgud? One of those two. "I'm Dr

Robert Epstein. How do you feel right now? Do you remember me?"

Charlie shrugged. "I've never met you before in my life."

Dr Epstein nodded. Looked to Charlie like he'd been expecting that answer. "I can assure you we've met," he said. "It's just the medication but it'll wear off. Not to worry Charlie, I know it's confusing right now, but it'll all make sense very soon."

Charlie felt as if somebody had shoved him halfway across the room.

"Medication?"

Dr Epstein cleared his throat before continuing. He was still clinging on to that tight-lipped smile for dear life. "Yes. Charlie, you're in a state of medically assisted forgetting. Okay? That's all this is right now, nothing more, nothing less. It's a combination of drugs, including beta blockers, that we've used to temporarily remove painful memories. It's intentional forgetting for therapeutic means. Short-lived, but the long-term effects can be beneficial. In truth, you don't really forget but it can push the memories away, just long enough so we can work on trauma."

Charlie continued to shield his eyes from the harsh light. "I didn't understand a word of that. What in the name of God are you talking about? Medically assisted forgetting?"

"You signed all the papers," Dr Epstein said quickly. "Everything's above board and perfectly legal, I can assure you. It was only supposed to blunt your memory. To last long enough for us to..."

Charlie's head was a dense, swirling fog. "For you to do what?"

"To do what needed to be done."

"Will somebody please tell me what the hell is going on here?" Charlie said, with an exasperated sigh. He looked back and forth between the doctor and the imposter. At the same time, he was becoming aware of more noises from elsewhere inside the house. Talking. Banging. Something big scraping off the floor. How many people were in on this thing? The privacy of the farmhouse was no more.

Dr Epstein dropped the reassuring smile. His shoulders loosened a touch as he pointed a finger at the man who'd called himself Ryker.

"Charlie – this man is an actor."

Charlie's eyebrows formed a stiff arch. "What?"

"You're not in Kintyre," Dr Epstein said. "You're in Edinburgh, in a therapeutic setting that we arranged together in the clinic. Do you remember yet? Is it coming back to you?"

Charlie looked around the sparsely decorated room. He was in...Edinburgh? What the hell? But this place looked identical to the living room in his Kintyre farmhouse. Everything was where it should be – the bookcases, the worn-out couch that he loved so much and had picked out from a British Red Cross shop in Campbeltown, the dreary wooden floor. Everything was here. The old box TV in the bedroom. Those were his things, weren't they? They were *his* things. Despite the renovation work he'd undertaken in Kintyre all those years ago, Charlie had insisted on keeping the farmhouse as basic as possible in terms of interior furnishing and accessories. He didn't see the point of getting away from the city and coming to a country house loaded up with all the same gadgets. Out here he could think. He could meditate. Catch up on his reading and basically just stay away from people. He sure as hell didn't want to Zoom anyone.

But no crumbs on the bedroom floor. Remember?

And that tap was running too well.

"I'm not Ryker Marshall," said the imposter. It was as if he felt the need to say out loud what by this point, was perfectly obvious. Maybe he wanted to say it to Charlie again. "It's like Dr Epstein said. I'm just an actor."

Charlie watched as the man pulled the black wig off his head. Maybe, Charlie thought, he should have noticed the lack of grey hairs on it. Would Ryker really have given up the world, his career, friends and family, but kept a hold of the hair dye? Doubtful. The actor's head sported a dark buzz cut. Looked to Charlie like his head had changed shape now that he'd lost the wig. More rounded, less angular. The facial resemblance to Ryker tapered off further, reminding Charlie that he'd seen his old buddy in this man only because he'd wanted it so bad. Was he really that gullible?

The actor tossed the wig onto the couch.

"Sorry man."

"Who are you then?" Charlie asked.

"My name's Graham Rice. I'm from Bishopbriggs, just outside Glasgow. This was a job for me mate – that's all it was. I was hired by the clinic to participate in your therapy session. To play the part of an older Ryker Marshall, one who's returned after twenty-five years."

"I don't get it," Charlie said with a shake of the head. "What was supposed to happen here? How was this scenario supposed to help me?"

Rice shrugged. "Catharsis, I guess. You were supposed to yell at me – that's what I was told to expect anyway. Verbal assault. You were going to scream at me. Unleash all your repressed anger about Ryker. You know? About how he walked out like he did and left you all hanging. I wasn't expecting a fistfight though. That wasn't in the contract."

Again, Rice looked at the doctor. Rubbed his fingers together.

Dr Epstein paid no attention to the imposter's less than

subtle hints about compensation this time. He chewed on his lower lip while he stared at Charlie.

"Charlie. Is it starting to come back?"

Charlie lowered his head. "I paid for *this*?"

"Yes."

"How much exactly did I pay?"

"You're in Edinburgh," Dr Epstein said, ignoring the question altogether. "It's important you come back to yourself now, Charlie. You're at the Dawson Clinic and at your behest, we're working on an experimental form of therapy. Like Graham said, it's been designed for you to achieve emotional catharsis in regards to your relationship with Ryker. Your *troubled* relationship. The risk of failure was always high but we didn't see *that* coming. It didn't occur to us for one second that there'd be an issue with Graham taking the glass in his right hand. We should have checked out the minute details in advance. Lesson learned. You do know your friend well, don't you Charlie? Even after twenty-five years."

Charlie replayed the critical moment in his head.

"Ryker would never reach over with his right hand. Not when there's a glass inches from his left one."

Graham stood by the couch, blushing. "Sorry. I'm super right-handed. Always have been and I didn't think it would matter for the job."

Charlie stood there, feeling numb. There were more footsteps in and around the farmhouse. The *fake* farmhouse. He caught a glimpse of shadowy figures hurrying back and forth on the other side of the living room window. Sounded like people whispering instructions to one another. Trying not to disturb what was going on in the living room itself with Charlie's emotional recovery. Were they dismantling the set already because the 'experiment' had been a colossal failure? Charlie felt dizzy, his reality changing as it was poured too fast into a different-shaped glass. Even the ground under his feet felt like it was about to open up and reveal a gaping black hole.

"I did this?" he said, looking at Dr Epstein. Looking at the imposter. Looking at the...studio? "I chose this?"

The doctor nodded. "You did."

"Why? Why would I do this?"

"You wanted to talk to Ryker," Dr Epstein said. "This scenario was originally scripted by you – a scenario where Ryker would show up at your house in Kintyre, knocking on the door in the dead of night. You said you'd dreamed about it once, not long after his disappearance in 1997. You dreamed about getting answers. The Kintyre scenario was a good one. It was private, just the two of you. It would give you a chance to let loose and even after the drugs wore off, you'd feel the benefit of having unburdened yourself from all the pent-up emotion. It's a heavy weight you've been carrying Charlie."

"Sounds crazy," Charlie said. "I can't believe I bought into this bullshit. It's crazy."

"Experimental," Dr Epstein said, the pursed smile back on his face. "Possibilities were discussed and you gave us written permission to proceed with memory blunting. It was all designed in accordance with your therapist, Dr Ritchie."

"Ritchie? I don't even remember him."

"*Her.*"

Charlie's head felt like it was about to burst open. "Let me get this straight. I planned all of this, paid for all of this, just so I could shout at someone? Someone, *anyone*, I believed was Ryker?"

Dr Epstein lowered his clipboard. "Charlie, it's not as ridiculous as it first seems. You're angry at Ryker for walking out like he did. You're *furious*. You, like other people who knew him back then, feel betrayed and have done so for the past twenty-five years. And now we have the twenty-fifth anniversary coming up. I know this time of year is particularly difficult for you Charlie. He was twenty-four at the time he went missing, right?"

"Right."

"And now he's been gone twenty-five years."

Charlie nodded. He heard the doctor's muffled words in his ear and wondered if whatever pharmaceutical cocktail he'd taken had begun to wear off. It still felt mighty foggy up there in his skull. He turned to the actor, Graham...what was it? What was his name? Who was that standing beside the couch again? Charlie spoke in a quiet voice, lost in the clutter of noise around him as workers in the clinic continued to take the set apart.

No. He was back in the farmhouse.

In Kintyre.

"I'm not sure what I was supposed to say to you," Charlie said. "I guess I would have gone full-on batshit angry."

He took a step closer to the couch.

He could see Ryker again. Ryker was back, after all those years in the wilderness of God knows where.

The man backed off, threw a worried look at the doctor. "Hey. I don't think he's fully out of it yet doc."

"What happened to you?" Charlie said, peering at the blurry shape through narrow eyes that fought against the light. "Where did you go? You weren't taken by anyone, were you? You walked out. Right? You walked out on us. Couldn't take it anymore, eh? Fame was too much? So where did you go? Somewhere quiet? Questions, questions – all I have are questions. Do you have any idea what that was like for the rest of us? Discovering that you'd gone. Living with it for twenty-five years. Has it been that long?"

"Charlie," a distorted voice called from another dimension. "Charlie, it's too late. This is Graham, remember? He's just an actor."

But Charlie kept moving towards the blur. Towards Ryker.

"Well," he said. "You're here now. Do you know what happened to Sally?"

Charlie stopped dead. He blinked and saw a vision of himself sitting in a white-walled Edinburgh office building. Sunny day outside, but the room was cold. Powerful air-conditioning. There was a glass of water sitting on a clear glass table. In the vision, Charlie was shaking hands with a man. With Dr Epstein. There was a woman there too, tall and attractive. Looked like a professional. Another doctor?

Everyone was smiling.

Client discretion is of paramount importance, Charlie. Nobody will ever know about this.

"Charlie," someone said.

The man with the clipboard – it was Dr Epstein – stepped in between Charlie and the blur that wasn't Ryker but a jobbing actor. "I'm sorry but it's too late. At least this time. We didn't know that Ryker's left-handedness would be the deciding factor. That it would lead to such a premature and unsatisfactory ending to the scenario. This is over for today."

"He still looks pretty stoned doc," said the actor.

"He'll be fine."

Charlie shook his head. That last blast of whatever drugs he was on had been powerful, but it was gone now and it felt like his scrambled brain was coming home at last. He looked to his left. Saw someone in a white lab coat walk past the door. A woman – looked like the therapist, Dr what's-her-name? She didn't look back. Charlie's head hurt. Maybe that was a sign that things were clearing upstairs. Yes, it was starting to come back. The truth. The arrangement. He'd been so optimistic about it at the time. About seeing 'Ryker' and saying all the things he needed to say, even if it was just an exercise in catharsis.

Another white coat walked past the door, carrying what appeared to be a portable fan. So, Charlie thought. That's where all the cold 'Kintyre' air had been coming from.

"Charlie," Dr Epstein said. He was leaning in closer. Almost whispering in Charlie's ear. "If you want to try again next year or even sooner for that matter, I'm willing to offer a twenty percent discount on behalf of the clinic. Things didn't work out this time but I still believe this *can* work. That it can help you overcome your burden."

Charlie looked at the man. "Do this again? You're joking, right?"

"I'm quite serious."

"I'm never doing this again," Charlie said with a firm shake of the head. "That much I can promise."

Dr Epstein sighed. He took a step backwards towards the door, that tight-lipped smile re-emerging on his face. "I understand. But..."

"But what?" Charlie snapped.

"That's what you said last year."

5

The Broken Gods
(First international TV interview)
VH1

Two fresh-faced, twenty-one-year-old men with Beatle-style mop tops are being interviewed on VH1. Charlie Lewis and Ryker Marshall are the faces of The Broken Gods, a rock band from Glasgow, Scotland, whose first album (Bad Money), has skyrocketed to the top of the charts in the US. Their second single (Poppers), is also number one at the time of the interview.

This is their first major interview outside of the UK.

Both men are slickly dressed, wearing Lambretta shirts inspired by the mod scene that took Britain by storm in the 1960s, along with tan-coloured chinos and penny loafers. Ryker sports a pair of big, black sunglasses that cover half his face. His trademark fedora rests on his lap.

The interviewer is Gary Lyndhurst – a square-jawed, perma-tanned music journalist with a vague resemblance to Tom Cruise.

GARY: Alright, here we go. Very excited to talk to you two fellas today – Charlie Lewis and Ryker Marshall in the studio with us here at VH1. It's no exaggeration to say that these guys are the leaders of a movement that's starting to look, to my eyes at least, a lot like another British invasion to the US. How did you two first meet?

Charlie and Ryker are silent, allowing for a long pause to filter through the studio. They look at each other and smile, as if waiting for the other one to answer the question. In the end, it's Charlie who yields. His youthful, high-pitched Scottish accent is soft and musical.

CHARLIE: We were about four and well, believe it or not, we met in a sandpit in our local kindergarten. That's what our parents tell us anyway. Can't say if we hit it off immediately, eh? Can't really remember but that's how we met. In kindergarten.

GARY: In a sandpit?

CHARLIE: Aye.

GARY: And you've been inseparable ever since?

Ryker answers. It's the sound of a painfully shy kid who doesn't like talking too much. His Glaswegian accent, the rhythm of speech and delivery, mirrors Charlie's to perfection. They could almost be the same person when they talk.

RYKER: Not really. We didn't get to know each other that well until later on. When we were in school.

CHARLIE: I used to protect Ryker from the unwanted attention of bullies in secondary school. He had a weird attitude to other kids, like he couldn't be arsed with them for the most part. Bit of a loner. He had a funny name too. Not a lot of Rykers walking around where we grew up, you know? Plus, he was into weird stuff. Art. Literature. Strange, avant-garde music. He was ahead of his time and unlike the other kids, didn't give a shit about Rangers and Celtic or any sort of sport for that matter. Bit of a goth too, which meant he was an easy target for the idiots. And there were a lot of idiots at our school.

GARY: (*to Ryker*) Is that true?

RYKER: (*nodding*) I was a sensitive boy, aye. Charlie had a lot more swagger than I did back in the day. He used to act like he knew Kung-Fu but in reality, he was just jumping about hitting thin air.

CHARLIE: Kept the bullies away though, eh?

RYKER: It did, aye. Kept the girls away too.

CHARLIE: He's still a sensitive wee boy by the way. Go easy on him Gary, eh? No tough questions or he might cry.

The two bandmates laugh. Ryker picks up the bottle of Heineken at his feet and takes a hefty gulp. Then he lights up two cigarettes and passes one to Charlie. Charlie takes it with a nod. Ryker offers a smoke to Gary who politely declines.

GARY: And so this friendship developed throughout school and of course, led to the creation of The Broken Gods.

RYKER: The friendship bloomed naturally. We bonded over everything, me and Charlie. Everything. Music, politics, art and of course we both had the same desire to escape the dead-end life that awaited us if we towed the line and did what everyone else was doing. If we did what our parents and career advisors told us to. We don't come from money so the opportunities looked bleak for people like us. They told us take whatever job we could get. To have no ambition. But we always knew we were going to do something big. We just didn't know what it was. Not until music.

GARY: So, how did the band get up and running?

CHARLIE: (*shrugs*) Just kind of happened. At some point we found out that we were both writing songs but separately, you know? We were too embarrassed to admit what we were doing to anyone else but each other. Writing songs, it was weird. Who did that in our wee circle? No one. It was all football, pubs and drugs where we came from. With me and Ryker, it was two outsiders coming together. I didn't know Ryker even had a guitar at first, him being left-handed and all. I didn't know they had guitars for lefties. Neither did he and that's why he learned to play right-handed at first.

GARY: That's incredible. There can't be many people in the world who can play both right-handed and left-handed guitars. At least, not to your level.

RYKER: (*shrugs off the compliment*) Like Charlie says, no one inside our circle was writing songs. Anyway, we started working together. Welding his ideas and mine together. Eventually we got Tommy and Bobby in and it just went from there. Started off slow, stayed slow for a long time but eventually it skyrocketed. Just like we always knew it would.

CHARLIE: We don't mean to sound arrogant. It's just that we always we knew it was meant to happen.

GARY: You guys, more than any other group I can think of, have rejuvenated a tired rock and roll scene on both sides of the pond. In fact, you're already being compared to that other famous L/M songwriting team, Lennon and McCartney. Do you foresee the writing partnership lasting a long time?

Charlie and Ryker wait in silence, hoping the other will answer first. Again, it's Charlie who gives in.

CHARLIE: I don't know about the writing partnership, eh? But I do envision the friendship lasting a very long time.

Ryker blows a cloud of smoke in the air. He lifts the fedora off his lap and puts it on, tilting the hat slightly to the right.

RYKER: Brothers forever. To me, that's even more important than the band. We go back a long way together. Tighter than blood. We're always going to be there for one another, no matter what happens.

CHARLIE: Soulmates, that kind of thing. We're like lovers without the shagging.

RYKER: Ha-ha. I've tried but he won't have it.

They laugh.

CHARLIE: No matter what happens, that connection between Ryker and me is always going to be there. Like he says, brothers. I guess it started in the kindergarten sandpit all those years ago. We're on the same wavelength. And just like it was back in school, if somebody hurts him, I'm going to hurt them back.

RYKER: With your shite Kung-Fu?

CHARLIE: Aye.

GARY: I can feel the love in the room guys. That's awesome. Alright, well it's been great to meet you both. Best of luck with your upcoming tour which kicks off with a special warm-up gig at the Whisky a Go Go tomorrow night. I think I speak for the entire nation when I say that we in America can't wait to see more of you guys up close and personal.

CHARLIE: Cheers Gary.

RYKER: Cheers man.

Clip ends.

One week until the anniversary of Ryker Marshall's disappearance...

6

Saturday 15th April

Charlie was expecting the call from Annie Marshall. Sure enough, it came through in the week leading up to the anniversary.

He'd been keeping a low profile since his return from the Dawson Clinic. What a monumental fuck up and waste of money that exercise had been. If only he could get another cocktail of drugs to forget it. *Thousands. Tens of thousands.* Might as well have flushed the cash down the toilet for all the good it had done Charlie in terms of catharsis. Turned out it wasn't the first time that, despite having his memory blunted, Charlie had shot himself in the foot by noticing little things about the actor that weren't 'Rykerisms'. Happened every time, according to the doctor. Charlie knew his old friend too well. There was always a moment at the beginning of the exercise where Charlie accepted the actor as Ryker because of how much he wanted to see Ryker in the room with him. Then it happened. It could be something as simple as a facial expression that wasn't right. Sometimes it was the voice. Using his right-hand when it should have been the left. Sooner or later, Charlie always spotted the mistake.

No more, he told himself. No more Dawson Clinic. He'd get a punch bag and beat the crap out of it for thirty minutes a day. That would relieve the tension, at least on a short-term basis. Plus, it was cheaper and better for his health. Maybe he'd work on that biscuit belly and get back to being skinny Charlie. If that was even possible.

Since coming home, he'd hunkered down in his terraced house in the affluent Kingsborough Gardens section of Hyndland in Glasgow's west end. It was that time of year. The anniversary. God, Charlie *hated* the anniversary. He'd faced twenty-four of them so far and instead of getting easier, it had become progressively harder. Every time, the build-up felt like a slow, neverending fall into a black hole. Hopelessness. Helplessness. After all these years, he was still unable to do anything for Ryker. And these feelings were always accompanied by the expectation that something disastrous was going to happen to him too. That it was Charlie's turn to vanish, die or make the headlines for all the wrong reasons. It had started off as a vague, uneasy feeling after Ryker's disappearance. Charlie had dreamt of his own vanishing on multiple occasions. It came in many forms but usually he was jumping off a tall bridge and falling towards black water. Ryker disappeared. Why does Charlie get away with still being here after all these years? They were partners. It happened to Ryker and sure enough, whatever cosmic force had taken his friend would come for Charlie too. *Brothers forever*. They were glued together by an unbreakable, timeless thread. This vague uneasiness about his own fate had flowered over the years, nourished by Charlie's increasing paranoia. He'd stopped drinking and smoking weed. Still, he couldn't shake off that feeling.

Something was coming.

But what?

(ridiculous, you're being ridiculous)

Could it be death? Assassination by some crazed fan? That had never quite sat right because that's not what happened to Ryker. It was the vanishing. And the vanishing left nothing but questions behind. Charlie couldn't escape the feeling that he too was going to vanish like his songwriting partner. It was a big stretch and yet over the years, the inevitability he felt had only solidified. Paul McCartney, George Harrison and Ringo Starr must have felt vulnerable in the years after John Lennon's assassination. They didn't fear being kidnapped. They feared being shot. To make it worse, the bastard who squeezed the trigger that cold December night in 1980 was famous. The nobody was somebody. Imprisoned yes, but famous. Universally despised yes, but famous. The world was full of nobodies who could become somebodies by committing a simple act of brutality.

Charlie was convinced that Ryker had vanished willingly. He hadn't been kidnapped. He'd walked. It was obvious to everyone who knew him back in 1997 that Ryker was wilting under the pressure of fame and so he disappeared. Whether he jumped off a bridge or started a new life in the Himalayas, nobody knew for sure. Call it survival instinct, but he'd disappeared by choice. Charlie didn't want to take off. He wasn't going to leave his two boys behind wondering what had happened to their dad, even if they did prefer spending more time with their mum and stepdad these days. So how would it happen?

Someone was going to kidnap Charlie.

(you're paranoid)

That would make it nice and symmetrical. Both halves of the Lewis/Marshall partnership disappearing twenty-five years apart. Charlie had always feared the twenty-fifth anniversary most of all because he'd clung to one of those damn lyrics that Ryker had written years ago for the Gods' biggest hit – 'Coming For You.'

It's a sick twisted joke,
Truth's lying to you.
Get out while you can,
Go run with the few,
'Cos in twenty-five years, they'll be coming for you,
In twenty-five years, they'll be coming for you.

Just words, Charlie told himself. He'd been telling himself that for years. Just words. Lyrics chosen to fit the melody. They didn't mean anything.

In twenty-five years, they'll be coming for you.

The anniversary was next Sunday. Charlie wanted to sit that day out. All he wanted to do was hide in the house, wait it out with a blanket over his head and keep the doors locked. Maybe keep a knife within grabbing distance. Apart from that, take it easy. Eat junk. Watch TV. Keep the lights off even when day turned to night. Forget about what day it was. Turn off the phone. But retreat was out of the question. The Dark Stars had three gigs to play in Scotland over the weekend – the final three shows on their Back-To-Basics tour. There were also a couple of rehearsals scheduled at the local studios during the week. It was a busy stretch leading up to the anniversary itself.

Charlie wasn't sure how he was going to get through it.

He didn't ignore Annie Marshall's call when it came. He hadn't heard from Ryker's older sister in almost three years but he guessed she was back in Glasgow for the big anniversary, back in town to see her mum and to take up duties as family spokesperson for any media requirements that would come up. And there'd be a few of those, especially this year – the year that marked a quarter of a century since Ryker's disappearance. Charlie took the call and it was a brief conversation. Annie wanted to meet up for an hour, grab a drink, maybe a bite of lunch. Too long, she said. It had been too long since they'd seen one another.

Charlie said yes.

They arranged to meet for a drink in a small restaurant on Argyle Street, directly across from Kelvingrove Art Gallery and Museum. The restaurant's owner, Jack Graham, was an acquaintance of Charlie and was only too happy to offer some private space at the back of the restaurant, partitioning it off so Charlie wouldn't be bothered by autograph hunters or the occasional idiot who thought they could gawp at him for as long as they wanted. Like he was a waxwork.

Before going out to meet Annie, Charlie put on a cap and pulled the visor low over the top half of his face. He ran a hand over the dark shadow of stubble on his chin, wondering if he should have shaved or not.

Too much effort, he thought.

He pulled out his phone. Booked an Uber to take him to the restaurant by one o'clock. When the car pulled up at his gate, Charlie walked outside and greeted the Lewis Loyals, a small cluster of fans, who followed him everywhere. They usually stood on the opposite side of the street, keeping a respectful distance from the house. Today was no different. As he approached the car, Charlie recognised most of the Loyals across the street: Ginger and her posse of girlfriends –

a group of twenty-something indie rock chicks who thought it was still 1996 and the glory days of British guitar bands. The lads were there too, most of them dressed in Lambretta or Fred Perry polo shirts even though it wasn't the warmest of weather and even though those tight-fitting shirts weren't the most flattering fit on their middle-aged bodies anymore. Blondie, he was one of the lads. Friendly. Talkative. There was a new guy there who Ginger had previously introduced as Chunky. He was bald-headed, short and stocky with a protruding gut that tested the elasticity of his red Fred Perry top. Chunky was pretty shy. The new ones always were.

And of course, there was Ronnie.

Charlie didn't miss Ronnie, standing behind the group. Always slightly apart from the others, as if he didn't quite belong. He was a skinny guy in his mid-to-late forties, with long blackish-grey hair and a scruffy beard that gave off serious Charles Manson vibes. Like Blondie and Ginger, Ronnie was a long-time Lewis Loyal who'd been there for years but he rarely ever said a word or called out to Charlie like the others did, even the newbies who still felt a bit awkward hanging around outside his house. Ronnie just stood and stared. Charlie had always been a little freaked out by him.

Maybe he was shy. Maybe he couldn't help acting like a creepy bastard.

As always, Charlie kept his interaction with the Loyals brief. A few pleasantries were exchanged from opposite sides of the street. As he climbed into the back of the Uber, somebody asked him where he was going. Charlie called over. Said something about meeting an old friend in the southside – a flimsy diversion strategy targeted at any of the Loyals who planned to follow him. The Loyals were good trackers. With any luck, they'd strike out. Maybe they wouldn't even bother to follow.

It was a short journey to Argyle Street. When Charlie reached the restaurant, he had a polite conversation with Jack at the bar. While he was talking, he saw several photos of himself and other celebrities who'd frequented the restaurant over the years. Jack led Charlie to the partitioned area where Annie was already waiting behind the curtain. Upon seeing Charlie, Annie stood up from the table and Charlie fell into her open arms. Jack left them to it while they stood there, locked in each other's grip.

It was a little after lunchtime and the restaurant was quiet. There were only a few scattered groups in the main dining area, none of them having noticed Charlie's quiet entrance. He still had the cap pulled low over his eyes. It'd be a few hours yet before people started showing up for dinner at Jack's place and filling out the empty space.

They sat down at the table. As it turned out, neither Charlie nor Annie were hungry enough to order food. Annie ordered a glass of Merlot and Charlie settled on a Coke. They made small talk for a while, catching up on the banal before the subject inevitably turned to the anniversary.

"I didn't think there'd be so much coverage," Annie said. "But it's everywhere – on the radio, TV, podcasts. I can't believe there's still such a huge interest."

Charlie nodded. He smiled as Annie talked. She hadn't changed much since he'd last seen her three years ago, apart from giving up the black hair dye and allowing her shoulder-length mane to resort to its natural silvery-grey. Looked good on her, Charlie thought. She wore a slim-fit black pleather jacket and blue jeans. Her skin was nicely tanned. As Charlie recalled, Annie worked as the head teacher of a primary school located about eight miles north of Glasgow, something that amused him whenever he thought back to the wild and rebellious teenager he'd known in the late eighties and early nineties. Drink, drugs, boys, shoplifting – Annie had been there, done it and her face was plastered all over the t-shirt.

"After so many years," she said, "you think that maybe they'd forget about Ryker."

Annie's tight-lipped, awkward smile was identical to Ryker's. Charlie didn't know whether to be thankful for or horrified by these moments of recognition and remembrance. Likewise with Ryker's mother – occasional flashes of her son would appear in Heather Marshall's eyes. It was there and then it was gone. Almost as if Ryker was looking back at Charlie through his mother. Just for a second or two.

Sometimes, Charlie had to look away.

The guilt he felt was too much.

"It's a mystery," Charlie said, glancing through the window at the steady flow of traffic on Argyle Street. He saw a section of the museum across the street, its familiar red sandstone a defining feature of Glasgow's Victorian era architecture. "People love a good mystery. If Ryker had been shot by a lunatic, hit by a car, died of a drugs overdose or something like that, it wouldn't have such a hold over them. It would be case closed and that's that. But when there's no closure..."

Annie nodded. "Every theory, no matter how wacked out, might be the right one."

"Exactly. And there's some wacked out theories about what happened to him. I like the one where he's spying for the Chinese in Tibet."

"Oh God," Annie said. "You're kidding?"

"Nope. It's not the most popular fan theory but it's out there."

Annie sipped her wine.

"How's it going with The Dark Stars?"

Charlie sighed. He picked up his glass, took a sip of Coke and realised how much he hated the black, sugary poison from Hell. The problem was, when he was out, he didn't know what to order when he wasn't ordering beer. Water was boring. He didn't like orange juice. Non-alcoholic beer was pointless.

His leg was shaking under the table.

"Not so good."

"How come?"

He shrugged. "It's not the same thing, Annie. I wanted to put a band together after doing the solo thing with session musicians for years. But it's just not happening. There's no spark between me and Darcy and Hutch, not in the studio and definitely not on stage during this tour. No chemistry. It was an interesting experiment, picking up two buskers off the street and seeing what would happen. I was trying to get that old Broken Gods magic back into my life. But the experiment failed."

"I think The Dark Stars sound great," Annie said. "For what it's worth. The reviews are positive too. For the albums, the gigs."

"You been checking up on me?"

She smiled. "Of course I have. I've always taken an interest in your solo work. I think it's great you're still out there Charlie. You've got more talent than most of these acts today have in their little fingers. The music industry needs you. Who gives a shit if you're nearly fifty?"

Charlie grinned. Like he needed reminding of that last

part. "I seem to remember Annie, back when I was nineteen, you told me not to give up the day job."

"Have you ever had a day job, Charlie?"

"Nope. You still said it."

"I said a lot of things back then. How could we ever have known what the future had in store for you guys?"

"Aye."

"So," Annie said. "You're not happy with the band?"

Charlie shook his head. "They hate my guts."

Annie frowned. "Darcy and what's-his-name? They hate your guts?"

"Yup."

"I must be watching a different band," Annie said. "Looks to me like the three of you are having a blast on stage."

"Maybe at the beginning," Charlie said, following a loud sigh. He fell back in his seat. Picked up the Coke and immediately put it back down again. "I don't know. It's different now. I think they know that the writing's on the wall."

"And what does the writing on the wall say?"

"That I'm breaking up the band," Charlie said. "After these shows are over at the weekend."

"Oh wow. I'm sorry to hear that."

"Thing is," Charlie said with a lazy shrug of the shoulders. "I haven't actually told them yet. I haven't told anyone, not even Dennis."

"Dennis?"

"Dennis Walsh – remember him? Short, strawberry blond hair. He's got a long beard that sort of makes him look like a biker in a banker's suit. He was a roadie back in The Broken Gods days. Now he's managing The Dark Stars. He's a good talker. Anyway, I'll have to tell them all sooner or later. Was planning on doing it after these gigs are over."

Annie took a long-delayed sip of wine. "The Back-To-Basics tour didn't work out then?"

"Nah. Load of shite."

"I thought it sounded like a great idea," Annie said. "Getting back to small audiences – playing the pubs, clubs and town hall gigs again. The critics agree Charlie because the reviews have been glowing since the European leg."

Charlie nodded. He was aware of the positive reviews in the press and on social media in general in regards to the tour. The critics had been kind to him, declaring that Charlie was writing, playing and singing better than at any point since peak Broken Gods era, circa 94-97. Sobriety agreed with him, according to the music press. Charlie agreed with that last part. But sometimes he wondered if he was getting an easy ride from the press because of Ryker's disappearance. *Go easy on him, he's lost his wee pal. Must be hard. It's just great that he's still out there trying his best. He's almost fifty after all.*

He still wasn't feeling the music though. More than ever, he missed playing with Ryker and the natural connection they had both on stage and working together in a recording studio. One mind in two bodies. They understood each other perfectly. Charlie wanted to know what it would feel like to play with Ryker as two middle-aged men, thinning hair and expanding waistlines, in an industry that worshipped youth. Could they still cut it?

"It's a nightmare," he said to Annie. "Travelling around all these cities in small vans, stuck to each other like we're a bunch of nineteen-year-olds. Back-To-Basics was a good idea on paper but it's a pain in the arse to execute. Everything's bare minimal. No tour buses, just these tiny little transit vans split between band and crew. Thank God, I still get a hotel room to myself and we're not all sleeping on top of one another in the back of the van. We've been at it for months now. Three more gigs and it's over."

Annie's face was a mask of calm concentration. She nodded as Charlie spoke. "If you break up the band, what happens to your bandmates – to Darcy and Hutch?"

Charlie was looking across the street at a young couple sharing a picnic on the grass outside the museum. As they sat there eating sandwiches and sipping something hot out of a stainless-steel flask, it looked like they didn't have a care in the world. At the same time, he couldn't see any Lewis Loyals loitering near the restaurant. Hungry-eyed. Waiting for a glimpse of their ageing hero. That was a minor victory.

"I can't babysit them forever."

"That's true," Annie said, nodding. "But does that mean they have to go back to busking for a living?"

"They might get work elsewhere."

"They might. But you're right – it's not your problem. So the tour's almost over? You must be happy about that then?"

"Thank God," Charlie said. "We've had a couple of weeks off since the English and Welsh gigs and that's been a welcome break. Now we've got three Scottish legs to finish up with – Glasgow, Edinburgh, then it's Inverness on Sunday. That'll be the last Dark Stars gig ever, but right now you and I are the only people who know that for sure."

"So you're playing on the anniversary itself?" Annie said.

"Yep. Last thing I want to be doing."

Charlie was getting fidgety. Drumming his fingers off the table. He found himself craving a cigarette and that didn't happen often anymore. But there it was, that restless gnawing in his gut, an old sensation returned from the past. He'd been off cigarettes for at least six years and joints for almost the same length of time. Right now, he missed the old vices. Missed the refuge they offered.

He grunted out a laugh. "You know something, Annie. No matter what I do this week, all anyone will see is Charlie Lewis up there on stage getting old while Ryker stays young, immortal and mysterious."

"Do you resent him for that?"

"Maybe. I don't know."

Annie leaned over the table and gave Charlie's hand a squeeze. She locked eyes with him and Charlie saw the lines mapping her face and wondered where the years had gone. He recalled the tall and leggy teenage girl who'd been a constant feature of his visits to the Marshall house, located two streets along from the Lewis home in the east end of Glasgow. Charlie's earliest sexual fantasies had been about Annie and her friends. Their short skirts. Swelling breasts. They'd been his local goddesses, so near and yet so far. To them, he'd been nothing but a daft, drooling boy but he'd never forgotten those girls and the way they made him feel. If pressed, he could probably name every single one of them. Describe the way they'd looked back in the day, what they'd worn and how they'd treated him. Some had smiled. Some had ignored him. But Annie had always been the first.

"We've known each other a long time Charlie Lewis," Annie said with a smile. "You can tell me. Not that I can't see it written all over your face."

"See what?"

"You're pissed off at Ryker. You're angry at him. It's okay, so am I. He walked out, left us all and did what he had to do to stay sane. But he didn't say goodbye because...well, we wouldn't have let him go. So he went and you're justified in feeling the way you feel. It's okay to be angry at him – that's what I've been telling myself all these years."

"I doubt he was in his right mind," Charlie said.

Annie shrugged. "Or maybe he was."

Charlie felt his guard slipping. "I resent him for a lot of things Annie. Walking out is one thing but when you add Sally's fate into the mix, it's nothing short of a fucking tragedy. He never would have walked if he'd known how it would end for her. I keep envisioning him in some sort of hippy commune in India, no contact with the outside world. That's the sort of thing he would've done. I wonder if he even knows she's dead."

Annie nodded. "I hate this time of year."

She picked up her glass and tapped the rim off Charlie's Coke. "You ever hear from Sally's family? Her mum? Brother?"

"Fletcher?"

"He was your first roadie, right?"

Charlie nodded. "Aye, they made a good team. She booked the gigs and Fletcher tuned the guitars. We'd have been lost without them. Nah, I haven't kept in touch with the Darbey family. Haven't seen Fletcher or his mum in years. I get the feeling they'd rather keep a low profile, especially around this time of year."

"Sometimes I wish Ryker had been a normal guy," Annie said, staring out towards the museum. "But then he wouldn't have been Ryker, would he? He had a way of mesmerising people, you know? He always did. When he spoke, you listened. When he did something, you paid attention. Sally adored him. You and I adored him. Jesus, the world adored him and it was too much. Not long after he disappeared, Sally told me that she believed he'd joined a cult. Or a commune, like you said. But as the years went by, her thinking changed. She lost hope. She couldn't accept that he was alive because he hadn't tried to contact her. So, she believed that he was dead. That he really had jumped off Erskine Bridge. And that his body just vanished."

She hesitated.

"I suppose it was her way of following him."

Charlie nodded.

"I'm sorry," Annie said, furrowing her brow. "Oh God, I know it's a horrible story. Reliving it all in conversation – well, sometimes it feels like there are only a few people who understand the loss. And you're one of them."

"I hear you."

Annie sat up straight and picked up her wine glass. "Anyway," she said, wrenching a smile onto her face. "I'm sorry to hear about the band. I hope, if nothing else, that the last three gigs go well."

"Aye," Charlie said. "Thanks."

They made small talk for a few minutes and Charlie felt a flicker of relief when Annie said she had to get back to her mother. They stood up. Charlie looked at his glass on the table. He'd taken about three sips of Coke and that was three too much. Annie's wine glass was empty. He offered to walk Annie to her car, which was parked at the back of the restaurant in the staff parking area. Charlie had arranged this in advance so that Annie wouldn't get a ticket if she parked elsewhere. Saved her a walk too. As they passed through the still-quiet restaurant and made their way towards the back door, Charlie shoved the wrinkled khaki cap back onto his head, pulling the visor low. He thought about the Lewis Loyals. Hoped that none of them had tracked him down to the restaurant.

Especially Ronnie.

It was a short walk to Annie's car – a silver Mondeo backed up against the wheelie bins.

Standing beside the car, they embraced again.

"It's been good seeing you," Charlie said, taking a step back. "Listen, I hope everything goes well at school and well, you know. I hope you guys will be okay on Sunday. You doing anything special for the anniversary?"

Annie laughed softly. "Just taking Mum and Auntie Alison out for tea. We'll go for a wee walk or something afterwards. Keep them occupied, you know?"

"Give my love to them," Charlie said, thinking of Annie's mother, Heather. It had been a long time since they'd last seen one another. There were cousins and other loose family connections that Charlie hadn't seen in a long time too, but it was Annie who he'd kept in touch with.

He was about to walk away when Annie grabbed his arm.

"Before you run off," she said. "I have something for you."

"For me?"

"Yep. It's in the boot of the car. Just hang on a second, will you?"

Charlie frowned. "What is it?"

Annie smiled, but she didn't answer the question. She walked around to the back of the Mondeo and opened up the lid of the boot. As Charlie stood there, he glanced left and right, still wary of the Lewis Loyals showing up. He wouldn't have minded too much as long as they kept their distance and didn't hassle Annie. Still, he felt exposed being outside like this. But it was nothing he wasn't used to.

Annie rummaged around loudly inside the boot. After about a minute, she walked back to where Charlie was waiting at the bonnet. She was carrying a guitar case and she held it up at chest level, offering it to Charlie with a grin.

Charlie's insides swirled around like clothes in a washing machine.

"This has been sitting dormant in Mum's house for too

long," Annie said. "It's too good for that. It should be out there making music and doing what it was made to do."

Charlie knew what was inside that battered case. And yet he tried to feign ignorance, putting a dumb look on his face that wasn't fooling anyone, least of all Annie.

"What is it?"

Annie put the case down on the bonnet and with a sweeping hand gesture, invited Charlie forward. "Open it."

Charlie trudged forward like he was walking through quicksand. He flipped the latches, lifted the lid and peered inside. Knowing what was in the case was one thing. Seeing it, after all those years, was something else. "Oh shit."

"Yep," Annie said.

Ryker's 1965 Fender Telecaster was strapped up neatly inside the case. The guitar was legendary, spanning the entirety of The Broken Gods' story from spotty garage band losers to rock and roll heroes. The guitar had originally been painted black but at some point in the early nineties, dissatisfied with its appearance, Ryker had stripped it back to its classic rosewood colour. He'd bought the guitar in a Merchant City music shop as a teenager, having saved up months of earnings from a part-time job in a DIY superstore. Ryker had loathed that job (customers! sales!) but he stuck it out for the guitar. The Telecaster was unique in the sense that it was a right-handed guitar and Ryker was a natural leftie who'd learned to play right-handed before switching back to left-handed instruments later on. There weren't many ambidextrous guitarists out there who could play equally well as a righty and leftie. Ryker made it look easy. This guitar had always maintained a special place in his heart and its bright, chirpy tone was sprinkled over every Gods album from 1994-1997.

Charlie couldn't speak. It might as well have been Ryker

himself lying inside the cushioned interior of the case, grinning up at Charlie and yelling 'surprise'.

"This belongs to you," he said to Annie. "To the family."

Annie closed the lid over and locked up the case. She forced the handle into Charlie's reluctant grip. "You *are* family Charlie. Ryker didn't have any kids and I sure as hell don't want it – it's weird but I find it unsettling."

"What do you mean?"

The tight-lipped smile was back on Annie's face. "Ryker told me once that his soul was inside this guitar. He meant it too. *Really* meant it. Like a samurai who believed that the sword represented his soul – you know? Well, that's how it was. Ryker kept banging on about it. I can't look at it anymore. Mum feels the same. Will you take it?"

The handle was burning hot in Charlie's hand. "Are you sure you don't want it?"

Annie nodded. "He'd want you to have it. He'd want you to *play* it. Take it out on tour this weekend and he'll be with you in a way."

Charlie stared at the case. "He told me about all that samurai shit too." He saw his smile reflected in the car window. Looked more like a grimace.

"Thanks Annie."

She gave him the hard stare. "How you doing Charlie? How you *really* doing? We've done the small talk, all the bullshit, the catching up and that's fine. But I hear things, you know? I know you've been having a hard time with Jenna and the kids. I was sorry to hear about the divorce – how she got custody of the boys and a new husband. Must hurt. And now today you tell me that The Dark Stars are on the verge of breaking up. You used to love music Charlie. It's what you lived for but looking at you, it's like the light's gone out in your eyes. No offence. And of course, there's the anniversary hanging over everyone's head – yours included. I don't like to think of you being on your own right now."

"I'm fine," Charlie said, avoiding her eyes. "I've got these gigs to keep me occupied. Wish I didn't but at least they'll keep me busy."

The hum of traffic filled the gap in between conversation.

"I better let you go," Charlie said.

"Aye, okay."

They embraced again and Charlie was about to leave the car park with the guitar case when he stopped. He turned back to Annie. She was standing at the driver's door as if she'd been expecting one final exchange.

"I miss him," Charlie said. "I miss what we had back then. I was too young and stupid to appreciate it."

He laughed.

"You know, I've been thinking about getting a punch bag and putting a picture of Ryker's face on it. Might make me feel better."

Annie wiped something from the corner of her eye. "I used to punch him in the face for real when we were kids. It was quite satisfying."

Charlie laughed. He glanced at the guitar case in his hand and couldn't quite believe what was in there.

"I just want to talk to him again," he said. "I want to bounce ideas off him. I want to know what he thinks about the solo stuff I recorded. About The Dark Stars. What he thinks about my failed marriage and an ex-wife who hates my guts. About my kids who I hardly ever see. Ryker never liked Jenna, did he?"

Annie shrugged. "She was a rival for your attention."

Charlie stood there, weighed down by the past. He

tapped a finger off the side of his head. "My therapist thinks there's a lot of unresolved anger up here."

"I'm sure there is," Annie said.

"Oh God, you wouldn't believe the things I'm doing Annie – some of the elaborate bullshit I've been conjuring up with my therapist. Wasting thousands of pounds in Dawson Clinic just so I can have an imaginary conversation with Ryker."

"Really?"

Charlie nodded. "Please don't ask for the details. I'm embarrassed enough as it is. I'll see you Annie, okay?"

She smiled.

"See you later Charlie. Take care fo yourself."

He waved one last time before walking away with Ryker's guitar.

7

Charlie returned home from the restaurant and the first thing he did was call Jenna, his ex-wife. It was a mistake. He knew it was a mistake when he picked up the phone. It was still a mistake when he found her in his contacts. Then he hit the call button.

Another mistake.

Now he was pacing the bedroom. Back and forth, back and forth. Sweating like a fat man in a sauna. It was a solid workout and Charlie would even venture out into the upper hallway and spare bedrooms before coming back to his room. At the same time, his body trembled in that uncontrollable way, something that only Jenna could get out of him these days. His voice was on the brink of cracking.

"Two weeks," he barked into the phone. "Two weeks at the start of June, that's what we agreed upon at the start of the year. Correct?"

"Yes," Jenna said. "That's what we agreed *then*. But now..."

"Bloody hell Jenna, I'm only calling to confirm and now

you're telling me that it's off? That I can't take the boys to Ireland this summer?"

"Charlie, if you'd just listen for a second then..."

"No," Charlie snapped. He knew that getting this angry was a bad idea. That it would lead to him saying something he'd regret and also that it would make *Charlie* look like the unreasonable one, even when it was Jenna calling the shots. But it was like hot lava in his guts and it wouldn't go down.

"I'm the one calling you and that's how I find out my holiday's off? I have to call *you*? What the fuck Jenna? We agreed months ago that I'd get the boys for the first two weeks of June this year. That was set in stone. Fourteen days. You know I had plans. The Irish road trip – I told you all about it. What the fuck?"

"And what have you done so far, Charlie? Booked any flights? Hotels? Hired the car?"

Jenna's matter-of-fact tone was infuriating.

"Yes," Charlie lied.

He heard her sigh down the line. She knew he was bullshitting. "Things change Charlie. I *was* going to call you, okay? So please calm down. And no, it's not cancelled. I'm only asking you to push the Ireland trip back to the end of July. I want the kids with Roger and me when we go to his house in Lake Garda this summer. We asked the boys first, okay? They both said yes. They want to meet Sofia, Roger's daughter who's at uni in Milan. Look Charlie, at the end of the day, it's up to the boys. That's fair, isn't it?"

"Considering I'd made plans," Charlie said, "no it's not fair. You didn't think it was worth a call to let me know *before* you asked them? A text?"

"I've been busy."

"Booking more plastic surgery?"

"Don't go there Charlie. We can still talk like grown-ups, can't we?"

Charlie's free hand was balled into a tight fist. "I want the boys in June. We agreed and this time I'm putting my foot down. Italy can go fuck itself."

Another sigh from Jenna.

"The boys are coming to Italy with Roger and me. Then they'll go to Ireland with you later in the summer. I know you haven't made any concrete plans, Charlie."

Charlie felt a full-on blowout coming. *Breathe, breathe, breathe*. And yet despite his attempt to pretend otherwise, it wasn't like he'd booked the Irish trip. If only he'd booked one hotel or the car or something, then he could send her the confirmation and show her how unreasonable she was being. It was shameful how little he'd done in terms of prep work, despite being excited at the thought of going away with the boys. It was pretty much the only thing he was looking forward to. Still, despite the fact he hadn't booked any hotels or flights, Charlie wasn't ready to lie down. Lying down would send the wrong message to Jenna. That she (and Roger the twat) could mess him around whenever she wanted.

"Correct me if I'm wrong," Charlie said, jamming the iPhone in between his ear and shoulder while he picked up some crumpled t-shirts off the floor and tossed them onto the top shelf of the wardrobe. That was where all of Charlie's clothes went to die. "Don't I still give you money for those boys every month? Don't I still pay for their upkeep even if Roger the sugar daddy is trying to take my place? I'm still their father. Me, Jenna. I still get a say in their lives."

"They haven't heard much from you lately."

Charlie felt like she'd punched him in the guts. How did she always know what buttons to push? He sat down on the bed next to Ryker's guitar case. His breath was shallow and frantic as he picked at the corners of the tattered exterior.

"You know perfectly well I've been on tour," Charlie said. "I've been busy for the past three months travelling up and down the UK, Ireland and Europe. The boys know what I do for a living. You better not be poisoning their minds against me. Where are they now? I want to talk to them."

"Oh Charlie."

Jenna must have been thinking the same thing that Charlie was in that moment. How on earth did it come to this? They'd made the perfect couple once. Soulmates, that's how it seemed at the time. They met through work. Jenna had worked for a London-based graphic design agency that The Broken Gods used in the mid-nineties for their interior album art. There was a big launch party in a giant artsy-fartsy warehouse in Shoreditch and the electricity between Charlie and Jenna was instantaneous. Pure chemistry, beyond anything that Charlie had ever experienced before or since with anyone else. He was going to spend the rest of his life with this woman. No question about it. They'd been inseparable after that first night following the launch party and for the first time in his life, Charlie knew what it was to be in love. And it was everything they said it was.

The relationship moved at a lightning-fast pace: moving in together, marriage, cars, houses and holidays in the sun. They'd decided against kids, mostly due to their busy lifestyles. But when the marriage began to grow stale, they tried to fix it by starting a family. That didn't work, poor damn kids. Both Charlie and Jenna were bored. With boredom came temptation and both succumbed to it in the end. There were also plenty of stimulants to fuel the mutual suspicion that grew as they finally accepted the fact that they were no longer enough for one another. Falling in love had been a whirlwind. Falling out of love had been a slow, terminal illness. The idea of Charlie and Jenna as soulmates ended up as a twisted joke. A warning about the risks of rock and roll marriages. In the end, for the boys' sake as well as their own, they'd divorced.

"Hold on," Jenna said. "I'll see if they're in their rooms."

"Fine."

Charlie sat on the bed, staring at the tired-looking guitar case. It was as beat up as he felt. He hadn't yet lifted the lid for a second look at Ryker's pride and joy, the rosewood Telecaster. Charlie wasn't ready for a second glimpse. Not yet. But the thought of seeing it again was seriously freaking him out. Just thinking about it made the bedroom spin.

A drink would fix things. Just one.

Take the edge off?

No. The desire to disappear back down a bottle was gone as quickly as it had appeared. But that's how it came – in spurts. If Charlie ever fell off the wagon, it wouldn't be because of Jenna. He wouldn't give her the satisfaction. Besides, Roger would love hearing that story. That the boys' old man was back on the sauce.

Charlie's not safe for the kids to be around. Is he Jenna darling?

"Hello? Dad, are you there?"

Charlie flinched when he heard his son's voice. It was his eldest son, Jake, calling him back to Planet Earth. At fifteen years old, Jake had two years on his younger brother Matt. Out of the two boys, Jake was a dead ringer for his father while Matt, the fairer of the two, resembled his mother. But it was Matt who was taking an interest in the guitar, much to Charlie's concern. He'd rather the boy did something else. Anything else.

Charlie slid forward, his backside hovering on the edge

of the bed. He did his best to sound cheerful. "Hi son. How are you doing?"

"Okay."

"So what's all this about Italy?"

Jake piped up with excitement. "Yeaaaaahh! Can't wait. It's going to be amazing."

"Is it?"

Charlie listened as Jake listed all the things they were going to do at Lake Garda – diving, kitesurfing, visiting theme parks. It *did* sound amazing. Roger and Jenna sure made excellent promises. There was no mention of Ireland at all and Charlie, hearing how enthusiastic his son was, decided against bringing it up. Clearly, the boys had embraced the idea of going to Italy in June with their mum and her sugar daddy husband. Maybe they'd simply forgot about Ireland – it wasn't like Charlie had brought it up lately.

"Sounds great, son."

It was all he could say.

He should have talked to the boys earlier and found out what they wanted to do with their summer. *Weren't on the ball with this one, were you Charlie boy? Weren't even on the fucking pitch you idiot.* If he'd got in there quick enough, he could have been the one going to Italy and doing all those fun things with Jake and Matt. A proper dad would have got it done. But even if he had been on top of things, Charlie thought, Jenna would still have found some way to sabotage his plans. That's because she hated him. They'd fallen out of love and in hate with one another. Charlie still couldn't fully accept it. What the hell had happened to the woman he'd adored so much it drove him crazy? Day by day, she was turning into someone else and no doubt, Charlie thought, it was at Roger's behest. Jenna was changing on the outside, almost as much as she was on the inside. She was destroying her beautiful face. She'd never been interested in cosmetic surgery before but what the hell? It was her body and she could do what she wanted. But was it as Charlie suspected? Was Roger trying to sculpt a beautiful woman into an expressionless doll?

"Dad?"

"What was that son?"

Charlie was staring at Ryker's guitar case again. He felt a strong, underlying anxiety and yet he couldn't pin it down. Why was he so out of sorts? Was it the anniversary? The guitar? Was it the fact that his ex-wife hated his guts and seemed intent on sabotaging his relationship with his sons?

How did he fix this?

"Dad?" Jake said. "Are you still there? Do you want to talk to Matt?"

Charlie tried to declutter his mind. He stood up off the bed and walked towards the open wardrobe. He slid the door closed, sparing himself the sight of that chaotic top shelf and the graveyard of clothes. "Next time, okay pal? Tell him I said hi. Put your mum back on for a minute, will you?"

Jake signed off and Charlie heard him calling for his mum to come back to the phone. As he waited for Jenna, Charlie's thoughts returned to the three Back-To-Basic gigs starting on Friday. Glasgow, Edinburgh, Inverness. Three more gigs and the tour was over, thank God. Charlie wanted to call it off now. Quit the tour. He wanted to take a step back, spend more time with his kids doing the little things that would become their nostalgia in later years. A terrible thought occurred to Charlie. What if the adult versions of Jake and Matt looked back and saw Roger in their childhood memories?

Silvery, sugary Roger.

"Twat," he hissed.

He could do it, couldn't he? Charlie could cancel the gigs, make up a health-related excuse and say they were *postponed.* Meaning cancelled. That would mean he didn't have to venture out on Ryker's anniversary and...

"Jesus!"

Charlie almost dropped the phone in horror. There was a flicker of movement in the corner of the room. Something moved. Something just *moved.* It looked like, whatever it was, it had just shot across the bed towards the window.

Light, he told himself. It was just the light. A reflection – something like that.

Charlie stared at the guitar case. Felt his heart thumping in his chest.

Just a trick of the mind.

Just the light.

The anniversary.

In twenty-five years, they'll be coming for you.

Oh and by the way, his ghost lives in that guitar.

"Charlie? Are you there?"

Jenna was on the other end of the line. She sounded pissed off.

"Charlie are you there? I can hear you breathing for God's sake, will you just answer me please? I don't have all night."

"I'm here."

"Listen to me, okay? For all I know, you were going to cancel that Ireland trip anyway. Don't think I've forgotten what it's like being married to you. You might have said you were taking the boys away, then disappeared into a recording studio for five weeks and broken their hearts."

"Bullshit," Charlie said, talking through clenched teeth. "When have I ever let the boys down like that?" As he spoke, he glanced around the room. At the bed. The window. The guitar case. He didn't dare blink. *Trick of the light, trick of the light, trick of the light*. He was tired. He wasn't getting enough sleep but what else was new? Exhaustion was always an issue leading up to the anniversary of Ryker's disappearance. No wonder Charlie was seeing things.

It's his ghost.

Three gigs to play. Three gigs and then it was time for a holiday. Ireland. He could still do Ireland later in the...

"Charlie!"

"I'm here for God's sake. Stop shouting."

"Why do you keep zoning out like that? Are you on something? Are you back on drugs for God's sake?"

"Of course not. Listen Jenna, I'm not twenty-four anymore. And yes, I might not work a nine-to-five but just because my job takes me away for weeks and months at a time, that's no reason to push me away from the boys. They're *my* boys."

"I know that."

"Well, make sure Roger knows that. And stop pushing me away."

"I'm not pushing you away Charlie," Jenna said. "You do a pretty good job of that all by yourself."

Charlie spat out a bitter laugh. "Jenna – don't piss down my back and tell me it's raining. I know you and Roger want to take the boys away from me. Be one big happy family. It's not going to happen. You should be happy that I want to spend time with Jake and Matt. It means more freedom for you and the sugar daddy. You can jet off to the Caribbean whenever you want and act like you're still seventeen. Not long till your birthday now, eh? What's he getting you this year? New lips? A Barbie doll face?"

"You're treading on thin ice."

Charlie's emotions had spilled over the brim. He knew that he was being a hurtful prick, saying horrible things and yet no matter what he said, he felt powerless against this woman. "What sort of example are you setting for our boys, eh? Thank God we don't have a daughter, that's all I can say. She'd think you have to be plastic to be fantastic. Can I ask you something Jenna? Does Roger make you get all this work?"

"It's none of your business," Jenna snapped. "Welcome to the twenty-first century Charlie, now get the fuck off my back, will you? And don't talk to me about setting an example for the kids. What example did you set our boys when we were married? Remember? When you fucked everything that moved."

"And you didn't?"

"Yes, I did it because you made me feel like I was invisible. Like I was a babysitter for your sons while you were out on tour."

"Jenna, you're talking about the old Charlie. About a man who doesn't exist anymore. I'm almost fifty for God's sake."

"Charlie," Jenna said. "It doesn't matter to me who you are now. I don't care – really. You're just bitter because you're alone. You're a sad old man and you're all alone. There's nobody there when you get home and close the door. There's no one beside you in bed when you turn off the light at night. Why is that? Why don't you take a look in the mirror for God's sake? Fix yourself before you start..."

Charlie ended the call. He'd heard enough. Heard it a hundred times before and she always won, like she did this time. Jenna was right. He was a mess. He was alone. Without thinking twice, Charlie flipped the lid of the guitar case open and pulled out Ryker's Telecaster. He sat down on the floor, held the guitar tight to his chest. Strummed an E major chord and it was hideously out of tune.

He knocked on the wood next to the pickups.

"Are you in there?"

Charlie laughed and then felt a sudden desire to put the guitar down. To step away from it. It was as if he could feel Ryker's presence in the room. He thought about the thing he'd seen. The flicker of light. Or whatever it had been.

In twenty-five years, they'll be coming for you.

"Ryker," Charlie said, lowering the guitar onto the floor. "I'm sorry."

8

Darcy Doyle's Video Diary
Sunday April 16th

Darcy Doyle, lead guitarist for The Dark Stars, is walking to Berkeley 2 rehearsal studios in Glasgow city centre.

She's a striking-looking girl, tall and pretty with light-brown skin. Twenty-seven-years-old, sporting a towering Afro. Some of the people on the street recognise her from the band and wave. Darcy waves back to all of them. She gives them a smile. There's a guitar case strapped to her back and a small Reebok rucksack draped over her right shoulder.

Darcy's happy with her lot in life. But she didn't always have it so good. She survived a tough upbringing in Crumlin, Dublin, growing up with an Irish father and Nigerian mother, both with their fair share of substance-dependency issues. As well as coping with problems at home, Darcy endured her fair share of racial abuse from the local bullies. 'Fookin' half-caste' was the soundtrack to her youth. Friends were few and far between but there was always her dad's guitar, a Gibson Les Paul copy, to keep her company. When she was seventeen, Darcy moved to London with that same guitar to pursue a career in music but struggled to land a break. She busked as a solo guitarist for many years, surviving occasional stints of homelessness along the way before one blessed day, Charlie Lewis, scouting for raw and unpolished talent in London, decided to pick her for his new band.

Darcy lives in London but she's staying in Glasgow for the two rehearsals ahead of the final Back-To-Basics gigs. The record company have put her up in a lovely two-bedroom apartment in the west end.

She walks with a phone attached to a selfie stick. As she turns left onto Lancefield Street, she hits record and waves at the camera.

DARCY: How's it going everyone? Darcy Doyle here, guitarist for The Dark Stars, checking in from the not so sunny streets of Glasgow. So, you might be asking – what am I doing with this filming bollocks, right? Well, I've been meaning to keep a diary for years. I was even going to do it the old-fashioned way, you know? Pen and paper. *Jaysus*. But I know what I'm like. I'll never stick to writing something at the end of the day. I'm going to give this a go instead. A video diary. A vlog or whatever the feck it's called. Not sure if I'm going to publish it on my channel or keep it private – we'll see how bad it is when I watch it back. See if I stick at it. Now, before I talk about what's happening today, you might be interested in my motivation behind keeping a diary. Yeah? No?

She laughs, then shrugs.

DARCY: That's a no, is it? Well, I'll tell you anyway. A friend of mine, Iain McDonald, died recently in a car crash in the States. Just outside LA. He was only twenty-three. A boy for God's sake. A talented artist, street art, that kind of thing, you know?

She shakes her head. Flicks a peace sign at the camera.

DARCY: Love you Iain. Miss you man. God bless your sweet heart and I'll say this much – you've inspired me to start documenting my life because well, that funeral two weeks ago, it hit me hard man. Life's too damn short. Made me realise that I need to jot down the memories while I can. Look at me – I used to sleep on the streets in East Ham for God's sake. I was always hungry. Always had nothing. Now I'm a full-time musician. I play in The Dark Stars with Charlie Lewis. *The* Charlie Lewis who played in Broken Gods. I'm playing gigs. Making albums. Getting paid good money. I'm living the dream man and one day, when I'm old and wrinkled, I'll want to remember the good times. Iain, you didn't get the chance to look back as an old timer. I'll do it for both of us brother. I'll make videos and you can be the angel-director on my shoulder.

She looks at the sky for a moment. Blows a kiss and then walks down a quiet stretch of road. The studios are nearby.

DARCY: Anyway, that's my motivation for doing this vlog. I'm telling you guys – some days I wake up and literally pinch meself on the back of the hand. Fucking hell, it's jarring like. Being homeless one minute and then the next, you're playing in a band with the great Charlie Lewis. The guy's a legend and guess what? He's my bandmate. He picked *me*.

Darcy stops. Looks further down the road She waves to someone in the studio car park.

DARCY: Hutch! You alright mate? Be there in a second.

She waves again.

DARCY: (*to camera, speaking in a hushed voice*) Speaking of Charlie, he's been acting a bit funny recently. You know?

Not funny, ha-ha. The other one. Funny strange. I don't know how to explain it to be honest and I don't want to sound negative, especially on the first vlog. Right Iain? The Dark Stars have been together for two and a half years now and I'm telling you, sometimes I feel like I don't know Charlie. Not one little bit.

She stares into the camera. A thoughtful expression on her face.

DARCY: I'm not going to be negative today. Not about Charlie and not about the session either. We're going to have a great rehearsal. Charlie is *not* going to be weird and sulky or any of that shite. Now, we *have* to have a great rehearsal because we've got three shows coming up this week and after that? Well, to be truthful, I don't know. A lot of people have been asking me what comes after the gigs at the weekend, but I'm in the dark on that one. We're still waiting to hear from Charlie about what's next. Probably another album. After that, a bigger tour. A world tour. I just want to keep playing, you know?

Okay, I'd better go. That's it for the first entry in my video diary or whatever this is. I have no idea if it was shite or not. I'll watch it back later for a giggle, yeah? Anyway, over and out and I'll see you after the rehearsal for a quick update, alright? Take care.

Clip ends.

9

Charlie was sitting on the toilet in Berkeley studios. Lid down. Trousers pulled up. It wasn't biological necessity that brought him here – he didn't need a number one or number two. Didn't need to throw up. Nothing like that.

He was hiding.

As he'd learned over the Broken Gods years, when dressing rooms became a bit too crowded with press and hangers-on, the bathroom was the only reliable place of refuge. Somewhere he could go and be left alone. And right now, Charlie needed to be alone.

He'd locked the cubicle door and had the sole of his boot pressed up firmly against it for good measure. It was an uncomfortable sitting position to say the least, but it made Charlie feel better to keep his foot there so he did it, even though his leg was stiff and the tension in his joints unbearable.

The band had just completed a gruelling six-hour rehearsal in studio four. Charlie's vintage Fred Perry polo shirt clung to his skin to the point of choking him. The sweat on the shirt had cooled, leaving an unpleasant dampness to linger on his upper body. Charlie was convinced that he'd have to be surgically removed from the shirt later.

The rehearsal had been an unmitigated disaster. Charlie performed every song with all the heart and soul of a robot fit for scrap. And yet the others kept telling him how good it sounded. Bullshit. Why didn't he just cancel this tour? Call Dennis, get it out there quickly so people could come to terms with it. *No, you can't.* Three nights, starting on Friday in Glasgow. It was a chilling thought. Everyone was expecting Charlie Lewis to be there and to be the guy he used to be. Rock star Charlie. The public version of Charlie, a far cry from the reality of the man these days. All the people who'd bought tickets wanted him to go ahead with the tour. All the people whose income relied on The Dark Stars, they definitely wanted Charlie to be out there.

It was settled.

He *had* to be there.

Charlie had walked out of studio four after they'd finished the last song, mumbling something to Darcy and Hutch about going to the bathroom. He'd been so desperate to get out of there. He was hot and thirsty. They'd said something about waiting for him. Charlie shook his head. He'd paused at the door, told them to go whenever they were ready. Not to wait. But he knew they'd wait anyway, for a while at least.

Ten minutes, Charlie thought. Have I been in here ten minutes yet?

More like five.

The Dark Stars had become a prison. And Charlie was a man trapped behind the bars of his own legend. Why on earth had he formed this godawful band in the first place? Picking out street buskers in London, overly pleased with himself for trying something different and letting everyone know how fucking cool he thought he was. Charlie had hoped that all the disparate pieces of the puzzle would come together and form something whole, something special and most of all, something that could compete with the Gods in his heart and take him back to a time that was gone. It was okay for a while. And Darcy and Hutch had been grateful. They'd slept in the gutter and woken up in the stars and it was all thanks to Charlie. They'd been so excited to find themselves in first-class recording studios in London, New York and Los Angeles. Sitting on a luxury tour bus. Sleeping in a five-star hotel with everything they wanted at their fingertips. It was a gig that most top-flight musicians would have sold their souls to be a part of.

The band was decent. But, Charlie felt, they were stale. And already plummeting from those mediocre heights.

In twenty-five years, they'll be coming for you.

Charlie groaned when he thought about that song. He'd struggled with the lyrics of 'Coming For You' during the rehearsal. Especially that part about twenty-five years. The words got stuck in his throat and Charlie noticed his two bandmates giving him strange looks. Why did Ryker choose twenty-five years? Why that number? Why not twenty? Why not thirty? It had to mean something, right? They'd written 'Coming For You' in the back of a transit van one freezing cold winter's night in 1992. This was before the band was big-time, middle-time or even small-time. They'd sat together on the hard floor, two broke musicians with guitars working under a dodgy light bulb that flickered constantly like something out of a horror film. Their breath was a fine mist as their cold fingers ironed out the chord changes. Charlie recalled how they'd worked long into the night. Took them about three hours to nail the whole thing from start to finish. It was Ryker who'd penned the line, 'In twenty-five years, they'll be coming for you.' It just happened. Charlie didn't ask about it at the time, but he'd always wondered if it meant something. Twenty-five years. Why twenty-five years? He'd always believed that the vast majority of The Broken Gods' lyrics didn't mean anything.

He wasn't so sure anymore.

Charlie looked at his phone. How long now? Fifteen minutes?

Would they be gone yet?

He sat with his head lowered. Charlie felt old and tired. He was aware of his gradual decline as a singer, musician and songwriter. The magic wasn't there and he sounded so vanilla these days it made him sick. Why did everyone lie to him? Friends, critics – why did they say he was still good? Better than ever. Hadn't they noticed what was obvious to Charlie? He was straining to reach high notes that he'd nailed with ease in his twenties. He'd peaked too young, that was the problem. As a singer, musician, songwriter. He wasn't going to get any better in his fifties and if he stuck around for too long, he was destined to become little more than a tribute act to his younger self.

Cancel it.

Cancel the rest of the tour.

Call Dennis and do it now.

But it wasn't that simple. He *had* to finish the Back-To-Basics tour. Everyone had to get paid while Charlie went out there and played the ageing rock and roller while Roger the twat got to stay at home and play 'Daddy' to Charlie's kids.

He pressed his foot harder against the cubicle door.

"Five minutes," he said. "Then stop hiding in the toilet for God's sake."

The world looked at Charlie and saw a man who had everything – money in the bank, worldwide fame, respect and recognition from his peers, and the sort of life experiences that most people could only dream of, including travelling the world many times over. All of it meant nothing if there wasn't happiness. Charlie would've traded all his experience and riches if it meant getting off the crazy train for good and grabbing a little peace of mind. If it meant getting Ryker back.

Twenty-five years. Ryker, what happened?

He couldn't shake off the anxiety he felt about the anniversary.

Sunday night.

That feeling - what was it trying to communicate?

Charlie and Ryker. Ryker and Charlie. Brothers forever.

It's my turn next. And you know, deep down you know, that this is the time.

There was a voice at the back of Charlie's head (it sounded like his mother's voice) screaming at him to stop this. You're being ridiculous, he told himself. Locking yourself in a toilet for God's sake. Three gigs. It was only three gigs. He didn't even have to leave Scotland this time like with most other tours that involved long stretches of travel. This was a piece of cake. Glasgow, Edinburgh, then three hours up the A9 to Inverness on Sunday night.

In twenty-five years...

Charlie froze as the bathroom door swung open. Loud, plodding footsteps approached the urinal. He sat still on the lid of the toilet, listening to someone whistle 'There She Goes' by The La's while they pissed out an entire swimming pool. He only relaxed after he heard the whistler walk out without washing their hands.

Was Charlie really going to sit here for much longer? Waiting for his bandmates to leave the studio before going back out there? How the mighty had fallen. The men's toilets smelled foul, a pungent cocktail of piss and chemicals intermingling into one hell of a rancid smell. Smelled more like the public toilets inside a train station and that was a surprise to Charlie, considering how well maintained the rest of the studios were. But Shane, the owner, couldn't be expected to stay on top of everything. Charlie knew as well as anyone that musicians, especially young male musicians, weren't the most hygienic bunch. Most of them were allergic to soap and deodorant.

"Twenty minutes," he whispered.

Darcy and Hutch would have left the studios by now, wouldn't they? Surely they'd be gone. Hutch had said something earlier about an interview he was doing for some YouTube drumming channel. That was taking place in an Argyle Street music shop, not far from the studios. With any luck, Darcy would tag along for the rid. She'd tried to probe Charlie again during the session, asking about the future of the band. It was always Darcy that kicked off and then Hutch would zone in on Charlie. He'd seen the look in their eyes. Desperate.

After the tour. That's when he'd tell them.

How would they take it when Charlie told them it was over? It would be especially hard for Darcy and Hutch to hear, even if they did know already as Charlie suspected they did. He was sending them back to busk on street corners.

How would you take it Charlie boy?

Charlie pulled off a long sheet of toilet paper and dabbed it off his damp forehead. The gnawing thirst inside was getting worse. He hadn't drunk enough water during the rehearsal and now he was paying for it. It was the sort of thirst he felt in the old days when the hangovers had been so bad, he'd literally wept at the pain in his head.

Of course they'd smiled. Darcy and Hutch. They'd smiled when he'd delayed the conversation about the band's future. Acting cool. Sunshine and rainbows.

How desperate were they?

Charlie didn't know what was going on with those two. They gave the impression of being easy-going kids, grateful for their lot in life and they kept talking about how excited they were for the last three shows, particularly the Inverness gig. *Why that one?* And they were also excited, they'd said, for whatever shows and recordings would come after the Back-To-Basics gigs. Their grins were a little too forced when they said that. Excited for Inverness? *Why that one?* Yeah, particularly the Inverness gig. Why was the joint anniversary of Ryker's disappearance and Sally's suicide such a big deal for Darcy and Hutch?

Twenty-five years, Charlie.

They'd been given a taste of that sweet glittery fruit at the top of the tree. Charlie knew better than most how intoxicating that fruit was, especially in the early years. Life was easy. The privileges were many. It was only natural that two ex-buskers wanted to keep their place at the top of the tree. What were they willing to do in order to stay there? Charlie was the big branch holding them up. They didn't write the songs. They didn't have the star power.

He controlled everything.

You cool with that Darcy? Going back to the streets, playing screeching Hendrix riffs outside Sainsburys and living off the few coins that land in your guitar case? Guess you could always get a REAL JOB. How about you Hutch? Okay with hitting the drums outside the post office and dreaming of someone giving you the sort of money that folds instead of the jingle-jangle kind?

Damn it, Charlie thought. He stood up off the toilet seat.

They have to stay relevant.

It's dangerous Charlie. They're dangerous.

They'd learned how to play the game fast. Both Darcy and Hutch had YouTube channels and a growing presence on social media. But they weren't big enough to make it on their own yet. Not even close. Shit, Charlie thought. What are they so excited about Inverness for? They *did* know he was quitting the band, didn't they? And they were going to do something about it.

But what?

Charlie felt a cold, creeping sensation in his bones. Like he was dead already and Darcy and Hutch were dancing over his grave.

The cubicle walls began to shrink. With his heart racing, Charlie unlocked the door and leapt out of the confined space and back into the main bathroom. He took a deep breath, barely noticing the smell of stale piss anymore. Charlie stood in front of the mirror, running the cold-water tap and splashing a handful onto his face. It was good. Icy-cold. He turned off the tap. Took a step back and took in his reflection. He studied the way his hairdresser, Tracey, had styled his hair at the house last night. It was back in the Beatles mop top style that he'd worn in the mid-nineties. Only he'd dyed it jet-black so he resembled Ryker. He was also wearing a waistcoat like Ryker used to back in the day. And of course, he'd been playing the Telecaster.

The only thing missing was the fedora.

Charlie felt a little dizzy. Time to go home, he thought. He walked out of the bathroom and trudged on heavy legs back down the corridor to rehearsal room number four. He pushed the soundproof oak door open and to his relief, saw that his two bandmates had indeed taken off with all their equipment.

"Thank God."

Charlie breathed a loud sigh of relief. He stepped back through the door and lingered in the corridor like someone who didn't know where he was supposed to go. He stole a glance towards the office where Shane worked. To the front door beside it, leading out to the car park.

Was it too late to talk Dennis into cancelling the gigs? He didn't want to see those two vampires again, not tomorrow, not ever. More than ever, Charlie was sure they were up to something. Why hadn't he just hired session musicians? People who did the job, got paid and then went home.

Charlie jumped when he heard a sudden explosion of electric guitar behind him. He stood there in the corridor, rooted to the spot in terror as a monstrous, winding roller-coaster of a riff split his head open like an axe. A riff that Charlie knew well.

It was the intro to 'Coming For You.'

His jaw hit the floor. Slowly, Charlie turned his head around. Looked at the door to studio four. The rehearsal room was empty, wasn't it? Charlie had just been in there and there was no one inside. There was only...

Ryker's guitar.

Sitting on the floor.

Playing all by itself.

Charlie felt sick. He was about to brave the door when another door swung open. It was the door leading into the neighbouring studio, number five. At the same time, the 'Coming For You' riff swelled in volume and to Charlie's eternal relief, he realised that the music was coming from next door.

He felt his face burning with embarrassment. As if the world could read his thoughts.

A young lad with long brown hair poked his head through the gap in the studio door. He couldn't have been much more than eighteen-years-old. The guy saw Charlie and his eyes bulged like an overexcited cartoon character. He turned his head back, signalled inside the studio to others. The splitting guitar riff stopped and seconds later, five young men rushed through the door and spilled into the corridor. They were all dressed in Lambretta and Fred Perry tops, and they gathered around Charlie like starving lions who'd surrounded a fat zebra. They looked at him, awestruck. For a moment, none of them spoke.

Charlie took in the scene, still trying to hide his embarrassment after thinking that Ryker's guitar had...

It was like looking at a young version of The Broken Gods. They had everything – the mod-style clothes, the hair and one of them even had a Fender Telecaster strapped over his shoulder; it was the perfect replica of Ryker's classic guitar, albeit this one was in better shape. Charlie wondered what this little group would do if they knew the original Telecaster was lying on the floor in the next studio.

"We're a tribute band," someone said.

The speaker stepped forward. He was a stocky guy, clutching a pair of Vic Firth drumsticks in one hand. A cluster of acne peppered his chin. The rest of his ghostly white face remained hidden behind sweaty curtains of ginger hair. "Shane told us you were in today and we asked, well begged, if we could get the studio next door."

The floodgates opened after that. The band barraged Charlie with enthusiastic requests for autographs. They wanted him to sign their books (Ryker and Charlie biographies mostly), CDs, vinyl records and their musical instruments. They wanted selfies. They wanted Charlie to answer all their questions about the Gods. They wanted to know if there was any way they could get on the guest list for the Glasgow gig on Friday night. Or the Edinburgh one on

Saturday. They'd even go up to Inverness if there was room. Charlie had to explain that there wasn't a guest list, although he didn't know if that strictly true. Most likely, there was a guest list. But he had to say something to fend them off.

As the young musicians swarmed around him, Charlie stole another brief glance towards the office. Towards the front door. He was talking to the boys, giving them the attention they so badly wanted. But his eyes kept returning to the door.

Why Sunday?

Why were they so excited for *that* gig?

10

Darcy Doyle's Video Diary

Berkeley 2 Studios.

Darcy and Benjamin 'Hutch' Heikkinen are standing outside rehearsal room four. The two musicians offer tight-lipped smiles to the camera as Darcy begins the second instalment of her video diary. Their foreheads gleam with fresh beads of sweat.

Behind them, we can just about see into the spacious rehearsal studio. The Yamaha drum kit sitting at the back of the room with the drumsticks resting on the snare. There's a guitar (a Fender Telecaster) on the floor. Usually it's leaning against the amp when not in use – but not right now. The walls are covered with panels and acoustical foam to soundproof the room.

DARCY (*to camera*): Hi there. This is Darcy's vlog and we're coming to you from inside Berkeley studios, Glasgow, Scotland. We've just finished a solid six hours of rehearsal, going over a two-hour set twice and fixing little bits and pieces here and there that needed working on. All in all, it was a good day's work and I think we smashed it. Not bad at all, eh? How about you Hutch? Good session?

Hutch is a big man, broad shouldered with short blond hair, milky-white skin and piercing blue eyes. He speaks in a gruff Finnish accent.

HUTCH: Was good today. We were rocking hard.

The drummer looks at Darcy, his deadpan expression like a faceless mask.

HUTCH: Well, *we* were rocking.

DARCY: Yep.

They exchange awkward looks. Darcy leans her head past Hutch's shoulder, stares down the corridor as if to check who else is around. She turns back to the camera. Lowers her voice.

DARCY: Well, it happened. Charlie was acting weird again today, even by Charlie's standards. Don't you think Hutch?

HUTCH: Charlie's always weird.

DARCY: (*to camera*) Don't get me wrong. We're ready for the three gigs this weekend. Musically, at least. We've got one more rehearsal scheduled ahead of Friday's gig here in Glasgow but that's just a formality. We're ready. Charlie's going through some stuff right now. Get this – he brought Ryker's old guitar into rehearsal today. *Jaysus.* I must admit, that freaked me out a bit. The right-handed Telecaster. I even got to play it on a couple of songs. Sounds good but still, it's kind of weird having Ryker's guitar there for a Dark Stars rehearsal. What do you think, Hutch?

HUTCH: (*nodding*) He looked like Ryker today.

Darcy nods.

DARCY: Yeah, his brown hair's dyed jet-black and he's got the waistcoat thing going on. You wait and see – he'll be wearing a fedora hat at the next rehearsal.

HUTCH: Maybe it's, how you say, tribute for this weekend?

DARCY: (*shrugs*) I hope that's all it is. We played 'Coming For You' this afternoon and Charlie totally fluffed the lyrics at the end of the chorus. Not great. It's not that hard, is it? 'In twenty-five years they'll be coming for you.' One line but he keeps missing it over and over again. What was that about?

HUTCH: Anniversary thing.

DARCY: Suppose.

HUTCH: He keeps staring at me. You see that, Darcy?

DARCY: What's that?

HUTCH: I catch him *staring* at me sometimes, usually in between songs. It's the way he's staring at me – like he hates me or something. Like he's thinking to himself, what's this fucking busker doing here in the room with me? *I'm Charlie Lewis!* Oh man Darcy, I'm not looking forward to being in that little van with him going to Edinburgh and Inverness. Not looking forward to it at all.

Darcy gives an embarrassed shrug of the shoulders.

DARCY: Yeah. That's the thing with Back-To-Basics. No tour buses, no big crew. Two vans – one for the band and one for the roadies and the tour manager. We're pretty much driving ourselves around this weekend.

HUTCH: Where is Charlie anyway? Where he go?

DARCY: Dunno. He said he was going to the toilet but that was ages ago.

She looks at the camera.

DARCY: Yeah, we're not trying to be bitchy or nothing like that. Charlie's a good guy and he's having it rough at the moment. But he kinda walked out on us. He put down the guitar and just marched out, said something about going to the toilet, I think. That was fifteen minutes ago. Poor bugger. I hear he's got some domestic issues flaring up. Ex-wife. Kids and all that. He's not a happy man right now. You can see it on his face. And then there's the anniversary. *Jaysus* – poor bastard.

The two musicians turn back towards the rehearsal room.

DARCY: We'll give him another five minutes. After that, we'll just go to your interview Hutch. Leave him to it, eh? Okay, see ya diary. Signing off until later.

HUTCH: Bye-bye!

Clip ends.

11

STV

Six o'clock News Report

Monday 17th April.

The sky over Bridge Street, close to the main shopping area in Inverness, is blanketed with grey and angry-looking clouds. Heavy rain is forecast as dusk descends over the 'Capital of the Highlands'. The air is unusually warm and clammy for this time of year.

STV reporter, Hugh MacFarlane, is standing outside The Hoot and Annie, a well-known pub and live music venue. The Hoot (as it's referred to by the locals) has been a popular gathering point for thirty-five years and counting. Passers-by glance at the STV camera as Hugh prepares to go live. Some of them wave and say hello. Some pull comical faces but MacFarlane, a professional journalist with over forty years of experience, doesn't miss a beat. He doesn't even flinch when his ginger combover flips up in response to a sudden gust of wind.

HUGH MACFARLANE: Good evening from Inverness.

This weekend, something very special is happening in the pub behind me. Now, on any normal Sunday night, you'd be more likely to find Charlie Lewis playing a gig in a massive indoor arena in London or at a stadium gig in Los Angeles or New York. But not this weekend. This Sunday, Charlie's coming right here to Inverness. Right here to that pub behind me, The Hoot and Annie. The stage is downstairs. The capacity is a whopping five hundred and the lucky people with a ticket will bear witness to the hotly anticipated final leg of The Dark Stars' Back-To-Basics tour of the UK, Ireland and Europe.

The broadcast cuts to a brief montage of clips taken from various stages of Charlie's career – music videos, live gigs with The Broken Gods, his solo career and then his later work with The Dark Stars. The montage freezes on a shot of a young, smiling twenty-four-year-old Charlie with his arm wrapped around his best friend, the fedora-wearing Ryker Marshall.

Cut back to MacFarlane on Bridge Street.

HUGH MACFARLANE: There's a certain poignancy to Sunday night's concert as the date, April 23rd, falls on the twenty-fifth anniversary of the mysterious disappearance of Ryker Marshall. For those who don't know, Charlie and Ryker were best friends and partners in the cultural phenomenon that was The Broken Gods. But twenty-five years ago, Ryker disappeared without a trace. And he hasn't been seen since.

Behind MacFarlane, a wiry forty-something man is edging ever closer to the camera. The man is accompanied by a lanky teenage boy who waves at the camera and has a toothy grin on display. The older man is wearing a navy and cream t-shirt with The Broken Gods' logo emblazed front and centre.

MacFarlane notices their less-than-subtle approach. Instead of glaring at them or shooing them away, the ordinarily gruff reporter encourages the pair to come closer. He thrusts the microphone towards the older man.

HUGH MACFARLANE: What's your name sir?

Both man and boy gawp like rabbits caught in the headlights. They continue to inch forward on the pavement as if traversing a minefield.

The boy's still waving.

MAN: Jimmy Watt. Ma name's Jimmy Watt and this here's ma wee boy, Jimmy Junior.

HUGH MACFARLANE: Let me guess Jimmy – you're a Charlie Lewis fan. Am I right? I don't think it's a coincidence you're standing outside the Hoot wearing that t-shirt, eh? Tell me, did you manage to get tickets for Sunday night?

JIMMY WATT: Oh aye. Me and ma mates, we're aw going. We were Broken Gods mad back in the nineties. Absolute mad about that band, so we were. Ah know every song, every lyric – ah could probably sing them backwards, eh Hugh? Anyway, aye, we're aw going on Saturday and I'm just so excited to see Charlie playing live again. Ah want to shake his hand. Ah want to look that man in the eye and say thank you for aw he's done for me in ma life. For aw the music which has got me through many a rough patch in ma life.

HUGH MACFARLANE: Well, I wish you all the luck in the world Jimmy. I hope it's a success. Hope you get that handshake.

Jimmy gives a thumbs up to the camera.

JIMMY WATT: Cheers Hugh.

Macfarlane resumes his report as another gust of wind lifts his hair.

HUGH MACFARLANE: It's been said that Charlie has never recovered from his best friend's disappearance. No doubt then, it's going to be an emotional night here in Inverness on Sunday. But it's a night that will see Charlie doing the very thing that brought him and Ryker Marshall to the forefront of pop culture in the mid-nineties. Playing music. Keeping the crowd happy. It's set to be a thrilling, emotionally charged weekend here at The Hoot and the people of Inverness are coming out in droves to see Charlie Lewis in their backyard. I'm expecting something very special indeed.

This is Hugh MacFarlane, standing outside The Hoot and Annie pub in Inverness. Back to you in the studio Pam.

Clip ends.

12

Tuesday 18th April

Darcy is in the living room of her flat in Glasgow's west end, conducting a live Zoom Q&A with fans on The Dark Stars' official YouTube channel.

The host, Brian Ortega, is from Sacramento, California. Brian, 32, is a die-hard Broken Gods fan with his own YouTube channel dedicated to Charlie Lewis, Ryker Marshall and everything Gods related.

After talking to Darcy about her early days in Ireland, her homelessness and busking on the streets of London, Brian throws in some questions from the live chat box.

BRIAN: Okay Darcy. Before we start with the questions, let me say a big thank you for your time today. For talking to us about your life, which has been fascinating to say the least. Are you ready for the quickfire questions?

DARCY: For sure, I'm ready Brian. Let's do this.

BRIAN: Cool. We've got a lot of questions popping up in

the chat box so I'll try and get through as many as I can before we wrap up. Apologies if I don't get to your question – we're running out of time fast. We could literally be here all night but that's not possible because as we know, Darcy's got a big weekend ahead of her. Three shows that are going to be EPIC.

Darcy laughs.

BRIAN: Okay. Are you ready?

DARCY: Still ready.

BRIAN: Here we go boys and girls. The first question is from Stacey in Dublin. A fellow Irishwoman for your Darcy.

DARCY: Hooray. Dia dhuit Stacey!

BRIAN: Whatever that means. Ha! Okay, Stacey's question is: How's the band sounding in rehearsal ahead of the shows this weekend?

DARCY: The band's sounding great Stacey. We've been running through the setlist, a slightly different setlist from the one we played in England and Wales, and I'm telling you guys, it's tight. The band sounds deadly. Here's the thing – people think I'm mad when I say that The Dark Stars are every bit as good as The Broken Gods. But we are. Especially when it comes to playing live. We're up there with the Gods, no question about it. I might be a busker at heart but I belong up there with Charlie and so does Hutch, who by the way, is the best feckin' drummer I've ever seen. Guy's a beast.

BRIAN: Alright, thank you Stacey for that question. We've got another one here from Danny. Danny's in Cooperstown, New York and his question to you Darcy is – will you marry me?

Darcy pretends to vigorously fan herself.

DARCY: Wow, Danny. Bit soon, no? Listen, I'm an old-fashioned girl at heart and I'd like to be courted, you know? Having said that, Danny and Darcy – that sounds pretty good, doesn't it? Fair play to you Danny, we'll see how it goes. Send me a photo, yeah?

BRIAN: Okay, good luck with that Danny. Moving on. The next question comes from a gentleman called Robert White. Robert lives in Derby, England, and he wants to know what's next for The Dark Stars. That is, what's happening with you guys after the gigs this weekend? I'm sure you're aware of the rumours swirling around the gossip mill, right Darcy? Some people are saying that The Dark Stars are on the verge of splitting up. Now, say that happens. Is that a massive concern for you? What's next for you personally if the band's days are numbered?

DARCY: Listen, I'm not worried about the future of the band. And thanks Robert for your question by the way. Cheers. Look, whatever happens next, it's been a blessing. As we talked about earlier, I've had my ups and downs in life. Things got rough at home. I was busking in Dublin, then London and then I was homeless for a while and at my lowest ebb. Charlie saved me and it's incredible what's happened since. Unbelievable. I'm gigging and recording with one of the rock and roll greats in some of the best recording studios in the world. I have a beautiful home in London. I have friends and money and I can buy a nice guitar if I want one. I've been touring the world. *Jaysus*, life's good. It's bloody good. Now, to answer Robert's question – no, I don't think it's over. To tell you the truth, I think we're going to be working on another album very soon. Maybe even adding more musicians to the mix. Horns, keyboards, that kind of thing. Spice things up a bit, yeah? I'm looking forward to whatever happens next. This is just the beginning for The Dark Stars.

BRIAN: But are you worried that Charlie wants to move on?

DARCY: No. Charlie knows how good we are.

BRIAN: (*laughs nervously*) You got plenty of money in the bank anyway, I guess?

DARCY: I'm doing alright.

BRIAN: Alright, moving on then. Running out of time here folks – again, sorry if I don't get to your question before we have to quit. Okay, this is from Cathy in Sydney, Australia. She asks, Darcy, do you think that Charlie's performance over the weekend will be affected by the anniversary of Ryker's disappearance? Yeah, that's a question we're all asking. I mean, it's gotta be tough for the guy, right? Twenty-five years, oh man. He's going to see a lot of Ryker t-shirts, posters, banners and God knows what else in that crowd on Sunday night. Probably on Friday and Saturday too. Reminders everywhere. I wonder if that'll help him or make things harder, you know? Charlie's always been open in the past about how much he struggles mentally at this time of year.

DARCY: Charlie's having a rough time of it right now. I'd be lying if I told you that things weren't weighing heavily on his shoulders. He's got his demons. Twenty-five years, *Jaysus*. I can see it in his eyes, you know? The love he had for Ryker. His brother from another mother. Those guys were tight back in the day and so yeah, Charlie's in a wee bit of pain right now. Hutch and I get it. We're doing our best to empathise. I know Charlie's apprehensive about the gigs, especially Inverness.

BRIAN: Especially Inverness? He said as much?

DARCY: Charlie isn't exactly an open book at the best of times if you know what I mean. He's almost fifty and Ryker's been gone for so long now. But it never gets easier. He misses his friend. He was good friends with Sally Darbey too, Ryker's girlfriend, and we all know what happened to her, right? Bloody tragic. It's just dark times, you know? He's in a bad place. And the thing is with Ryker – nobody knows what happened to him. There's no closure for Charlie or for any of Ryker's family in this matter. There's only the bizarreness of it all and it just goes on and on. The stories, the legends. It's one big mystery. And as we all know Brian, the world loves a good mystery. Right?

13

Charlie woke up, his heart pounding like a drum. He was in bed, staring up at the darkness, at the ceiling that emerged from the black fog of sleep.

Why was he awake?

What had disturbed him?

He'd dreamt about a choked screaming sound, one that shot out of his mouth like a jet of steam escaping from under a kettle lid. Who was screaming? Was it him? Ryker? Sally, as she jumped off Erskine Bridge in the dead of night and realised too late that she didn't want to die after all? Was it a dream? Charlie wasn't so sure. He knew that something was wrong and that it was wrong inside the house. Inside the bedroom. This was pure instinct. And yet, in those first few moments after waking up in bed, Charlie lay there in absolute blindness. It felt like he was falling.

Then he screamed and knew for sure that it had been him all along. A strong pair of hands was clamped around Charlie's leg at the ankles, locking in a vice-like grip. Someone was pulling him out of bed.

Chaaaaaarlie.

Charlie screamed again and again. He kicked his leg free of the icy-cold grip that, despite its coldness, felt like it was pulling him down to the fires of Hell. Then he flipped over on the mattress, rolling to the right and tipping over the edge. The short-lived terror of falling. Charlie hit the wooden floor, registering the impact with a wince but the pain, if there was any, was lost in the adrenaline rush of the moment. He spun around, sat up with his back facing the wall, his eyes labouring to adjust to the gloomy darkness.

"Who's there?"

Was it Ronnie? Was creepy Ronnie finally inside the house after all these years? Standing at the edge of the bed, leering at Charlie with a hungry machete in his hand? Slowly pulling down the zip on his jeans. *I want you to do whatever I tell you to do, Charlie.*

Charlie sat up further, keeping his back to the wall. He was naked except for a pair of boxer shorts. He called out again, demanding to know who was in his bedroom, but no one answered. When nothing else happened, he told himself it was just a nightmare. Nobody else was in the bedroom. Of course not. He had a seriously high-tech alarm system installed after all and it hadn't been activated.

The house was silent.

A nightmare. Just a vivid nightmare.

Charlie's brain was still half-asleep, his thoughts trapped like feet in quicksand. He rubbed his eyes. It still felt so real.

"Is someone in the room?"

His voice sounded different. It sounded like Charlie was talking to himself from the other side of the house.

He flinched at the sound of someone breathing. *No, Charlie boy, you're not alone.* There was no mistaking that sound, *in-out, in-out, in-out*. Hoarse, laboured breathing. It was coming from the far corner of the bedroom, next to the door that was sitting semi-ajar. A door that Charlie was certain he'd closed over before getting into bed. Of course, he thought. That's where the Fender Telecaster was. It was sitting in the guitar stand over there. For some reason, Charlie had wanted it close.

"Ryker? Is that you?"

The grainy outline of a man rose like billowing black smoke from the floor and came to a stop about ten metres from where Charlie had fallen off the bed. Then it inched backwards, slithering like a cloudy snake onto the wooden chair that was propped up against the bedroom wall. Now it looked like it was sitting down. The Telecaster was perched on its lap. Charlie could hear the faint strumming of an unplugged electric guitar. Whispered notes, coming in and out. Stop-start, stop-start. Chord patterns shifting from major to minor and forming familiar progressions – progressions that Charlie hadn't heard in a long time. These were songs that had once belonged to The Broken Gods.

The guitar-playing silhouette didn't have a face. The slender, fragile shape was hunched over the guitar. Humming quietly, fishing for melody.

Hello Charlie.

"No," Charlie said, shaking his head. "I'm not going to accept this. You're not real. You're not here."

You're in danger. You need my help.

Charlie coughed out a painful-sounding laugh. "I'm in danger? Is that right?"

Yes. You already know that.

"And you want to help me, do you?" Charlie said. "Is that what you were doing? Dragging me out of bed in my boxer shorts at ridiculous o'clock? Hmmm, interesting. Tell you what old buddy – why don't you shove your help up your non-existent arse? You're not here!"

I know what's going to happen to you.

"Aye? Got a crystal ball, have you?"

Watch out Charlie. When the anniversary comes around...

Charlie felt his insides clench up and it was a short, sharp jolt of pain. It felt like he was a rubber ball being squeezed in a merciless grip. He sat up further, leaned his shoulder off the wooden bedframe for support. Everything was starting to hurt. He could feel his left knee throbbing after the fall out of bed.

"I'm losing my mind, aren't I?"

No. You've been right all along.

"About what?"

C'mon. It's me Charlie. Your best friend in the world.

"My best friend in the world?" Charlie said, cackling with laughter despite the terror he felt at the very real possibility of grief-induced insanity encroaching upon his mind. "That's a good one Ryker. The same best friend who walked out on us back in 1997 because he couldn't hack fame and fortune? That one? What I want to know is, were *you* in your right mind when you left your car at Erskine Bridge? Were you so far gone that you didn't think about what you were leaving behind? About the consequences? Who would ever have thought that we'd both lose our minds, twenty-five years apart?"

Charlie closed his eyes. He could still hear the delicate strumming of the guitar.

You knew what you were doing when you took the guitar home. That's why you hesitated when Annie showed you the guitar case. Because you knew what it meant. You knew exactly what you were letting in.

"It's just a guitar," Charlie said. "There are no haunted guitars."

Then why did you hesitate?

"Because it's hard enough as it is," Charlie snapped. He hammered the side of his fist off the floor. "I don't need any more reminders of you."

You don't know what happened.

"Most people think you're dead but I don't. I think you're alive and living it up in Israel or Argentina or some other far-flung corner of the world where you got to start over with a clean slate. Having fun, are you Ryker? What name do you go by these days? What do you look like now? I envision long hair, a long beard, robes and someone who's happy. I bet there's a glow on your cheeks. A twinkle in your eyes. Are you happy? What do you do all day?"

It's me Charlie. I'm here.

"Fame was hard for all of us," Charlie said, cupping his sore knee. It wasn't as bad as he'd first thought and he could feel the pain diminishing. "For *all* of us. Aye, it got crazy. It was anything but healthy. But the rest of us didn't crack up, did we? We didn't check out of the Marriott and park our cars by a bridge and then pretend to the world that we'd topped ourselves just to throw everyone off the scent. Did you really think people would fall for that? That's what you did, didn't you? You were always a smart fucker but never as smart as you thought you were. You're alive. You're a monk. You're living in a cave. You're in Antarctica. To hell with everyone else, right?"

Charlie...

"What do you want?" Charlie said, his voice crackling with anger. He could feel the blood bubbling in his veins, coming to the boil. Sore knee or not, he was on the brink of jumping to his feet, charging across the room and snatching the Telecaster out of Ryker's shadowy grip and smashing him over the head with it until something shattered into a hundred pieces. "Why did you come here? What the hell do you want from me?'"

We're friends.

Charlie shook his head. "Friends don't walk out on friends. Do you know what happened to Sally?"

Charlie.

"What?"

They're plotting against you. You know that, don't you?

Charlie shook his head.

Don't doubt your instincts.

"No," Charlie said. "I hear this stuff swirling and swirling around in my head but I know it's all nonsense."

They'll be coming for you.

Charlie put his hands over his ears, pressing down hard. In that moment, he felt like a child who refused to listen to his parents telling him to go to bed. He didn't want to hear this. Charlie wasn't crazy. He wanted to cling to the calm voice of sanity that was still there at the back of his mind, the voice that told him he was wrong about his bandmates. *Dead wrong.* Of course he was wrong. Plotting against him? Oh God, he had to get his shit together and fast. Maybe he'd be the one parking his car at Erskine Bridge next.

But the shadow kept talking.

You made a mistake Charlie. Plucking two penniless buskers off the street and thinking there wouldn't be consequences. You pulled them out of the gutter. Showed them the stars. If they get sacked after the Inverness gig, they go back to being nothing. What were you thinking? You think they're just going to lie down and take that? They're street punks for God's sake. They probably have criminal records, you know? God knows what they're capable of.

"Go away Ryker."

Only they've figured it out. Haven't they? They know their golden goose has had his fill. And now what? Now they're scrambling to find a solution. And guess what Charlie? They've found it. They've worked a way around the problem and this opportunity they've uncovered, it's going to cost you everything.

Charlie felt like he was sinking into the floor. He knew everything that Ryker was about to say. They'd always been tight, since back in the good old days. Since forever. Charlie and Ryker. On the same wavelength ever since that first encounter in the kindergarten sandpit.

Brothers.

Dead Charlie is worth a lot to Darcy and Hutch. But you know what's even better than that?

"Shut the hell up Ryker. This is fucking mental man."

What's better than dead Charlie?

Dead Charlie.

"Fuck off."

What's better than dead Charlie?

"FUCK OFF."

Missing Charlie.

Charlie felt a myriad of knots tightening in his chest. *Yes, missing Charlie.* It was getting hard to breathe in the stuffy bedroom and at the same time, it was getting hard to deny the conclusion of Ryker's logical thinking. Charlie longed to poke his head out the window and inhale some fresh air. But he didn't dare move. His bones felt like matchsticks that would snap at the slightest provocation.

"I'm not listening to this."

Missing Charlie. That's what they want. Your bandmates can build a very nice career around missing Charlie. They can go for years riding the coattails of that one. Look at what happened to Tommy and Bobby after The Broken Gods ended. What have they done since musically? Nothing. Not a damn thing. But they've done very well out of my disappearance, haven't they?

They've written books, partaken in speaking engagements, documentaries, television interviews and all the rest of it. Professional leeches sucking on the blood of tragedy. Raking in the cash. That's it – that's their career and it's a damn good one. People love a good mystery, don't they Charlie? Darcy and Hutch aren't stupid. They've seen what Tommy and Bobby are doing. They've seen the possibilities of being attached to a story about another rock star's disappearance. They won't have to work a day in their lives ever again, not as long as they have their own legend to cling on to.

"Are you finished?" Charlie said.

It's easy money brother. Fame. That's a helluva drug and becoming a professional leech is a lot better than going back to the streets and busking for fifty quid a day, isn't it? Deep down, you regret pulling those musicians off the street. Don't you?

Charlie shrugged.

These kids don't care about anything except getting ahead. Look at what's happening on social media – they'll do anything for fame and gain and influencer status. Darcy and Hutch – they're not willing to lose what they've got. Think about it. You've seen the way they look at you in the studio. Right? On the tour bus. On every stage you've ever played with them. They're terrified of the hold you have over them. You have all the power Charlie. You have all the power and they know you're about to pull the plug. You can end The Dark Stars whenever you want, at the click of your fingers. But you drop big crumbs Charlie. And scavengers can be ruthless.

Charlie nodded. He knew that look in their eyes. Like vultures circling a wounded animal. Waiting for the right moment.

Charlie Lewis goes missing on Sunday, April 23rd. I GUARANTEE it. In twenty-five years they'll be coming for you. This is where it all leads. Me, back then. You, this weekend. Symmetry, you know? But I don't want you to join me. Maybe it's not too late old friend. If they can hide your body and keep it hidden so that no remains are ever found then they're set for life. The world loves...

"...a good mystery," Charlie said.

That feeling you feel in your guts – listen to it. That's nature's warning. That's why I'm here. To give your head permission to listen to your heart. You know they're up to no good. Darcy's all over the Internet talking about future albums but she's full of crap. She knows it's over. No more albums or tours. She's just putting on a front, her and the fat drummer. I'm your friend, Charlie. I'm here to help. They'll play the three gigs with you and then afterwards, Charlie Lewis will go missing forever. Mark my words. They'll say you cracked up and took off because of the pressure. Maybe they'll plant drugs and make it look like you relapsed. Don't wait for it to happen. Don't let it happen. You're just a cash cow to them, dead, alive or vanished. We both know what it feels like at the top. The pressure. It's unbearable at times. I had to get away Charlie...I had to get away.

Charlie pushed himself back up to his feet. His knee wasn't too bad but the room was spinning.

"Ryker," he said. "About what happened back then. We need to talk..."

But the shadow was gone. The bedroom was cloaked in silence and Charlie saw the Fender Telecaster sitting back in the guitar stand. But there was one last whisper and he heard it over the sound of his racing heart.

We're friends Charlie.

And friends forgive one another.

14

Friday, April 21st
First gig
Glasgow (King Tut's Wah-Wah Hut)

Charlie could hear the crowd screaming his name. It was so loud that it felt like his head was going to split open. Wouldn't that be a hell of an encore? A thousand meaty chunks of Charlie-brain splattering off the wall.

"*Charlie! Charlie! Charlie!*"

It was a mindless chant that bounced off the walls, floor and ceiling of the sweaty cauldron that was King Tut's in the aftermath of The Dark Stars gig. Already, the chant had burrowed its way into Charlie's mind, sure to resurface later and haunt his dreams. He was drenched head to toe in sweat, having just come off stage. To call it a hot one was an understatement. Charlie could literally see a plume of smoke rising off his shirt at the shoulders.

He was trying to get out of there before the overexcited

fans tore him apart limb by limb. That's how crazy it was. Tut's was a tight, small venue. There wasn't much distance between crowd and band on stage, which was great for atmosphere but not so great for post-show survival and rapid-fire exit strategies. Charlie was surrounded by a small posse of security men dressed in black suits, each one a man mountain and a stereotypical, square-jawed bodyguard minus the dark sunglasses. They were trying to carve a path through the swarm of bodies that currently blocked the route to the stairs. They *had* to get to the stairs. The main bar was down there. The front door was down there too and outside, that's where the car was waiting to speed Charlie away to the hotel. Getting out felt like a long shot. The people were ecstatic. Still buzzing. Still singing the songs as if they were trying to blow the roof off the venue.

Charlie, shielded by his pack of security, made his way through Tut's at speed. He felt hands grabbing at his hair, clothes and hands. They didn't care. Tonight, he was just a thing to be picked at and they wanted a piece of him to take home. Any piece would do. Large or small. Take a souvenir, why not? They'd paid their money.

"Charlie, where you going mate?"

"Charlie, want a beer mate?"

"Charlie, I'll suck your dick!"

They rushed downstairs. Charlie's exhausted legs barely held him up but he couldn't slow down or the security train would lose momentum. And then the world would fall on top of him.

There was a scream of recognition inside the main bar as Charlie and his team landed. The roof-raising chant from upstairs followed them as he neared the front door. The Charlie hunters weren't giving up anytime soon. That much was clear. Squeals of excitement trailed after him. Boyish roars. Bellowing drunks desperate to be heard. "CHARLIE!" It was like being chased by an angry tribe who could only say one word – his name. Cannibals, every single one of them desperate for a bite.

The security posse pushed their way forward with a renewed sense of urgency. They hurried towards the door.

Charlie couldn't take the heat inside Tut's. The air was scalding hot. Felt like he was trapped in an oven with hundreds of other people all jostling for space. White spots danced in front of his eyes. He was on the brink of passing out as they yelled from the sidelines.

"Charlie! Sign my boobs!"

"Charlie. I love you!"

"Charlie, can I get a selfie? Pleeeeeaaaaase!"

Security ignored all cries for attention. They yelled at people to get out of the way and to do it now. Some swatted at the more stubborn of the Charlie-hunters, urging them to clear the route to the door. That's when Charlie heard the first boos. The mood inside the cauldron was turning unpleasant. Charlie's legs were spent but he pushed towards the door. Towards the car on St Vincent Street.

The people in the downstairs bar continued to cheer and yell and boo and sing songs. It was a cacophony of noise that rattled around inside Charlie's head. The security train slipped through the front door at last. They were outside. There were more people gathered out there, smoking and somebody on the street was singing 'Coming For You.' Charlie almost tripped on the short staircase that led up towards the street. Towards the bright lights of Glasgow on a Friday night. The security team shielded him from another barrage of hands and faces.

"Charlie, great gig man! Any chance of a photo for my Insta?"

"Charlie, can I get an autograph?"

"Charlie, you want any drugs man? Want to come back to a PAAAARTY?"

More of the cheers turned to boos as Charlie ignored them. Security increased the pace of the escape train. They steered Charlie towards the black BMW waiting at the kerb with the engine running. Charlie didn't care about the boos ringing in his ear. He'd heard it all before. Someone opened the car door and Charlie fell into the back seat. More white spots. God, he was thirsty. Several of the security personnel climbed in after him, giving the driver the all-clear to go. The BMW sped away, driving north and leaving Tut's and the crowd in the dust.

Charlie's head fell back onto the headrest. He could hardly breathe. Felt like he was drowning in sweat. One of the security mountains leaned over and asked him if he was okay. He nodded. It was all he could do.

One down, he thought, watching the bright lights of the city go by.

Two to go.

15

Sub Club, Glasgow
The Dark Stars Official Afterparty
Darcy Doyle's Video Diary

The Sub Club is Scotland's most famous underground music venue. Tonight, the main floor is crowded with sweaty, writhing bodies. Blinking neon lights. Fast-twitch electro beats, blasting out of the speakers at lethal volume.

Darcy walks through the crowd, her phone once again attached to a selfie stick. She's livestreaming the afterparty for her daily vlog and YouTube channel. She's no longer wearing her stage clothes and is instead, dressed in a white singlet, jeans and high-heeled boots.

She greets a group of suits from the record company. They're standing at the bar and they shake her hand, tell her how great she was tonight. Darcy smiles and moves on. An overexcited fan approaches, pats her on the shoulder and yells in her ear about how amazing the gig was. He tells Darcy she's the best guitarist she's ever seen live. Darcy is beaming with joy. She politely refuses his offer of a drink and moves on. Next, a dark-haired woman of about forty approaches, leans into Darcy's ear and asks a question. Darcy's smile fizzles out. She frowns, says something in response and after a brief exchange, she walks off and finds a sozzled Hutch at the bar. She drags him away by the arm. The guitarist and drummer make their way through the crowd to a small dressing room at the back of the venue. It's a private space for the band and record company people. Right now, it's empty. There's a long, wooden table covered in wine and beer bottles. Snacks. Fruit. Behind the table, a large mirror reflects Darcy and Hutch as they close the door behind them. The thumping beats are instantly muted.

The two musicians flop onto the couch. Hutch leans over to his right, picks up a bottle of water off the table and unscrews the lid. Darcy adjusts the camera. Both she and Hutch are clearly in shot.

DARCY: Alright Hutch, look lively fella. We're live on YouTube, coming to you from the King Tut's afterparty right here in the Sub Club in Glasgow.

HUTCH: (*after a long slug of water*) We're on YouTube?

DARCY: We sure are buddy. Two and a half thousand people watching so best behaviour if you please.

Hutch empties the water bottle. He lets it fall onto the couch, then glances at the door, then back at Darcy.

HUTCH: Why did we leave the party? What was it you said at the bar? You said you had something to say?

DARCY: *We've* got something to say. That's why you're here buddy. And I want us to say it together on camera because I've just been asked for the hundredth time out there where Charlie is. You know what I'm saying? Where's Charlie? Why isn't he coming to the party? People want to know why he just took off like that tonight like the building was on fire. Especially when the show was so great. And it was – it was a deadly gig. The three of us played a blinder back there.

HUTCH: (*waving to camera*) Hello! Where are you, Charlie? We love you man. Hey Darcy, you think he's watching us on YouTube?

DARCY: I doubt it.

HUTCH: Guess if he wanted to see us, he'd have been here.

DARCY: You think?

HUTCH: (*to camera*) Charlie, why'd you take off like that? Didn't you see the crowd? Eating out of your hand, big man. I never even had the chance to give you a sweaty hug after the show. Tell you how great you were tonight. Darcy, did we do something wrong?

Darcy sighs. She sits forward, bringing the camera closer.

DARCY: I'm worried about you Charlie. Like, I'm just gonna say it. I don't get it. We're a great band and yet you've been so distant with us lately that it's starting to sting a little mate. You know what I mean? You're thinking about Ryker and about the anniversary and that's okay. But you don't have to push us away. We're here for you mate. We're here *with* you. I'm worried that you'll...nah, never mind. I'm not going there. Hopefully we'll see more of you after the Edinburgh and Inverness shows though, yeah? Come hang with us brother. We do love you, just know that. Okay?

She blows a kiss to the camera.

Clip ends.

16

Charlie's ears were ringing after the gig. He could still feel the crowd pulling at his hair and clothes. *Charlie! Charlie! Charlie!*

He was back in his hotel room, sitting at a small coffee table beside the second-floor window. Charlie had drunk six tall glasses of water (filled to the brim) since getting back from the gig. He was on his seventh now and he still felt dry. All the lights in the room were switched off. A warm glow from the streetlights found its way through a gap in the floral-patterned curtains. The external light seeped gently into the spacious suite.

Even though Charlie didn't live that far away from the hotel, he'd reluctantly agreed to stay with the rest of the touring party in the five-star digs in the city centre. The reason for this, according to management, was so that the band and crew could get an early start in the morning. There was a lot to do in Edinburgh before the gig tomorrow night. Media commitments. A brief photo session at the castle, something Charlie was determined to get out of. Dennis told Charlie it was easier if the small touring party was in the same place. It was a nice hotel but Charlie longed for home.

Would he ever see it again?

He leaned towards the gap in the curtains. Looked down onto Blythswood Square.

King Tut's Wah-Wah Hut was barely a five-minute walk from the hotel and you didn't have to be walking fast either to make it in that time. If there was any post-gig racket drifting uphill from St Vincent Street, it was drowned out by the rest of the Friday night noise coming from Sauchiehall Street, another short walk from the hotel.

Blythswood Square, where the hotel was located, was fairly quiet. Once upon a time, Charlie would have been elbow deep in the afterparty that was taking place at the Sub Club. He'd have been as wasted as anyone.

Tonight, there was only his seventh glass of water on the table. And he was alone. That would have been unthinkable in the nineties.

Charlie peered through the gap and looked outside. A small cluster of Lewis Loyals had gathered directly across the street from the Kimpton Blythswood Square Hotel. According to the brochure on the table, the Kimpton was Glasgow's only five-star hotel. Charlie had to admit it, despite his desire to go home. The hotel was pretty gorgeous with its elegant Georgian architecture, recently renovated rooms and as far as the service went, Charlie had no complaints so far.

As he watched the Loyals, he kept himself hidden behind the curtains. Leaning his head forward just enough so he could peer down at the dimly lit street. How long had they been standing out there? Had they been at the gig? Inside? Outside? Tickets were hard to come by. Maybe they stood outside all night and waited – that's what they did after all. They'd have seen Charlie leaving early in a hail of cheers and boos and *Charlie, Charlie, Charlie!* Had they gone to the Sub Club, thinking that he'd attend the afterparty? Realised he wasn't there and then followed him to the hotel? Charlie had to give it to the Loyals. They always knew where to find him. Charlie didn't know where the band was scheduled to stay in Edinburgh and Inverness over the weekend, but he was willing to bet that the Loyals knew everything – hotels, media obligations, gig-times. Everything.

He saw Ginger, the tall redhead, standing on the kerb. She was chatting to the two brunettes that were always beside her. Her lieutenants. What were their names again? Alice? Rachel? The women looked so casual, standing outside the hotel as if stalking other people was the most natural thing in the world. The Beatles had their Apple Scruffs and Charlie had the Lewis Loyals. He didn't see the appeal. Didn't they ever get bored? All that waiting around for a thirty-second glimpse of someone walking from a door to a car.

The guys were out tonight too. Charlie counted five of them standing next to the three girls. He saw the bald-headed newbie, Chunky, still wearing that polo shirt and no jacket. Blondie was there, a freakishly tall forty-something man. He and his two middle-aged mates were dressed in Ben Sherman jackets and wearing Kangol bucket hats. Looked like they were about to go to a festival in the nineties. And of course, Ronnie was there. Charlie felt a flicker of discomfort and then he quietly scolded himself. Was he giving the guy a bad rap for nothing? Some people were just quiet. Intense. Ronnie was leaning against the metal fence on the other side of the street, dressed head to toe in Fred Perry gear. He was still trim compared to most of the other guys in the group who'd succumbed to middle-age spread. But his resemblance to a young Charles Manson was off-putting to say the least. Charlie couldn't let that one go.

Was anyone waiting for these people at home? What sort of partner would put up with their other half stalking a past-his-prime rock star?

Maybe they were alone. Just like Charlie.

Despite his reservations, Charlie was glad to see them tonight. They were reliable, like a faithful old dog that didn't judge or expect too much from him. Whoever had coined the term Lewis Loyals (it might have been Charlie himself) got it right. They were a strange bunch but they were *his* bunch. They didn't question his behaviour. He was certain that none of them had booed when he'd walked out of the gig early. They didn't seem to want anything except to be close to him. To be close to what Charlie represented to them. Something lost. Their youth, perhaps. Long gone summers tramping around festivals. Bonfires and celebrations. Happier days, taken for granted and never to return.

He kicked the chair back and stood up. *What the hell?* Charlie pushed his way past the flowery curtains, unlatched the window and opened her up. He poked his head outside, leaning over the edge. It was a mild spring night in Glasgow. Not the worst weather for standing around outside a hotel, if that's your thing. The scent of spicy food was in the air, cruising up from Sauchiehall Street.

He waved down to them.

"Hey guys."

Charlie's voice was scratchy after the gig. He'd gone all out on every song, purposefully trying to wreck his throat so that the Saturday and Sunday gigs would have to be cancelled. Couldn't blame him for that, could they? No such luck. The critics were right – his voice *was* in better shape than it had been since the peak Gods era almost thirty years prior. That's what he got for giving up drink and drugs.

He waved again to the eight people standing with their backs to the fence.

"Hello!"

They didn't seem to register at first. Then a couple of bemused glances shot his way. One of the brunettes strained her eyes and let out an excited squeal. The noise was so high-pitched it might have shattered every window on every building in Blythswood Square. Charlie waved for a third time. He heard his name uttered amidst a flurry of excited chatter.

"It's Charlie," Blondie said, waving up towards the second-floor window with both arms. The man's face lit up like a kid on Christmas morning. "Alright Charlie? How you doing mate?"

Charlie nodded. "All good. How's it going down there?"

At first, Charlie couldn't hear a thing as they talked over one another. Even Ronnie looked like he was trying to speak, although he quickly gave up when he realised that he couldn't compete with the volume of the others.

In the end, Ginger won out.

"How was the show tonight?"

Ginger was the unofficial spokesperson of the Lewis Loyals, if there was such a thing. She did most of the talking and to Charlie's relief, there was no hint of overly-crazy about the woman. She was always respectful of distance. Always polite. Always mindful not to barge into Charlie's personal space whenever he walked down the street or left the house. He couldn't imagine the Loyals without her.

Charlie shrugged. "I've played better."

Blondie had by now taken up position in the middle of the road. He held up his phone, pointed it at the second-floor window and for a second, Charlie thought he was trying to take a photo. Then he saw a pinprick of light on the screen. Microscopic flashes of colour, followed by the crackle of tinny dance music.

"What's that?" he asked.

Blondie checked both ways for traffic before answering. A little too late considering he was already standing on the road. "Darcy's livestreaming from the Sub Club. I've been going through the comments and everyone's saying it was amazing man. The gig, you know? One of the best Dark Stars gigs ever, that's what I'm hearing. Scottish gigs are always good though, eh? Got a few clips posted on YouTube already. Smoking Charlie, totally smoking mate. Vocals sound incredible."

"You didn't go to the Sub Club then?" Charlie asked.

"What's the point?" Ginger asked, a satisfied grin emerging on her face. Of course, Charlie thought. They knew he wasn't partying like he used to. That he was more likely to go back to the hotel. They *were* good. Lewis Loyals indeed.

"We went to the venue for a while," Blondie said. He spoke at rapid-fire speed and in an accent that sounded like it came out of east London, at least to Charlie's ears. "Obviously never got tickets man. Sold like hot cakes, didn't they?"

"Next time I play Glasgow," Charlie said, "you're all on the guest list. Least I can do."

They yelled out their thanks but Charlie knew it was a hollow gesture on his part. He felt guilty even saying it because at this point, he didn't know if he'd play another gig after Inverness. Plus, if his suspicions about Darcy and Hutch were right then there was a good chance he was about to perform a Ryker-esque disappearing act. And even if he did make it back from the Highlands and do another tour at some point in his life, was he really going to reach out to the people who stalked him on a full-time basis?

"Catch you guys later," he said. "Nice to see you again."

With a final wave, Charlie thanked the Loyals and closed the window over. He secured the latch. They waved back from the street and some of them started singing 'Good Night' by The Beatles. One of Charlie's favourite songs. He smiled, then pulled the curtains over, leaving no gaps this time. The room was plunged into darkness. He walked over to the bed, switched on the bedside lamp and sat down on the king-sized mattress.

It was quiet now.

Well, he thought. At least the Loyals know what window to look up at. He wondered if they'd stay out there on the street for much longer now that he'd spoken to them. What else was there for them to gain by sticking around? To Charlie's surprise, he found himself hoping that they'd stay a while longer.

He collapsed onto the bed, his head drowning in the five-star pillow. His eyes were heavy and slowly closed over...

Charlie! Charlie! Charlie!

The landline buzzed, pulling Charlie back from the brink of sleep. He blinked off the fog in his head. With a groan, he sat up on the bed. He reached over and grabbed the handpiece, cradling it on his shoulder.

"Hello?"

"Hello. Is this Mr Lewis?"

"Who's this?"

"This is Thomas from down at reception, sir. I'm sorry to bother you this evening but I have a call for you. It's a gentleman who claims to know you and he's quite insistent on speaking to you, even though I've tried to deter him several times now. As I said, he's determined. A most persistent chap. I just need your permission before I send the call up to the room."

Charlie frowned. "A call for me? It's probably a prank."

"Yes sir," Thomas said. "That's what I thought too. But he said you were friends many years ago."

"This isn't someone from the Sub Club, is it?"

"No, I don't think so sir."

Charlie groaned again. He'd been so close to passing out for the night and now what? He wasn't expecting any calls. "Who is it? Did you get a name?"

"Yes sir. Fletcher Darbey."

Charlie almost dropped the phone. Fletcher? Sally's younger brother and The Broken Gods' first roadie from way back at the beginning of the journey. Wee Fletch, as he'd been affectionately known by the group. Of course, Charlie thought. He'd been confused for a moment, but then it made sense. This was bound to happen as the anniversary approached. First, Annie had checked in. Now it was Fletcher's turn. The past was creeping up on Charlie and it was coming in thick and fast. That's what happened at this time of year. Everyone who'd been affected by the tragedy of Ryker and Sally was going through a hard time. Everyone was reaching out to somebody. Trying to form a clear picture, trying to make sense of it after all these years. But the clear picture never came. The pain dulled, but it never lessened. For Sally's family, it was the twentieth anniversary of her passing. A big number. Charlie knew that her death, as tragic as it was, was always going to be overshadowed by Ryker's disappearance. The vanishing and the wacked out theories that accompanied it were more media-friendly than suicide. It had to be hard for the Darbey family. To see their daughter's story reduced to the B-side of the tragedy.

It was a mess, Charlie thought. A total mess.

"Put him through."

"Yes sir, thank you."

Charlie heard a faint clicking noise in his ear. A moment later, a scratch. Then a nasal voice trickled out of the earpiece.

"Hello? Charlie?"

"Fletcher," Charlie said. "Is that really you?"

The voice lit up on the other end of the line. "It's me Charlie. How are you old friend?"

Fletcher's voice was exactly as Charlie remembered it. Slightly nasal, enthusiastic and good-natured. As Charlie sat up further on the bed, he tried to conjure up images of the young Fletcher as he'd been thirty years ago. He hadn't seen the guy in years. How many? It was three years since he'd seen Annie but a lot more when it came to Sally's brother. Fletcher had been a fairly small-statured man back in the day, lean, sporting an angular face with prominent cheekbones. Someone had once described him as looking like an elbow in a black wig and as cruel as it sounded, that description wasn't far off the mark. He'd been a good soldier for the band. He'd loved the Gods and delighted in dressing as they did, in acting like one of the boys. Fletcher was as loyal as they came. Had he possessed any musical talent, he would most likely have become the fifth member of the band. Ryker had a soft spot for him, perhaps because he was Sally's little brother. Charlie liked wee Fletch because he was enthusiastic, energetic and committed to getting the band out there. A good worker. Tireless.

"I'm good thanks," Charlie said.

"You've been going hard on the voice tonight," Fletcher

said. “I recognise that crackling sound in your voice. It was the same when you were twenty years old. You never did know how to hold back but I guess that’s what makes you Charlie Lewis, isn’t it? Don’t push it too hard Charlie – take some advice from an old friend. You’ve still got two shows to do.”

Charlie smiled. “Sounds like you’re still working for us.”

“A good roadie never leaves his musicians. Not until he’s called up to work at the great gig in the sky.”

“I’ll be fine for the other shows,” Charlie said. Unfortunately, it was true. His voice didn’t seem to be fizzling out like he’d hoped. “How did you find me?”

“You don’t mind me calling, do you?”

“Nah, of course not. I was just curious.”

“Well,” Fletcher said, “it’s no secret that The Dark Stars are playing Glasgow tonight. And they’re not exactly going to put you – the great Charlie Lewis – up in a Travel Lodge now, are they? Still, it was a hard task getting that snobby receptionist to believe that I was once co-manager of The Broken Gods.”

Charlie smiled. He was pretty sure that Sally had taken care of the managerial duties back in the early days. Fletcher was the roadie. But still, he thought, let the man have his fun. If he dined out on being the Gods’ former manager, who was Charlie to get in his way?

“So what are you up to these days?” Charlie asked. “Still in the roadie game? Or...management?”

Fletcher laughed. “Not quite. I fell back to Earth with a bang after the rock and roll lifestyle. These days, I own a pet shop in Motherwell.”

“A pet shop, eh?”

Fletcher let out another soft laugh. “Food, toys, accessories. It’s quite a big place, modern, clean of course, and we run adoption programs for kittens and puppies too. It's a simple job, a far cry from tuning guitars, but I like it."

"Sounds good man."

There was an awkward silence after that. Charlie sat on the bed and winced because he knew what was coming next. Small talk over, now it was time for the main event. He hadn't prepared for this. He had no idea how Fletcher or the rest of Sally's family had been coping in the build-up to the twentieth anniversary of her death. He didn't know how they'd handled all the previous ones either. He'd lost contact a long time ago. The odd phone call here and there, but not much. The least he could do was be there now. And listen.

"That time of year again," Fletcher said. His voice sounded like it had shrunk. "Never easy, is it?"

"It's not," Charlie said. "How are you guys doing? How's your mum and dad?"

There was a loud sigh on the other end of the line. Then, a moment of silence before Fletcher spoke. "It doesn't get any easier, even after twenty years. Does it? For any of us. You too, I imagine?"

"No, it doesn't."

"Twenty-five years since Ryker vanished," Fletcher said. "And twenty for our dear Sally. It's been so long now that, and this is a terrible thing to say, but it's like they almost never existed outside of photographs. But they did, didn't they Charlie? They existed. I had a sister. Oh God, how do you make sense of it? It's been twenty years and still..."

Charlie felt that sinking feeling in his guts again. "I don't know if you can."

"No."

"Your parents?" Charlie asked. "They're managing alright?"

Fletcher sighed. "No, I wouldn't say that. Sometimes my mum talks to the framed photo in the hallway, telling Sally all about her day. It's a recent thing but it shows no sign of stopping. And with Dad's dementia, well, I don't know how much he understands anymore."

"I'm sorry mate. You know, they're always welcome at my farmhouse if they want...well, if they want to get away."

"Thank you, Charlie," Fletcher said, his voice hoarse. "But it's best they're close to the nurses and carers right now. Anyway, I won't keep you any longer. I just wanted to reach out. It's been too long my friend and I'm still not sure how the old gang drifted apart all those years ago. Do you ever see much of Tommy and Bobby?"

"Not really. We lost touch after Ryker..."

"A shame. I hope they're both well. Must be tough for them too at this time of year."

"I'm sure it is."

Charlie didn't feel compelled to go into details about how he never saw his former bandmates anymore. The truth was that the remaining three members of The Broken Gods had simply outgrown one another. It happened. The same way the band had outgrown Fletcher several years before. Once they'd acquired a professional tech crew, there was simply nothing left for Fletcher to do. He'd shown up here and there at social occasions, awards shows, family gatherings. But it was like old school friends. People who're a constant fixture in your life one minute and then the next, they're an afterthought. Same thing happened with Tommy and Bobby. They'd been so close to Charlie once, like brothers, but the drifting apart after Ryker's disappearance had felt so natural. Without the band, they had nothing in common. Charlie had made no effort to keep in touch and likewise, Tommy and Bobby hadn't contacted Charlie in years. Did they resent him for that? Was it *really* tough for them at this time of year or had they put all that behind them?

"Everything happened so fast," Charlie said. "From '94 onwards, it was a whirlwind."

"The good old days Charlie, the good old days. Well, it's been lovely hearing your voice again. Best of luck with the gigs this weekend. I know you'll be in fine form in both Edinburgh and Inverness. And who knows? Maybe playing a gig on the anniversary will be good for you. Help take your mind off things."

Charlie doubted it. "Maybe."

"Take care."

"You too Fletcher."

Charlie put the phone down. He let out a long, gasping sigh. Everywhere he looked there were reminders of Ryker and Sally and they were bound to keep coming in until the anniversary was over. Who'd call next? Ryker's mother? Charlie stood up off the bed, walked over to the window. He poked his head through the curtains. Ginger, Blondie and creepy Ronnie were still out there, standing beside the gardens across the street. He guessed the others had gone home. Maybe they'd gone on a supply run for booze, snacks and cigarettes.

Charlie pulled his head back into the room before the remaining Loyals saw him at the window. He closed the curtains, fell back onto the bed and switched off the bedside lamp. The darkness was a thick, comforting blanket that surrounded him. Charlie was still fully dressed but he didn't have the energy to take his clothes off. He'd sleep like this. Who cared?

He was drifting off for a second time when he heard it. The sound of someone breathing from the other side of the room. *Charleeeey*. There was no fear, not this time. Charlie lifted his head off the pillow and as expected, he saw the slender outline of a man wearing a fedora and holding the Fender Telecaster that Charlie had insisted on bringing back to the hotel after the gig.

The chords floated in the air – *major-minor, major-minor.*

In twenty-five years, they'll be coming for you.

"How will they do it?" Charlie asked, letting his head fall back onto the five-star pillow. He stared up at the black void of a ceiling. "Do you know that much?"

The strumming came to a stop.

Listen to me, Charlie. You need to lock your hotel room door on Sunday night. Okay? Lock it and barricade it with furniture because they're going to come looking for you after the gig's over. When everyone else is drunk. When everyone else is stoned and tired and not thinking straight. That's their window. Got it? That's when it's going to happen. They'll be all smiles too. Maybe they'll offer you a drink and put something in it to knock you out. Or maybe there'll be no messing around, you know? Club you over the head in the dead of night. Beat you black and blue. Then they'll wrap you up, bundle you into the back of the van and drive you out of town. Deep into the Highlands. Burn the body and nobody will see them do it. And that'll be it – you'll be gone. That's the disappearance of Charlie Lewis. The vampires will feed on the legend for the rest of their life. Better that, than go back to the streets.

"Bastards," Charlie hissed. "Why can't they just leave me alone?"

Charlie?

"What?"

There's something else. Make sure you're...

"Armed," Charlie said, cutting in. "I know that. I'm way ahead of you."

What did you bring?

"I've got something wrapped up under a pile of clothes in my bag. It's on the floor over there – the Adidas bag. Maybe I'll surprise *them* after the gig."

The axe you were planning to take to the farmhouse?

"Yep."

I hope you're prepared to use it.

Charlie sat up, pressing his back against the ornate, hand carved headboard. "What's the best way to do this?"

Maybe you should strike first. To hell with hiding. Go after them.

Charlie didn't like the sound of that. He held up a hand as if to cut short any further suggestions. "But if I can run away, then surely that's the better option. Right? If I strike first, I'll get done for assault or murder or whatever. I can't prove what they were going to do. I *can* get out after the Inverness show. I walked out after the gig in King Tut's tonight. I can do it again, and once I'm back in Glasgow on Sunday, I don't ever have to be around those people again."

Those two buskers mean business. And it's MEAN business.

Charlie's arm shot out, found the switch and turned on the bedside lamp. He'd been hoping to catch a proper glimpse of Ryker. But there was no one there. The Telecaster was in the guitar stand where he'd left it and Charlie was still alone in the luxury hotel suite.

"I can't just attack them," he whispered.

Charlie shook his head. He grabbed his iPhone off the bedside table and hit the number for Jenna. As it started to ring, Charlie glanced at the digital clock and saw how late it was. The kids would be sleeping. There was no way he'd get to talk to them now.

"Damn it."

He killed the call. Dropped the phone on the bed.

Well done, Charlie thought. *Well done Charlie boy*. Now she'll see a missed call from him in the morning and see what a sad, lonely bastard he'd become. She knew that already but here was more proof. The pathetic ex-husband calling at all hours because, as she'd stated so many times before, he had no one in his life.

Charlie got up and paced the room. He felt the urge to smoke but thank God, he had no cigarettes in the room.

Soon, he was back sitting on the bed. Leg shaking. Beads of sweat running down his face. *I can't just attack them, can I?* He looked around for distraction. Grabbed the remote for the Smart TV off the end of the bed. Switched the TV on. Logged onto his YouTube account via the app. The first video the algorithm recommended was a livestream from Darcy Doyle, straight from the Sub Club.

DARK STARS AFTERPARTY!!

Charlie swore under his breath. He browsed the other recommendations, expecting a flood of Ryker anniversary content to flood his homepage. Sure enough, there it was. A video by Brian Ortega, a Broken Gods superfan who Charlie was vaguely familiar with. Ortega's video was titled: *Ryker and Sally – A Doomed Love Story!*

There was another video that caught his eye. It sported a colour thumbnail image of Ryker and Sally at the Reading Festival, perhaps in 1996. The video had been uploaded by a channel called Nineties Gold and it was entitled: *Ryker and Sally – Twenty-Five Years Later!*

Charlie hesitated. Then he hit play.

17

Nineties Gold
Ryker and Sally – Twenty-Five Years Later!
(Brand New Upload!)

Nineties Gold is a popular YouTube channel (725k subscribers) that celebrates the best of nineties music. The genres covered are mostly rock and pop. It's a long-term passion project created and presented by forty-five-year-old Alison Barker, a former music festival promoter from Cornwall, England.

As well as albums and individual songs, the channel also looks at the unique personalities that stamped their mark on that particular era.

Alison presents each video from a spare bedroom in her Cornwall house that she's turned into a shrine to the final decade of the twentieth century. A collage of posters can be seen on the wall behind her desk, featuring some of the best bands and solo artists from that era: Nirvana, The Broken Gods, Rage Against the Machine, Oasis, Guns N' Roses, Alanis Morrissette and more.

The wall is also peppered with used concert tickets.

ALISON: Hi everyone. Welcome to another edition of

Nineties Gold with me your host, Alison Barker. Today, I'm taking a brief look at one of the great rock and roll tragedies of not just the nineties, but of all time. This is the story of Ryker Marshall and Sally Darbey. Really guys, this one deserves a full-length episode and I promise I'll do just that in the future. As for today, I'm giving you a brief intro to the story because, as we all know if you're watching this just after upload, it's almost April 23rd. Which means it's been twenty-five years since Ryker's disappearance and twenty since Sally's tragic suicide.

Alison narrates the intro over a faded colour image of Ryker and Sally at the Reading Festival in 1996. They're walking hand in hand, unkempt and smiling. It's a rare, unguarded moment. A photo beloved amongst the fans because of how happy they both look.

Cut back to Alison in the studio.

ALISON: This story is a real heartbreaker guys. As you all know, I'm a massive Broken Gods fan and in particular, a Ryker Marshall fan. I think that Ryker was a bona fide genius in a time when that word – *genius* – is horribly overused and watered down. Ryker was the real deal but, as is so often the case with our creative geniuses, he was troubled. Deeply troubled.

Cut to a black and white shot of a young Ryker standing on stage in the middle of a gig. He's in his prime, playing guitar, head thrust backwards, beads of sweat flying off his brow. Sally is visible in the background, standing at the edge of the stage. She's staring at Ryker, holding her arms in the air and singing along to whatever song the Gods are playing.

Cut back to studio.

ALISON: Ryker Marshall and Sally Darbey first met in February 1990 when The Broken Gods were a rough garage band from the east end of Glasgow called Creative Differences. Despite their limitations as a band, Sally was one of the early believers. She said in later years that, despite their flaws, she saw the band's potential from the start. Diamonds in the rough, that's how she put it. Sally took up managerial and promotional duties, mostly because no one else could be bothered. She landed them a few gigs around Glasgow. The wheels started turning and Creative Differences eventually changed their name, at Sally's suggestion, to The Broken Gods. And while Sally was taking care of the business side of things, Ryker and his best friend, Charlie Lewis, were polishing their songwriting skills. Ryker's been quoted multiple times in the past saying that Sally was his rock and that if not for her faith and hard work at the beginning, the Gods would never have made it. Charlie's always said the same thing too. Sally wasn't just Ryker's girlfriend. She was crucial in terms of management and publicity. Without her, The Broken Gods would never have escaped the garage.

Cut to a montage of early Broken Gods clips.

The band members soundchecking while Sally and a short, skinny roadie stand watching from the sidelines. Sally's blond hair is clipped at the sides and she's dressed in a red Lambretta polo shirt. The roadie is also dressed in Lambretta gear. He's sporting a Ryker Marshall/Beatles haircut and is wearing a fedora tilted to the side. They both sing along enthusiastically, waving with embarrassed grins when they notice the camera pointed in their direction.

Sally with the band when they're doing interviews. Sitting in the background, watching and listening with rapt attention.

There's a clip of her at Glastonbury 1994 (The Broken Gods' first appearance at the festival) standing at the side of the stage. Gazing out in adoration. This is the gig from which the earlier black and white photo was taken.

Alison narrates over the clips.

ALISON: It's now common knowledge that Ryker Marshall struggled with depression all of his adult life. And despite extraordinary commercial success and critical acclaim with the Gods, Ryker's mental health plummeted during the mid-nineties. This wasn't helped by his excessive or as some might say, *legendary*, drink and drug intake. In particular, he had a superhuman cocaine habit and when Charlie saw how bad things were getting, he knew in his guts that the Gods were finished.

Cut to a clip from April, 1998.

We're watching a snippet taken from an old BBC documentary about the life of Ryker Marshall. The documentary was originally broadcast on the first anniversary of Ryker's disappearance and featured interviews with friends and family, as well as police detectives and private investigators who were still trying to find out what happened to him. There's also an interview with a heartbroken Sally, conducted at her family home. She looks like she's aged twenty years since those earlier clips with the band. She's skin and bones. Dark shadows dull her eyes. She speaks in soft voice. It's flat, lifeless and little more than a whisper.

SALLY: Yeah, it's true. Ryker was very quiet before he disappeared. The drugs, the depression, they had him by that point. He was distant. We weren't communicating like we used to. It was hard, watching the man I loved become a stranger. I leaned on Charlie a lot for support, but even he couldn't get through to Ryker. Charlie, Tommy, Bobby – they were starting to avoid him. I don't blame them. He was impossible to be around. Paranoid. He thought the world was out to get him. Sometimes he was angry and that anger seemed to come out of the blue, like for no reason whatsoever. It was just...exhausting.

Cut back to Alison in the studio.

ALISON: There'd been talk of marriage. Ryker wanted

children – lots of children. He spoke of retiring from the music industry at thirty and living off the grid in the Highlands. But none of that was meant to be. On April 23rd, 1997, Ryker Marshall left the Marriott Hotel in Glasgow, drove off in his car, a British Racing Green Mini Cooper, and then promptly disappeared off the face of the earth. Much of the cash that Ryker kept in his house was later found to be missing. And even though the Mini Cooper was found near Erskine Bridge, a notorious suicide spot in the west of Scotland, many people believe that Ryker wanted people to think he'd killed himself. In other words, it was a ruse. A vanishing trick. Many fans, myself included, believe that Ryker had simply had enough of the industry and recognised that it was destroying him. He felt like a burden to those around him, his mental health was declining and in a last-gasp effort to save his sanity, he decided to start a new life. So in a sense, Ryker Marshall did die on April 23rd. Wherever he is today, he's probably unrecognisable and living under another name. But where is he? Despite multiple alleged sightings across the world, nothing has ever been confirmed. We, the fans, hold out hope that he's still alive. That he's happy. And that he's at peace.

Cut to footage from an STV news clip (circa April 2002)

Grim-faced police officers block both sides of Erskine Bridge. We see the flashing lights of police vehicles on the ground and a swooping helicopter with a searchlight hovering over the river. A photo of Sally appears at the corner of the screen beside a headline:

Missing rocker's girlfriend believed to have jumped to her death

Alison narrates as the news footage continues.

ALISON: Sally's tragic suicide came five years after Ryker's disappearance. Details are few and far between but it's believed that she arrived at the bridge shortly after midnight. Sally, who'd never recovered from the loss of her soulmate, jumped over the railings. She was exhausted. Haunted by questions. Why did Ryker leave her? If he *was* alive, where did he go? Did he still think of her? Did he still love her? We don't know if it was a snap decision on Sally's part to end her life or whether she'd planned it in advance. What we do know is that she was exhausted and broken-hearted. And so it was, one of rock's greatest love stories came to an end that night. For many people who came of age in the nineties listening to The Broken Gods, it was the end of something much bigger.

Thank you for watching. I'll see you next time on Nineties Gold.

Clip ends.

18

Edinburgh Evening News
(Online article – April 22nd, posted 11:37pm)
By Colin Paterson

IS THIS GOODBYE, CHARLIE LEWIS?

The streets of Edinburgh were ablaze with excitement tonight as rock legend Charlie Lewis brought his three-piece band, The Dark Stars, to The Liquid Room, an eight-hundred capacity venue on Victoria Street. This gig was the band's penultimate stop on their Back-To-Basics tour, a stripped back concert experience that's been receiving rave reviews from fans and critics alike.

Last night was no different. This was an outstanding gig. There was a white-hot tension in the venue ahead of the show, the sold-out crowd doing their best to wait patiently through the local support bands' plodding sets. No disrespect to these young lads and lassies – the support was well-intentioned (young bands need platforms like these to get noticed) but some of these acts could have been better and more appropriate. *Electro punk?* Simply put, everyone was there for the main event. Everyone wanted to see The Dark Stars. Scratch that (and no disrespect to the guitarist and drummer), they were there to see Charlie Lewis.

And as expected, Charlie Lewis didn't disappoint.

The band was approximately thirty minutes late on stage but the crowd didn't give a damn about tardiness. This was a raucous event but Lewis, who'd always been the most amiable of the Lewis/Marshall songwriting partnership, was distant with the crowd. There was no nonsense. No talking in between songs. His hair was jet-black, styled much like his old friend's hair back in the nineties. Charlie also wore a black fedora. And as if that wasn't enough, when it was Charlie's turn to play guitar (handing bass duties to Darcy), he was playing Ryker's battered old Telecaster.

Yes, that one. A guitar that hasn't been seen on stage since 1997.

Seeing that was worth the price of admission alone.

The Dark Stars opened up with 'Night Train'. It sounded like peak Broken Gods to this overjoyed writer's ears. That opener was enough to unleash a frenzy of primal excitement in the Liquid Room. It was jaw-dropping. You had to be there because it was, and I don't use this word lightly, *beautiful.* I'm getting excited just reliving it for this article. The truth is that no words can hope to recapture the magic happening in between those four walls tonight. All I can say is that it took me back to the heady days of 1995 and beer-soaked weekends with teenage pals (some of them sadly gone too soon), following the crowds to see The Broken Gods play in a big tent at Irvine Beach.

After 'Night Train', it was all go in the Liquid Room. The crowd, myself included, were at the band's mercy and the three musicians played a blinder, taking those eight-hundred people to heaven and back again.

Darcy Doyle and Hutch Heikkinen (Darcy and Hutch? Seventies cop show anyone?) are excellent musicians. That said, it's Lewis, the nineties icon, who really delivered the goods tonight. His stage presence is unrivalled, even today. Charlie's got something you can't buy and it's something you'll never find on Britain's Got Talent. It's charisma. Pure, unfiltered genius. Perhaps a touch of madness too?

His vocals, bass and guitar playing were as good as they've ever been.

Complaints? Not enough Gods songs in the set. After 'Night Train', there were only a few more sprinkled here and there. 'Coming For You' was a massive favourite of course, even if Lewis fluffed the lyrics to the chorus. One has to respect Lewis's decision to play newer material but it was particularly disappointing considering that Lewis and Darcy Doyle were taking turns on Ryker's Telecaster and this writer knows for sure that the legendary guitar was begging to scream out the riff for 'Falling Upwards'.

The other major disappointment of the night was Lewis's noticeable absence after the gig. By all accounts, he left immediately after the Glasgow gig on Friday and the same thing happened here in Edinburgh tonight. While his two bandmates stayed behind to interact with the crowd, to fulfil media obligations and attend the afterparty, Lewis disappeared. There was no sign of him whatsoever. Allegedly, he went back to the hotel.

How times have changed.

His interview on Radio Forth was stilted. A photo shoot at Edinburgh Castle was, according to management, postponed for undisclosed reasons.

All of which begs the question – does Charlie still want this? Does he still want to be a rock and roll star?

His voice, musicianship and stage presence are as good as they've ever been. But it seemed to this writer like there was little warmth coming from Lewis. He was great up there tonight but that's not the Charlie Lewis of old. As mentioned, he barely spoke in between songs. The chemistry with his bandmates was non-existent. But let's not be too hard on Charlie. He's got a pretty good excuse for being off right now. As most of us know, the anniversary of Ryker Marshall's mysterious disappearance is tomorrow (April 23rd). It's a big one. Twenty-five years. Charlie Lewis hates the anniversary and no doubt, it's affecting him. But has it pulled him down further than we'd anticipated? Has it made him question his future in music as he approaches the age of fifty?

All of which begs one more question. Was this the last time we'll ever see Charlie Lewis on stage in Edinburgh?

This writer was fortunate enough to grab a quick word with Darcy Doyle, who generously gave her time for the fans. We asked her about Charlie's state of mind. First of all, we asked if he was okay.

Darcy – *Yeah, I'm getting asked this question a lot right now. Is Charlie okay? Should he even be out on tour right now? It's a tough one, you know? Even on the earlier Back-To-Basics gigs in England and Wales, it was clear that Charlie's been up against it. Fighting his demons. Honesty is best right now because we're being bombarded with questions. We're all sad that Charlie doesn't feel up to meeting his fans and thanking them for all the support they've given us over the years. I'm still optimistic about the future of the band but what I think we really need is to get this anniversary behind us and take it from there. Things will be a lot clearer after the twenty-third.*

Edinburgh Evening News – *So you do think the anniversary's affecting him?*

Darcy – *It's not affecting his playing. That's deadly. But his mental health is always ropey at this time of year. You know, it's understandable. He's thinking about his friend. And as we all know, there was never closure for the guy. No one knows what happened to Ryker and that's hard enough for the fans, let alone for Ryker's best friend. Someone who actually knew him. I think if there was a grave or whatever, it wouldn't be so bad. He could mourn. Move on with his life. Charlie's a pretty sensitive guy at the best of times but then you only need to look at his lyrics to see that. It's a tough time. Hopefully he'll be okay. But you know...*

Edinburgh Evening News – *Inverness tomorrow? That should be an emotional one, all things considered.*

Darcy – *Mega-emotional. But the three of us, we're going to get on that stage up there and give it everything we've got. For Charlie. For Ryker and Sally. Just like we did tonight – thank you again to the lovely people of Edinburgh for coming out to see us. What a great show.*

Sunday, April 23rd

The Anniversary

19

Charlie flinched when he heard the knock on the door. It was Johnny Henderson, the tour manager, letting him know that it was 8.15pm. Time to go downstairs, Johnny called out. Time to leave the hotel. Get in the van and go to the venue, The Hoot and Annie pub on Bridge Street.

"Showtime Charlie boy," Johnny said, knocking for a second time. "See you downstairs in the lobby in five, eh?"

Charlie didn't respond.

The third knock came quickly. Still, Charlie said nothing. The fourth knock was more urgent – the panicked rhythm of knuckles rapping off wood.

"Charlie? Are you okay in there bud?"

Charlie felt the first flicker of guilt in his mind. He knew that Johnny was worried about him cracking up on the anniversary. This was it. The big day had arrived and Johnny was on red alert. Charlie had seen the myriad of quotes floating around online about how hard this night would be for him. About how he was struggling on this three-day stint in Scotland. Seemed like the entire world and their dog was worried about him. *Charlie! Charlie! Charlie!* The rest of the band were (at least that's how they wanted it to look across social media). The skeleton crew on the road with the band were worried about Charlie. Management. All of them. They were freaked out by his behaviour so far – no talking in between songs. Running out when the gig was over. Steering clear of aftershow parties. What would Johnny do if Charlie didn't answer that fifth knock on the door? Break it down? Call the police? Poor Johnny, Charlie thought. The tour manager was having a tough time of it too, just trying to keep everything running smoothly. Charlie wasn't much help this time around. He'd been sitting in his hotel room in the Best Western ever since the band's arrival in Inverness that afternoon. Doing everything he could to avoid the others.

Vampires, he thought.

Tonight was the night. Darcy and Hutch would make their move but not if Charlie made his move first, as Ryker had suggested that night in the Kimpton. *Not Ryker. It's your crazy fragmented mind!* What would it be? Use the axe, strike first and hard, or make another run for it after the gig? There was still a part of Charlie that wanted to get away without this thing descending into some savage ritual of Tarantino-esque violence. He could've run earlier. Just walked out of the hotel and laid low until the anniversary was over. He could have hopped on a bus or a train and went out into the middle of nowhere where nobody would ever find him. And yet here he was, still in the hotel room. Still willing to do the gig.

Too late to run now.

It's showtime.

"Charlie?"

Johnny's voice was laced with panic. It sounded like he was starting to consider the possibility that Charlie wasn't there. Or worse – that he was there, lying dead on the floor, face down on the carpet, his lips purple-blue, his fingers clutching an empty pill bottle. Maybe a note for his boys propped up beside the fresh corpse. *Enjoy Italy kids. And tell your mum I'm sorry. That deep down, I still love her.*

Poor Johnny.

"Coming," Charlie said in a gruff voice. "Just give me a minute, will you?"

Johnny let out a deafening sigh of relief. He hit the other side of the door, maybe with a fist, maybe with an open palm. Sounded like he was going at it with a wooden mallet. "Bloody hell Charlie! Are you okay? I've been knocking on the door for God's sake. Where were you? I thought..."

"On the bog," Charlie said. "Taking a dump."

A pause. Charlie could just imagine Johnny trying to compose himself out in the corridor. He had a blond, Elvis-like quiff and he was most likely running his hand through it right now, composing himself for the night ahead.

"Okay – get you at reception in five minutes?"

"Aye, cool."

"Five minutes Charlie, not twenty. Not thirty. We need to go."

"Heard you the first time."

Charlie listened to Johnny's footsteps receding down the corridor. He stood there in the centre of the large hotel room. Saw his reflection in the full-length mirror on the door. By now, the resemblance to peak-Gods Ryker was undeniable. Beatles mop top. The bluish-black tint in his hair. The maroon shirt with the black waistcoat, along with the ubiquitous fedora. The fans would take it as a tribute to the missing man. Especially when they saw Charlie wielding the Fender Telecaster on stage in less than an hour from now.

He glanced at the Adidas bag on the floor, wanting to check its contents one more time before going down to reception. But Charlie had already checked the bag at least ten times since arriving at the hotel that afternoon. The axe *was* there. He'd even managed a few practice swings in front of the mirror. It was heavy, but he was getting quite good at it.

Charlie walked over. Picked up the bag.

As he stood there, he briefly considered making a run for it. This was his last chance. There had to be a back door to the building. Charlie could go there now, avoid reception, slip away from the hotel and call a taxi. Leave Inverness. That would mean he didn't have to do the gig. Didn't have to face Darcy and Hutch and whatever body-burning ceremony they had in store for him out there in the wilderness.

But he didn't move.

Charlie's five minutes were up.

It was time to go to work.

20

The Hoot and Annie was the smallest venue on the Scottish tour.

It was a traditional pub that, around fifteen years ago, had built a live music venue downstairs. The downstairs area had previously been used as a sort of games room – a space for playing pool, slot machines and there were big screens for watching sports. The live music venue had taken off and hosted a variety of acts, mostly local bands and open mic nights. Charlie and his band were a big win for the Hoot. The sound team had even invested in a new mixer and some other equipment for recording the gig. Johnny had already said something about this to Charlie and assured the singer that there were no plans to officially distribute the live material and that the recording was for private use only.

Charlie knew, in the age of the Internet, that the recording would be online in days. And that it would be billed, *The Ryker Marshall Anniversary Gig – You've NEVER heard Charlie Lewis sing with such emotion! Click now...click, click, click!*

The dressing room (or green room as the staff preferred to call it) was located at the side of the stage. It wasn't much of a room, more like a vacant space that might have once been used for storing cleaning materials and other odds and sods. A giant cupboard with concrete walls. The scent of chemicals and stale sweat was everywhere.

The walls in the green room were covered in graffiti. Most of it had been provided by the bands who'd played there over the years. Some of it was outstanding. There were well-crafted depictions of mythological three-headed creatures. Medusa was up there too with her snake hair. Marilyn Monroe. John Lennon. Elvis playing an iPhone instead of a guitar. There was a plethora of punk rock art and Banksy-like protest art. Band names scrawled in marker pen. There were a few lewd messages and of course, the mandatory ejaculating penis art.

It was fifteen minutes to showtime.

Everyone was there in the green room, counting down the clock. Band and crew crammed into the tight space, along with a few chairs and a wooden table covered in snacks and drinks as requested in the band's official rider. The rider was modest by rock and roll standards. It was certainly tame compared to the sex-shop obscenities requested by The Broken Gods back in the nineties. Usually, these items were requested as a joke.

Sometimes they got what they asked for.

Charlie, Darcy and Hutch had been in the green room for about twenty minutes. They'd entered the building through the fire exit at the back of the pub, which led directly into the green room/old storage cupboard. Johnny had driven the band from the Best Western, dropped them off along with the tour's chief sound engineer, Frank 'Baggy' Boyle. Johnny then parked both transit vans, band and crew, in the brick alley at the back of the pub, leaving the fire exit clear as requested. The alley behind the pub was narrow. It was also quaint, carpeted with cracked cobblestones and lined from top to bottom with wheelie bins that belonged to the other Bridge Street establishments – offices mostly, as well as a tea shop and bakery. The alley was blocked off at both ends by security guards.

As soon as Charlie had walked through the fire exit and into the green room, he'd felt a blast of industrial heat wafting off the old pipes on the ceiling. The heat was one thing (and it would only be hotter after the gig) but the tiny green room, rammed with bodies, would be a bigger challenge. The door that led to the stage was closed but that wasn't enough to stop the yells, cheers and whoops of the excited audience forcing their way into the green room. Sounded like the roof was about to blow off the place.

They were chanting his name over the warm-up tunes.

"*Charlie! Charlie! Charlie!*"

Here we go again, he thought.

Darcy and Hutch were busy with their warm ups. Pacing back and forth like prizefighters waiting for the opening bell. Darcy had her guitar, a red Gibson SG, strapped over her shoulder and she was loosening her fingers by running over a few scales. Hutch did what he always did before a gig. He drank a shitload of beer. He also tapped his drumsticks off the table, off the walls, off anything that would help him prepare for two hours of balls to the wall drumming.

The sound of it was maddening.

Charlie didn't warm up. He'd never warmed up in his life and he wasn't about to start now. Back in the day, he used to drink like Hutch. Nowadays, he never knew what to do with himself. He leaned his back against the wall, occasionally glancing at his bandmates. Did they look more nervous than usual? How much did they resent the fact that the crowd were singing *his* name and not theirs?

Charlie didn't know most of the people in the green room. Staff. A small guest list. Baggy's younger cousin, Emily, a gorgeous thirty-something brunette who lived in Inverness, was there too. She was talking to her cousin, trying not to stare at Charlie.

Someone walked past. Complimented Charlie on his outfit, saying that it was a beautiful tribute to Ryker and that he'd be proud. A friendly pat on the shoulder. A sincere smile. A few others in the room agreed and those who didn't say anything about his clothes must have thought that Charlie had parked in Cuckooville and left his keys in the car. If they'd read the articles about him being 'weird' at the last two gigs, that *was* the easiest scenario to believe.

He tried to smile at the compliments. In truth, he couldn't think of much to say. He didn't want to be here. He wanted to be on the road with his boys in Ireland, exploring the Ring of Kerry and the Dingle Peninsula. Walking down Grafton Street. Why hadn't he booked the trip before the Italy thing came up? If he'd booked in advance, made concrete plans, the boys would never have chosen Italy and Roger the twat. Why hadn't he confirmed with the boys that he'd take them later in the summer, in July, as Jenna had suggested? Why hadn't he booked anything for *that*?

"Ten minutes to showtime," Johnny said, glancing at his watch.

Hutch whooped and high-fived Darcy. He went back to drumming the table, eyes closed, singing the opening verse to 'Night Train.'

People kept coming at Charlie. They talked *at* him. They asked him if he'd sign this or that after the gig. Sign their books, acoustic guitars, old gig posters and whatever else they'd brought with them into the green room. Vinyl albums were shoved in his face. He looked at the covers and tried to smile. The Broken Gods, Charlie Lewis solo and Dark Stars. Covers he'd seen a thousand times before. Charlie wasn't stupid. He knew that most of these items, assuming he signed them, would be on sale on the Internet before the end of the night.

The air in the green room felt hot and regurgitated.

"Want me to take that bag off your hands, Charlie boy?" Johnny said, reaching for the Adidas duffle bag.

Charlie flinched. He'd been holding the bag for so long he'd almost forgotten it was there.

"I've got it."

"Aye cool," Johnny nodded, backing off. He ran a hand through his quiff. "You don't usually bring a bag to the gigs. What's in it anyway?"

"Change of clothes."

"Nae bother."

Hutch was squatting at the dressing room door. He peered through the keyhole into the venue. "Oh man," he said in an excited voice. "Crazy – it's crazy out there. They're going nuts when we go out, ya?"

Charlie saw the enthusiasm on the drummer's face as he straightened up and turned around. He tugged on his black Metallica t-shirt, letting the air in. Darcy and Hutch bumped fists. They looked enthusiastic and so...innocent. Charlie's brains were scrambled as he watched them. In a split second, he reconsidered everything. It was like he was seeing clearly for the first time in a long time and in that window of clarity, he saw the truth. He *was* crazy. *An axe in your bag! You've got an axe in your bag! You fucking maniac!* What was happening to him? Was it the anniversary weighing down on him? The end of his marriage? The fact that he was losing his beautiful boys to Roger the twat?

Was it all of the above?

Ryker was the only true friend he'd ever had.

In twenty-five years, they'll be coming for you.

No, Charlie thought. There's no one coming for you. But you need to get off the road and get somewhere healthy. Do this gig and run rabbit run. Go to Ireland anyway. This world, it's killing you the way it killed Ryker.

"Charlie," Darcy said, cutting off his train of thought. She took a step towards him. Spoke in a gentle voice, as if she recognised that his head was getting hammered with requests left, right and centre. "I know this isn't the best time to bring it up, but have you given any thought about what's next?"

"People keep asking us," Hutch said, bringing his warm-up to a stop. "Asking us if Dark Stars are over."

Darcy nodded. "We deserve to know Charlie. I know you're the man and all that, but it's our lives too."

Charlie glanced around the room. It wasn't just his bandmates who wanted a definitive answer to that question. The crew were curious. Johnny, who represented the record company, was more than curious. Everyone wanted to know what was happening next.

"We'll talk later," Charlie said. "Okay?"

The tension in the room seemed to ease off. Or maybe Charlie was imagining that too.

He glanced at the bag in his hand. What the hell was he supposed to do with the axe now? How could he make sure that no one found out?

"Wanna do any more Ryker songs tonight?" Darcy said. She was fiddling with the guitar, fretting a series of bar chords to stretch her fingers. "I'm sure between us we could pull off songs like 'Fugitive and..."

"No," Charlie said. "It's a good set the way it is. Let's play what we've playing for the past couple of nights. It works."

Darcy nodded. "You're the boss."

Johnny had a pained look on his face. "Charlie, are you going to talk about Ryker when you're out there? Are you planning on saying anything?"

"No."

"Really?" Johnny said, arching an eyebrow. "At the very least, shouldn't you dedicate the gig to him? Maybe, tell a few stories? At least talk to the crowd tonight, Charlie. It's not like you to be so distant with them."

"Did you know Ryker?" Charlie asked.

Johnny looked like he'd been slapped. "No..."

"Ryker wouldn't want me to say anything. He'd want me to play a great gig and that's what I intend to do. Now, are we going out there or what?"

Johnny nodded. Both he and Charlie glanced towards the stage door. The noise spilling into the green room from the crowd was a full-on earthquake of excited anticipation. The floor under their feet was vibrating.

Baggy was sitting on the table, eating a packet of salt and vinegar crisps. He smiled at the sound of the crowd. "It's going to be a good one."

Charlie wanted a drink. He wanted to smoke at least one cigarette, just to get through the night. But that was a dangerous door and he wasn't going to open it up. He wanted to be anywhere except in this tiny shoebox of a dressing room with these people. He should've been somewhere else, marking the anniversary of his friend's disappearance. With Ryker's family. With Sally's people. They should be talking, holding hands, remembering and laughing and crying as they told stories, not for the sake of entertainment, but so they'd feel closer to him again. Feel him in the room. That's what the stories were for. They weren't for public consumption. They weren't something to plug the gap in between songs. And yet here he was, Charlie Lewis, back on the racecourse with tired legs and nothing new to offer. Still doing it. Still performing the old tricks for money.

Charlie dropped the Adidas bag on the floor. Kicked it tight beside the wall, close to the fire exit.

Do the gig, he thought. Then get the hell out of here.

21

JIMMY WATT
THE MISSION

Jimmy Watt's YouTube channel has four subscribers.

The last two subscribers came in following Jimmy's unscripted appearance on Hugh MacFarlane's STV news broadcast (posted on Jimmy's channel) in which Jimmy declared to Hugh and the world that he was a man on a mission. His mission is simple – to get a handshake from his idol, Charlie Lewis, after the Inverness gig.

It's been a little over ten minutes since The Dark Stars walked off stage. Jimmy is standing on drunken legs outside the Hoot, livestreaming (with the aid of a tech savvy friend) on Bridge Street. There's a massive crowd outside the pub. This is Jimmy's first ever live broadcast and he's surrounded by a horde of rowdy music fans who've just spilled out of the venue, every single one of them singing the chorus of 'Coming For You.'

Jimmy waves at the camera. He's got a classic drinker's face. Red cheeks. Bleary eyes. His nose is bumpy and slightly purple in colour.

JIMMY: Hello world! How you doing, eh? Welcome to Inverness on a Sunday night. Ma name's Jimmy Watt and I'm the world's biggest...

Somebody yells 'wanker' before Jimmy can finish the sentence.

Jimmy signals to a friend.

JIMMY: Hey Duncan, are you sure this bloody thing's on? Ah'm no jist talking to maself here, am I?

Duncan Graham, fifty-two, is the tech savvy friend mentioned earlier. Ginger-haired and bespectacled, he can be seen laughing over Jimmy's shoulder.

DUNCAN: Aye, it's on ya daftie. Telt ye that already. No that anybody's watching. Who'd want to watch your ugly mug on the telly?

JIMMY: (*to camera*) It's no the telly though, is it? It's YouTube. Right here we go again, take two. Hello world! Ma name's Jimmy Watt and I'm the world's biggest Broken Gods fan. Seriously, I've been a fan of the band since 1994 when the first single came oot. Ryker Marshall, Charlie Lewis – legends. Bloody songwriting legends so they are. Tommy and Bobby, love them. Bloody love them.

DUNCAN: Get on with it.

Jimmy points his thumb towards the pub behind him. The lights are on and the music is blaring inside. Now that the gig is over, a DJ is playing a collection of nineties music and judging by the raucous noise coming from inside, it's going down well.

JIMMY: Amazing gig folks. Totally buzzing after that. But here's the thing – ah'm no satisfied yet. See, ah'm on a mission. Ever since ah booked ma tickets, ah've been telling everyone that ah'm going to shake Charlie Lewis's hand. They aw think ah'm talking shite. Now, listen up. ah've been watching the news and ah hear that Charlie's been running off early after the gigs. Well, that means ah need to get a move on. Ah need to get in there before he does a runner and buggers off back to the hotel. As far as ah'm aware, he's still in the building. Most likely, he's in the dressing room at the side of the stage. But we're ready to go. Me and ma boys have got our work van here. See? It's parked doon the street there.

The camera spins around. There's a dirty white transit van parked across the street. The words 'Watt Plumbers' are stencilled on the side in big black letters. The camera jerks around a bit more. It lands on a small group of about ten people standing near the pub.

JIMMY: See those people over there? Lewis Loyals. Die-hard Charlie fans like maself. Some of them have come up from Glasgow, Stirling, Edinburgh. They came up in a van and some of them drove up solo. Seriously. We're talking die-hards man. Ah don't think any of them even had a ticket, eh? They've just been standing ootside the pub.

The camera makes another dizzying swing to the opposite end of the street. It lands on another white van with a massive 'Lewis Loyals' banner hanging off the side.

Jimmy approaches the group.

JIMMY: Alright troops? Anybody manage to get in tonight?

The camera skims over the Loyals. They laugh and yell out greetings. Ginger and Chunky lean in closer and wave. Blondie's there too with his mates. Ronnie's lingering nearby with some other faces, not from the Glaswegian contingent of the Loyals.

GINGER: Nah, we didn't have a ticket. We're just here for Charlie. To show support, make some noise. Take it the gig was amazing, aye?

JIMMY: Amazing. Ah'm hoarse, know what ah mean? Singing ma heart oot, so I was. Charlie's still got it. Guy's a fucking legend, excuse my language to the viewers. What do you say big man?

Jimmy throws an arm around the latest Loyals recruit, Chunky. Chunky looks uncomfortable but he smiles nonetheless.

CHUNKY: Amazing.

JIMMY: You guys all travel up in that van?

CHUNKY: (*shaking his head*) I drove up. Ronnie drove up too. Everyone else was in the big Sprinter van.

JIMMY: Nice to see such dedication to Charlie. After all the great music he's given us, eh?

Jimmy turns the camera back on himself. His expression is drunk and yet serious.

JIMMY WATT: Okay troops, ah really need to concentrate on the job. Ah'm dead serious aboot getting that handshake. Positive thinking, eh? Ah'm getting that handshake. Ah'm *getting* that handshake. We need to start keeping an eye on the back alley behind the Hoot because if Charlie leaves and goes back to the hotel, that's where I'll catch him on the way oot. I've waited nearly thirty years for this moment. Whatever it takes, ah'm getting that bloody handshake!

22

"Charlie, you can't do this. You can't just walk out again!"

Johnny's bellowing voice brought all other sounds in the green room to a sudden halt. Those sounds had been happy ones: the whirr of excited post-gig chatter, the explosion of champagne corks popping and the joyous laughter that accompanied a job well done. The tension before the gig was gone. The show itself had been a tremendous success from the moment the band had walked onto the tiny, beer-soaked stage and played the opening notes to 'Night Train'.

The Hoot and Annie crowd had roared at the sight of Charlie dressed as Ryker Marshall. The floor and walls trembled. A chant had broken out – "*Ryker! Ryker! Ryker!*" They screamed when Charlie picked up the Telecaster. The Dark Stars songs, which made up the majority of the set, had gone down a storm but as with the two previous gigs in Glasgow and Edinburgh, the rapturous applause had been reserved for The Broken Gods numbers, especially 'Coming For You'.

Charlie sang and played like it was his last ever gig. As usual, when he was in the moment, everything else faded away. There was only the music and the audience. The songs. The lyrics. The next verse, next chorus, next song. It was a state of pure happiness where everything blended into one.

Afterwards, the green room was a dizzying swirl of noise.

The fluorescent beams pouring down from the ceiling were sickeningly hot. There were too many people in the room, more than before the gig, all of them talking at Charlie at the same time, talking so fast and not giving him a chance to recover after the show. Charlie trudged through the crowd, back and forth several times, trying not to engage with anyone for too long. His clothes were drenched in sweat. The fedora was gone after he'd tossed it into the crowd.

Charlie wasn't hanging around.

He'd already asked Baggy to pack up his guitars and load them into the back of the band's van outside. He wanted to drive home by himself. Right now, without even stopping off to pick up his things at the Best Western. Let Johnny do that and drop them off during the week. Just Charlie's gear in the van, he'd instructed Baggy. Darcy and Hutch's equipment was to go in the crew van. Baggy was perplexed at the instructions but at the same time he knew who was paying the bills. The roadie got to work while Charlie went into the green room and towelled off. He continued to shut down all attempts at conversation. Mostly, people were asking him to sign things. Charlie signed a few autographs, but he refused to sign memorabilia as he knew it was all going online for profit.

Eventually, he made the announcement to Johnny that he was leaving.

"What is it with you?" the tour manager yelled. His

cheeks were blazing red. "Are we that horrible to be around? Are we that fucking dull that you have to run off after every gig?"

Johnny was holding an unopened can of Stella Artois in his hand. Looked like he'd been on the brink of unwinding for the night. Helluva time, Charlie thought, to drop the bombshell.

Charlie shrugged. He glanced nervously around the room.

"I'm going home Johnny."

Johnny spun around. He slammed the Stella down on the table with such force that the wooden legs seemed to buckle.

"Charlie," he said. "Please man. You walked out after the last two gigs and we didn't say anything. Okay? You *can't* do it again tonight. The fans are here for you. For *you*. There are at least five local journalists who want to talk to you. Just a wee interview mate, you know? About playing in a small pub in Inverness and what it means to people who've waited years to see you. C'mon man. I've said you'd do it. Help me out."

Charlie glanced at the other two band members. At the rest of the crew, as well as the staff from the Hoot and everyone else on the guest list who'd squeezed into the overcrowded dressing room after the gig. Everybody was looking at him. Apart from a couple of people who were pretending to look at their phones.

"Charlie," Johnny said. His hands were clasped together as he approached the singer. "Please. Just stick around for an hour and then I'll drive you back to the hotel myself. One hour bud – that's all I'm asking."

"No."

"Forty-five minutes."

"I'm going home."

Johnny's shoulders drooped in defeat. "Charlie..."

"Please Charlie," Darcy said, taking up position beside the tour manager. She gave Johnny's forearm a gentle squeeze. Charlie narrowed his eyes. A gesture of support? He'd seen the way those two looked at one another. Was that another reason they wanted Charlie to keep churning out songs for The Dark Stars until the end of time? So that Johnny and Darcy could stay on tour together and sneak in and out of each other's hotel rooms?

"C'mon mate," Darcy said. "Hang around for a wee bit, will you? Johnny's right. How many times will the people around here get to spend time with a bona fide legend like Charlie Lewis? Throw them a crumb or two man. Throw Johnny a crumb. He works his arse off for us."

Hutch nodded before chiming in from across the room. "People love you, Charlie. We love you. Stay. Let's have some fun."

For a brief moment, Charlie saw a silhouette at the back of the room. No face, no eyes, but the distinct outline of a fedora hat and a guitar slung over the shoulder. His only friend in the world.

Are you prepared to use that axe, Charlie?

"Will you?"

It was Johnny's voice.

"Charlie?" Johnny said, clicking his fingers over and over again. "Can you hear me for God's sake? I asked you a question. Will you stay for thirty minutes at the very least? Thirty minutes, starting now. We can do rapid-fire interviews, give them about five minutes each. They're all out there, waiting to get in. Half-an-hour my friend. Then we're done. Then I'll take you back to the digs."

Charlie blinked the sweat out of his eyes. "I played the show Johnny. I did what I came here to do."

No one said anything.

Charlie squatted down and grabbed his Adidas bag off the floor. The axe inside felt heavier than he remembered. He walked over to the table, pushed past the empty crisp packets, and picked up the keys to the van. Baggy had finished loading the guitars and he was back in the green room now, acknowledging Charlie's decision to go with a curt nod of the head and a neutral expression. Charlie gave the veteran roadie a pat on the shoulder.

He turned to the others in the room.

"See you later."

Some of them said goodbye. Most were quiet however, as if they couldn't believe that Charlie was really leaving. Johnny's arm reached out to intercept Charlie's departure. For a moment, it looked like he was going to hold Charlie back. But then the arm flopped to Johnny's side. Limp and lifeless. "Charlie, please. Don't..."

"Sorry Johnny. I'll give you a call in a few days."

Charlie shoved the van keys into his pocket. He marched over to the fire exit, his legs numb with tension and most likely, exhaustion. It was the end of a very long tour. Sweat poured down his face and he wasn't sure if it was just the lights or something else making him leak. Felt like he was still up there on stage, all eyes on him. At least he had his bag. Now that he'd eliminated Darcy and Hutch from his crazed suspicions about kidnapping, he had to get that axe out of there before someone found it and put a straitjacket on him. Charlie glanced at his bandmates on the way out. Gave them both a nod. They looked sad. Betrayed. Did they know? *Why are you walking around with an axe in your bag Charlie?*

Charlie stopped at the fire exit. It was time to be straight with the poor kids. With everyone who needed to hear what he had to say.

"The band's over."

He wasn't expecting the hurt look on their faces. Anger, that's what he'd been waiting for. The inevitable lashing out. But there was only a quiet pain. It looked so genuine that Charlie felt a sudden stab of guilt about the way he'd treated his bandmates.

"I'm sorry," he said.

"Charlie," Johnny said, creeping towards the fire exit as if there were landmines peppered across the floor. He spoke in the soft voice of a parent trying to appease a temperamental child. "It's been an emotional night. I understand that. But now isn't the time to make rash decisions about the future, okay?"

"I made the decision months ago," Charlie said.

That seemed to knock the wind out of Johnny's sails. He'd tried his best, but now the man crumpled like a sheet of used paper.

Charlie gave the room one last apologetic look. Then he lifted the metal bar and nudged the fire exit open with his shoulder. He walked outside and inhaled the fresh Inverness air, enhanced by the distinct scent of whisky seeping out of The Hoot's back window and floating off into the night. He heard cheers from both ends of the brick alley where security guards held the fans back. Charlie's focus was on one step at a time. He walked to the van. A woman cried out at the top of her lungs, telling Charlie how much she loved him. Said she wanted a kiss. A man's voice roared from afar, saying something about a handshake. There was something about the Lewis Loyals but Charlie wasn't slowing down for anyone tonight, not even Ginger or the regulars from Glasgow. He hurried over to the two vans parked by the wall. Then he called over to the nearest security guard to let her know that he was about to leave and could they guide him out. The guard nodded and then proceeded to walk down to the nearest exit to let the others know that one of the vans was coming out.

Charlie unlocked the driver's side door and climbed into the cabin. There was a slight hint of body odour in the van, a reminder of the journey up from Edinburgh, and of Hutch who didn't believe in deodorant the way other people did. Charlie dropped the Adidas bag on the passenger's side footrest. Then he slammed the door shut. Oh boy, he thought, looking at the bag. He thought about what was in there and felt his face burning up. Thought about how close he'd come to snapping and what could have happened. Lesson learned, Charlie thought. It was all due to the stress of the occasion combined with all the rest of it – the end of his marriage, the loss of his boys, and the fact that he was falling out of love with life as a rock star – the only life he'd ever known as an adult. Had he really brought an axe to Inverness to kill his bandmates? It was blatantly obvious that Charlie was exhausted. Burned out, that was it. Thank God, no one had seen the axe. *Thank God, thank God.* He'd take it to Kintyre, hang it off the front door and maybe one day he'd be able to look back and laugh about what he'd almost believed. About what he'd almost done. As for right now, he'd go home. Then, next week, he'd go to the farmhouse and escape. Maybe then he'd laugh. Most likely, it would take a lot longer before he could do that.

Darcy and Hutch. He'd make sure they were okay for money post-Dark Stars. It was the least he could do for being such a prick.

Charlie wafted the body odour towards the back of the

van. He assessed the road ahead. The guards were already waving him forward. That was quick, he thought. He couldn't wait to take the van out of the alley, get past Bridge Street and turn it into an island on wheels on the open road. It was an easy drive back. Charlie figured he could reach the A9 without too much trouble from here. He'd be back in Glasgow in the early hours. Things would get better once the anniversary was behind him. He could think. Get his shit sorted. Maybe he'd even go back to therapy and try again.

The guard was still waving.

Charlie waved back. "Coming."

He thrust the key in the ignition and gave it a sharp turn. The diesel engine croaked to life and Charlie breathed a sigh of relief. He was about to lower the handbrake when he heard footsteps at the side of the van. Charlie held off on the accelerator, expecting one of the security guards to appear at the window, offering to escort him down the alley.

The passenger side door opened.

Charlie turned to the left, a polite smile on his face. "Thanks for the offer but I'll be okay to get..."

It was Hutch. He was standing at the open door.

Without saying anything, the drummer leapt into van. He shoved along the double passenger seat, coming to a stop in the middle of the cabin. The reek of his sweat was fresh now. Overbearing. His right leg rubbed against the gearstick. Darcy appeared at the door behind Hutch, a nervous look on her face as she glanced at Charlie, then down to security. Then she jumped in, taking her place at the window seat.

She closed the door. Put her feet on top of the Adidas bag.

"We're a band," Darcy said, after a long silence. "If it's

really over for The Dark Stars, then what the hell, right? We should take this last journey together."

Charlie's blood ran cold. Last journey?

He stared through the windscreen, watching as the security guard continued to signal that he was all-clear to go.

"You guys travel back with the crew tomorrow. I go back to Glasgow tonight."

Darcy shook her head. "Sorry Charlie. We're going with you."

She took a deep breath. Her legs looked like they were shaking and she grabbed a hold of her thighs as if to regain control. He'd never seen Darcy this nervous before. Never heard her voice shake like it was shaking now.

"You're not going home," she said.

"What...?"

Charlie stopped talking when he felt the pressure on his thigh. He looked down. Hutch had a knife at his leg. It was a big mother too with a serrated edge, those hungry teeth biting into Charlie's flesh.

Hutch pressed down harder with the blade. He swallowed, looking every bit as terrified as Charlie felt.

"She said you're not going home, Charlie. So, why don't you do us all a favour, okay? Let's make this nice and easy."

23

Charlie was given instructions to drive the van out of the alley. Go slow, they said. Keep the van at crawling speed and they instructed him to smile. Wave to the guards. Wave to the fans. Don't arouse suspicion.

"I was right," Charlie whispered. "I was right about you both."

"What was that?" Darcy asked, tilting her head in his direction.

Charlie didn't answer.

"Be normal," Hutch said. "We'll make this as painless as possible. Just drive, go where we tell you."

Charlie did as he was told. He drove the van over the cobblestones, his eyes darting back and forth between the road and the knife at his leg. Was he imagining this? No, it was real. Somehow, he managed to smile at the security personnel who, after ushering the crowd back towards the road, had opened up a clear route for Charlie to navigate the van onto Bridge Street. The road was mobbed by fans, most of them bouncing up and down in excitement, waving their hands in the air and singing the same songs that Charlie had been singing for the past two hours in the basement. When they saw Charlie and his passengers, they went ballistic. Some of them tried to climb onto the van. Security pushed them away. Some of the fans played air guitar in the middle of the road, demonstrating their imaginary skills for Charlie.

"Keep going," Hutch growled. "Don't do anything stupid man. No signals, okay?"

Charlie could smell the alcohol on Hutch's breath. Smelled like the big man had been hitting the bottle of Jack Daniel's on the rider, as well as working his way through the beers. He *had* been drinking more than usual, Charlie thought. Building up courage? Charlie gripped the wheel tight. Felt his arms shake from shoulder to wrist. It was hard to tell who was the most nervous in the little cabin. The security team walked ahead of the van, still sweeping the eager crowd aside. Considering how outnumbered they were, they were doing a hell of a good job keeping things in order. The fans thumped the side of the van as it cruised past them, working its way slowly down Bridge Street. They yelled for Charlie. Some for Darcy and Hutch.

Charlie glanced towards the sidelines. He saw contorted faces in the front row, bulging veins on their foreheads. They reached for him.

"CHARLEEEEEEEEEEE!"

Charlie wanted to scream for help. What would happen if he did? Hutch had shifted several inches to the right, as far as he could go on the passenger seat. He was leaning towards Charlie, pressing the serrated blade harder against his leg. There was a faint sting, but the growing sense of dread that Charlie felt numbed most of the pain.

It was hard work getting away from the pub. Away from the crowds. Charlie sat upright behind the wheel, his back as stiff as a board. He glanced at the people on the street yet again. The crowd was thinning out. He felt a fresh spurt of panic. Screamed for help with his eyes but of course, nobody understood.

"Charlie! Charlie Charlie!"

Charlie looked down at the passenger side floor. Darcy's feet were still on top of the Adidas bag and even though it was barely out of arm's reach from the driver's seat, the bag (and what was in it) might as well have been sitting on top of Mount Everest. Charlie had made a big mistake. He'd doubted his instincts at the very end. Sure, his instincts had manifested as all sorts of crazy shit, especially the figure of Ryker Marshall in his bedroom and hotel room. But whatever had fuelled that vision, it was correct. The warning had been spot on. He'd let his guard down and given them just enough time to ambush him at the last minute.

"Where are we going?" Charlie asked.

They didn't answer. Somebody in the cabin took a large gulp of breath as if they were about to jump off a diving board from a great height. Whatever this was, Charlie thought, Darcy and Hutch were clearly doing it for the first time. Whether that was to his advantage or not, remained to be seen.

The crowd thinned out further. At last, Charlie could see the empty road ahead of them and it was a chilling sight.

"Where are we going?"

To Charlie's surprise, Darcy shushed him. She was leaning forward, staring at Google Maps on her phone. Her face contorted into a frown as she studied the blue dot that represented the van and the surrounding territory around it. She mumbled to herself. Marked their location. Then she looked up, leaning her long body towards the windscreen.

"Take a right, Charlie. This one coming up here."

Charlie sighed. He turned off Church Street and drove onto Queensgate. Darcy told him to take another sharp right, taking them onto Academy Street. It wasn't long before Charlie realised that they were driving out of town. Away from the bright lights. Buildings became few and far between. Pedestrians, non-existent. Before long, there was a towering outline of treetops in the distance. It wasn't a welcoming sight and it only seemed to be getting bigger. They drove for about ten minutes. Charlie couldn't remember the last time they'd passed another car on the road. Sunday night. Everyone who wasn't at the gig was at home. His heart was thumping. His throat, dry and scratchy. The bright lights receded, giving way to miles of dark countryside ahead. To long empty fields, partitioned from the road by short wire fences that ran parallel along the western route. The roads were narrowing. The peace and quiet, which Charlie loved in Kintyre, was maddening.

He took a slow, deep breath. "Guess I could always reform the band."

"Wouldn't have mattered," Darcy said. "Don't beat yourself up about this, alright Charlie? Jaysus, this is hard enough. It was happening anyway."

"What is *this*?" Charlie asked. "What's happening? Can you tell me that much?"

His kidnappers exchanged tense looks.

"What happened to you man?" Hutch asked. "We're good fucking band, ya? You picked us off the street for a reason and what then, huh? You got bored with us?"

Charlie shook his head. "I thought you said this was happening anyway." He looked at them both. "I knew it. I fucking knew you were up to something."

"How could you have possibly known?" Darcy asked, looking up from her phone. "That's bullshit."

"I know desperation when I see it," Charlie said with a shrug. "So, what is it? Just couldn't bear to lose the fame? The recognition? Lifestyle?"

Hutch shrugged. "What do you mean?"

"It's addictive," Charlie said. "Isn't it? Hell, if I was young and desperate and fucked up enough, I'd probably do the same thing."

"And what exactly are we doing?" Darcy asked. "How much do you think you know, Charlie?"

Charlie nodded, keeping his eyes on the dark road ahead. "Let me guess. It's Ryker's anniversary today. You're going to complete the double act, aren't you? You're going to make me disappear. Just like he did. If I disappear, you can make money off that for the rest of your life. Unsolved mysteries have a long shelf life. Books, interviews, documentaries – whatever. What happened to Charlie Lewis? We ask those who were closest to him at the end...*kerching!* But for that to happen, I have to vanish. Right?"

"The world *is* fascinated by a good mystery," Darcy said. She went back to studying the map. "But you're wrong about one thing."

"Oh. What's that?"

"We're not the ones who're going to make you disappear."

Charlie arched his eyebrows. "What?"

Hutch pointed at the windscreen. "We're just the delivery service, ya? All we have to do is take you there."

"I don't get it," Charlie said.

"We're being paid," Darcy said. "A *lot* of money. So yeah, there's definitely an element of self-preservation involved in what we're doing. But your books, TV specials and whatever – all that can fuck off. The world won't be seeing much of me after this goes through."

"And you're okay with that?" Charlie asked. "Handing me over?"

"I am."

"Then why are your hands still shaking?"

Darcy threw him a filthy look. "Fuck off Charlie."

"Where are you taking me, Darcy? Hutch?"

It was Darcy who answered. "To someone who wants you very badly. Now, I'll be perfectly honest with you Charlie. I don't know what he wants to do with you. And quite frankly, I don't care. You had your fun with us, didn't you? Take two little buskers off the street and then throw them away when you're done. Send them back to the streets. Why should we care about you?"

"How much?" Charlie asked. He could hear the desperation creeping into his voice. "How much are you getting for this? Thousands? Tens of thousands?"

"That's a conservative guess. We're kidnapping you, Charlie. We're not doing it for chocolate buttons."

"Who is it?"

"A very rich man who's fucked in the head," Darcy said. "I mean, it's serious money. It's retirement money and all for a quick handover in the middle of nowhere."

"What's his name?"

"You'll recognise him when you see him," Darcy said. "This guy, he follows you about everywhere. He's..."

Darcy hesitated.

"He's what?" Charlie said, his eyes still clinging to the narrow, winding B-road through the windscreen. It felt like he was submerging into deep, black water. Where the hell were they taking him?

"Lewis Loyals," Hutch said, after giving Darcy a nod. "He's one of those little lovesick puppy dogs that stand outside your house."

Charlie's heart was pounding in his chest. The Lewis Loyals? What the...? He mentally browsed a gallery of faces. All the faces that stood outside his house. Outside the studios. Outside the hotels. It was a *he*? Okay. Forget Ginger and the brunettes and any of the other women who followed him around. His thoughts turned to the huddle of middle-aged men that stood waiting for him on a daily basis. His mind's eye ran over their faces. They were harmless, weren't they? Losers, but they adored him. So how could it...?

"Oh shit," he said.

His fingers almost slipped off the steering wheel.

Ronnie.

Charlie felt like he was about to throw up. There were some crazy people out there, he knew that as well as anyone. Crazy people did crazy things. *Ronnie, what have you done?* Charlie couldn't get Ronnie's black eyes out of his mind. The way he just stood there in the background all the time, peering through the dark slits carved into his head. It was right there, right there in the way he'd always looked at Charlie. Never talking, never asking for anything. Just looking.

Waiting.

"Don't do this," he said. "Please."

Hutch's response was gruff. "Hurry up Charlie. We're behind schedule."

"Drive," Darcy said. "Just drive. It'll all be over soon."

Charlie was shaking like a leaf, but somehow he was able to keep control of the van. What could he do? The knife was still pressed against his leg. They travelled north on the A96, away from Inverness and heading towards Culloden according to the road signs. The road seemed endless. A right turn took them south. They were on another narrow

B-road. Thick hedges on either side. Charlie felt like he was driving through the back end of nowhere. There were no other cars on the road. No people. No streetlights or sound apart from the muted growl of the van. His skin was hot and clammy with sweat.

Darcy sat forward, staring at the map on her phone.

"We're close. Slow down."

Charlie's foot touched the brake pedal. *Close.*

"Okay," Darcy said, about a minute later. "Bring her to a stop here. Pull in at the side of the road."

Charlie rolled the van to a halt. He sat there, an icy terror washing over him as they sat in silence.

Eventually, he had to speak.

"Now what?"

Hutch peered through the windscreen.

"There," he said, pointing a finger.

There was a sudden flicker of light on the road. Up ahead, just around the corner. Looked like a set of yellow eyes opening up against the black night. But Charlie knew those weren't eyes. Two headlights glared in their direction. It was a car, sitting on the next bend. It had been sitting there when they'd arrived.

Ronnie was waiting.

24

Charlie couldn't breathe. He couldn't stop the swell of panic rising up in his chest.

"Who is that?"

He watched as the other car crawled slowly around the corner. It turned onto the straight and the brakes let out a soft screech as it came to a stop about fifteen metres away from the van. Charlie stared at it. It was a Skoda hatchback, one of the sleek, newer models. Dark silver by the looks of it. The Skoda's engine was still running, its bright, crystalline-shaped headlights pointing at the van.

"Don't do this," he said.

Hutch finally removed the knife from Charlie's leg. Charlie felt a faint sting down there, a hot prickling of the skin, but he wasn't worried about that right now. He was thinking about escape options. And yet it seemed hopeless. How would he do it? He'd have to pull the door handle and leap out before Hutch grabbed him, dragged him back inside and then maybe this time he'd bring the knife to Charlie's throat. Give him something to think about. Hutch was nervous too. They were both nervous. And between Hutch and Charlie, the drummer was the younger and stronger man by far. If it came down to a physical confrontation, then Charlie stood little chance of winning.

"How much did he pay you?" Charlie asked, returning to the question of money. "Whatever it is, I'll double it."

They didn't answer.

"I'll triple it. I swear to God."

Charlie fell back into the driver's seat. He found it hard to believe that creepy Ronnie had that sort of money lying around but then again, what did Charlie know about this guy? Nothing. Ronnie stood with the Loyals (stood near to them anyway) and based on their earlier encounters, Charlie had put the guy in a neat box. Ronnie was a weirdo, that's all. A harmless weirdo. A Charles Manson lookalike who, after stalking his favourite rock stars, probably went back to his one-bedroom flat in Partick and hammered out songs on the acoustic guitar, songs about pulling the wings off insects and eating human flesh. Ronnie lived off microwave meals and supermarket brand lager. He was a dreamer who'd hardened over time, a failure who now took solace in music. Creepy, yes. Disturbed, probably. But wealthy? Fans came in all shapes and sizes, Charlie knew that much. They came with all types of income. Who's to say that Ronnie wasn't a millionaire? Lottery win? Superfans were a strange bunch but it was always the quiet, unsettling ones who prompted the most concern.

And Ronnie never said a damn word.

"Retirement money," Charlie said, spitting out a bitter and fearful laugh. Then he snapped. "How much for God's sake? How much is he paying you?"

Darcy and Hutch were too focused on the other car to

respond to his plea. They sat like statues. Eyes unblinking. Charlie knew they were frightened too.

"Rich enough to pay off a couple of buskers," Charlie said. "What did he give you? A hundred pounds each?"

Darcy pointed to the door handle on the driver's side. "It's time Charlie. Just go."

Charlie didn't respond. He didn't know what to do or what to say. This situation was far out of his control. He stared through the windscreen, narrowing his eyes at the blinding headlights that felt like lasers trying to get inside his mind. "The biggest mistake I ever made was picking you pair of dogshits up off the street. You're scum. You've always been scum and no matter what your bank account says, you always will be."

His face was a grim mask of loathing.

"Compared to the Gods, you were average."

He stared one more time at the bag with the axe in it. Charlie fantasised about bringing it down on both their heads.

"Go Charlie," Hutch said.

Charlie slammed a fist off the steering wheel. So much for keeping a lid on his emotions. He felt like crying but he wasn't going to give these bastards the satisfaction of watching him fall apart. He was in control of that much at least. One last idea occurred to him. He glanced at Hutch, then Darcy. Pointed at the Adidas bag under Darcy's feet. "Can I take my bag with me? I'm soaked with sweat. Change of clothes. Can't hurt, can it?"

Darcy shook her head. She couldn't even look at him. "Will you just hurry up? He'll be getting impatient. You don't want to piss him off."

Jesus, thought Charlie. He killed the engine and pocketed the keys, making sure that he was subtle about it. Then he reached for the door handle. The metal was cold and unforgiving to the touch.

He looked back at the others.

"I'll triple it."

But they didn't respond.

25

Charlie was the first one out of the van, followed closely by Darcy and Hutch who exited through the passenger side.

He walked towards the Skoda and its waiting driver, who was still a motionless silhouette inside the car. Charlie glanced up at the sky. The moon was a perfect white sickle above his head, the centrepiece jewel in a blanket of stars. It was a chilly night in the Highlands. The breeze cooled Charlie's sweat-stained clothes but that wasn't why he was shivering.

"Keep walking," Hutch said.

They were behind him, but they kept their distance. Why? What were they afraid of? Afraid that their benefactor would renege on the deal? Take them out after the handover?

The Skoda's engine hummed quietly in the background. Charlie's advance came to a halt and he found himself sandwiched in between the two vehicles, still wincing at the fierce outpouring of light in his face. There was a big fucker of a headache coming on. Least of his many problems. He stood there on the road, wondering when the other driver was going to show himself. Charlie wanted to see the bastard's face, to confirm his suspicions.

Darcy and Hutch had also stopped walking forward. Unlike Charlie, they were still closer to the van than they were to the car.

Maybe, Charlie thought, there'd be time to tackle the bastard when he stepped out. Jump him. Take him by surprise. Pound his head off the road, turning it to pulp and think nothing of it. Charlie was desperate and desperate people had the strength of ten men.

My boys. I have to get back to my boys. We've got Ireland in July to look forward to.

Charlie did have something to live for. Something to fight for. After about a minute, the driver's door opened. A shadowy figure stepped out of the Skoda. Charlie strained his eyes but the man's defining features were still out of reach. And for a moment, he just stood there, lingering beside the car. Almost as if he was unsure about proceeding with this plan.

Footsteps.

The man came forward at last.

Charlie's fists were clenched into two tight balls at his sides. *Calm. Stay calm.* He glanced to his right, then to the left. Options. Quickly. A short strip of wire fencing to the left, running parallel with the road. On Charlie's right, the crumbling remains of a stone wall that looked like a relic from ancient times. Beyond the fence to his left, what was out there? An open field that stretched into the night. To where? To the hills and a steep climb to the stars. Beyond the wall to his right, a few scattered ash trees were visible. Behind them? More green fields?

His abductors had picked a good spot for the handover. Quiet and secluded. Charlie's escape options were terrible.

"Hi Charlie."

Charlie gasped as he took his first proper look at the man who'd stopped in front of the Skoda. His captor leaned against the bonnet. The car dipped under the weight and even made a faint groaning noise as if to protest. It wasn't Ronnie, that much was obvious as soon as he'd stepped within range of the headlights. Ronnie was long and lean but this guy was short and massively overweight. His walk from the car door to the bonnet hadn't been much of a walk at all. More like a laboured waddle.

And then Charlie saw the bald head, as white as the moon. From where he stood, it looked like the man's eyebrows were missing.

"Chunky?"

The man waved, his hand moving back and forth like a pendulum. There was a wheezing sound as he breathed.

"Surprised?"

He stared at Charlie through the black holes in his head.

"What do you want with me?" Charlie asked. "Why am I here?"

Chunky made a faint gagging noise. Sounded like there was something caught in the back of his throat. "Charlie, Charlie. Don't you recognise me? I guess it *has* been a long time, hasn't it?"

"What are you talking about? I saw you a couple of days ago in Glasgow. Standing outside the hotel on Blythswood Square."

"No," Chunky said. "You didn't see *me*. You saw *Chunky*."

Charlie's terror bubbled up inside. It manifested itself into a surge of full-blown anger and it took whatever restraint was left to hold him in place. He stabbed a finger at the man standing in front of the Skoda. "Will you just STOP? Enough of the horseshit. What the fuck is going on here? *You?* You paid them a fortune to kidnap me and bring me out here to the middle of nowhere? Why? What the fuck is going on Chunky."

Chunky wagged his finger in the air. "*Chunky?* Didn't you hear what I just said? After all these years, don't you recognise me?"

"What? I don't know you."

"Look at me Charlie. *Look* at me. Yes, you do."

Charlie's voice was a hoarse and cracked mess. It sounded like he'd been gargling broken glass all night. "Who are you?"

"It's me."

Charlie's unflinching stare devoured every inch of Chunky's bloated face. Dead eyes, milky white skin, and a blank expression that shone otherworldly in the evil-eye crystalline headlights. Charlie had only ever glanced at Chunky a few times (at most) in the short period of time that the man had stood with the Lewis Loyals. Like Ronnie, Chunky had always shied away from too much eye contact. Was that a deliberate strategy? To remain quiet and unnoticed. To linger in the background. Not tonight. Tonight, Chunky couldn't take his eyes off Charlie.

And why was he smiling like that?

"Who are you?"

Charlie took a step forward, his head swirling under the influence of something that felt like horse tranquilisers mixed with vodka. But he hadn't been drugged, at least not to his knowledge. This didn't feel like drugs. This was pure, dizzying bewilderment. He concentrated on the pale, bloated shape. Stared until his eyes hurt. Until his head hurt. And then, the horror of clarity. No, he thought. *It can't be.* Charlie's mind rebelled against the myriad of revelations taking shape in his mind. And while his spirit recoiled from the unfolding recognition, his eyes dug deeper into the other man. *It's you.* It was the voice more than anything on the outside that convinced him. The familiar voice. He was looking at the shipwreck of a great vessel, all rotten wood, fungus and decay. Charlie couldn't believe it. Somewhere in the dark canyons of Chunky's eyes, Ryker Marshall was looking back at him.

He was barely able to summon his voice. "Is...it...you?"

"You see me now, don't you?"

Charlie nodded. He couldn't feel his legs underneath him. Couldn't feel anything.

"Ryker?"

That was when he heard gasps of shock from behind. He'd almost forgotten that Darcy and Hutch were there, still standing beside the van. Still afraid to get too close. Charlie realised they had no idea they'd kidnapped him on behalf of his old songwriting partner.

Charlie's thoughts were all over the place. Was this good news or was it bad? He didn't like the way Ryker was looking at him. That look was too...*hungry*. Didn't seem like there was a warm embrace coming anytime soon.

"Is this another one of your therapy treatments?" Ryker said, grinning. "Is that what you're thinking right now, *old friend*? Is this another expensive scenario conjured up at the Dawson Clinic to deal with repressed trauma?"

Charlie felt like he was swaying on his feet. Like he'd been punched in the face so many times that he was on the brink of being knocked out. "No. It's not."

"Do they help you?" Ryker asked, tilting his head to the side like a curious dog. "Your therapy sessions in Edinburgh. Talk to me brother. What is it you want to say to me?"

Charlie's tongue was paralysed again. All he could do was shake his head.

"Let me help you with your burden," Ryker said, lifting himself off the Skoda's bonnet. The car sprang upwards and this time, the groan it made sounded like a sigh of relief. Ryker approached Charlie, never straying from the path of the shimmering car headlights. The light distorted the man, turning him into a supernatural creature that floated. "Maybe you'd like to start by saying sorry."

Charlie cleared his throat, searching for his lost voice. "Sorry?"

"I know," Ryker said. "I know that you and Sally were sleeping together before I disappeared. Please don't try to deny it. The two people I loved most in the world. Trusted the most. And all those years ago, you were betraying me. Laughing behind my back."

Charlie spoke through clenched teeth. "Nobody was laughing at you. We both regretted what happened but you...you weren't innocent. You were distant. You were a nightmare. Lost in your ego, playing up to the tortured genius image – the same one that you'd encouraged in the media when we started out. You were full of crap. You'd even started to believe your own press."

Ryker's face was still blank. "So you stole the woman I love?"

"We fell in love," Charlie said. "Or at least, that's what we thought at the time. But it wasn't just a fling."

"It's still stealing."

Now it was Charlie's turn to laugh. But it wasn't convincing and quickly descended into full-blown rage. "You see what I mean? About ego? Who the fuck do you think you are? You pushed us all away back then and don't say we didn't try. Then you ran out on everyone who ever cared for you. You left us all to think you were dead. Your mother. Your sister. Sally for God's sake! And you come back like *this*? Kidnapping me? Dragging me out into the middle of nowhere and why? Because Sally sought out a little comfort somewhere else? You broke that woman. Fucking self-obsessed prick. I pity you. Where have you been for the past twenty-five years?"

Charlie saw a flicker of discomfort in the man's eyes.

"I don't need your pity," Ryker said. "I'm in control here Charlie, not you. Me. Now listen – this is what's going to happen. We're going to take a little drive together."

"Like hell we are," Charlie said.

"Easy now, *brother*."

"She never got over your disappearance," Charlie said. "All the questions you left behind, they drove her mad. She struggled with the guilt so much. She thought it was her fault. *Our* fault. You have no idea. We..."

Ryker's eyes narrowed. "What?"

Charlie lowered his eyes. "We went to Erskine Bridge so many times, just the two of us. Always at her request. Always on the anniversary. She wanted to go there, I didn't. She felt some kind of connection with you when she was there, looking down at the water. Just the two of us, standing at the railing, apologising. It was like confession."

"Were you there?" Ryker said. "Were you there, Charlie? When she jumped?"

Charlie nodded.

"Yes. Well, no. Not really."

"Tell me about it."

"It was just after midnight on the fifth anniversary," Charlie said. "That was a tough one for her – felt like the first big anniversary we'd faced. She was already broken. We were on the bridge again, arguing because I told her that it had been long enough and...I couldn't keep going there. It did nothing for me and I felt like it was doing Sally more harm than good. We weren't together by that point. But I told her she had to let you go. That she had to move on with her life. I'd been telling her that for a long time. But she didn't want to know. She still blamed herself."

Ryker's eyes bore a hole deep into Charlie. "Did you push her off the bridge?"

"What the fuck?" Charlie said, screwing up his face in disgust. "Are you off your head? Of course I didn't push her. I..."

He hesitated.

"I walked away. That's what I did. I walked away that night and..."

"You left her alone."

"How the hell did I know she was going to jump?" Charlie said. "We got into a stupid argument and I told her I was done with it. Going to Erskine Bridge every year at midnight, standing there like a prize tool and thinking that it meant something. I suppose I did push her in a way. Maybe if I hadn't said that..."

Ryker glared at Charlie. "Why didn't you tell anyone? That you were there."

Charlie felt like he'd been hit by a wrecking ball. "Because I know how the press work and they would've used it against me. It would've been a great scandal, don't you think? Did he push her or not? Would've gone on for years and tainted everything I did. I didn't want that. I don't think Sally would've wanted it. There were no cameras on the bridge at that time so I kept my mouth shut about being there."

There was a long silence. Charlie felt like a massive weight had been lifted off his shoulders and yet there was no relief.

"It's time for that drive, Charlie."

Ryker glanced over Charlie's shoulder towards Darcy and Hutch. "My friends, have I bought your silence? You're satisfied with the arrangement?"

"I'll be satisfied when we get the second instalment," Darcy said. There was a look of astonishment on her face as if she was still digesting everything she'd just heard. "You know what I'm saying? The big one."

"Paid them in cash, did you?" Charlie asked. "Didn't spend all that money you used to keep hidden under the bed?"

Ryker ignored Charlie's quip. "Bring me his things. His belongings. Clothes, bags, instruments – anything that can be traced back to him, no matter how small or seemingly insignificant it might seem. Load everything into the boot and make sure you bring the Telecaster too. I assume it's in there?"

"It's in there," Darcy said. Her voice still shook with nerves. "We'll get it, no worries."

"Quickly, if you please."

Darcy and Hutch hurried as they went about their business. It was clear they were desperate to get away and put all of this behind them. First, they opened up the double doors of the van and pulled out both Charlie's Rickenbacker bass and the Fender Telecaster. Baggy had packed both instruments in their hard cases and there was a flurry of movement as Charlie's former bandmates loaded them into Ryker's boot. Afterwards, they walked back to the van to get the rest of Charlie's stuff.

Charlie shook his head. "Where are we going Ryker?"

Ryker wasn't idle as Charlie's things were moved swiftly from van to car. As Charlie watched, Ryker poured a few drops of clear liquid from a glass bottle, letting the drops fall onto a frayed strip of cloth in his other hand. Ryker snapped his head back from whatever foul scent shot up towards his nostrils. Chloroform, Charlie thought. Or something else like it. Something to knock him out with.

Holy shit, he thought. What was happening here?

Charlie didn't know what to do. Run, fight or stand still? He felt boxed in by his surroundings. Trapped on that little stretch of B-road with nowhere to go. All the while, he was trying to figure out what Ryker wanted him for.

"I'm sorry," Ryker said, glancing up at Charlie. He nodded towards the chloroform in his hand. "But this stuff doesn't work the way it does in films. Sometimes it can take up to five minutes before you go to sleep. I'll ask the drummer, what's-his-name, to hold you down. We'll do the best we can."

"Ryker," Charlie said, trying to hold on to his nerve. "I swear to God, I didn't push Sally off that bridge. If that's the reason you're..."

"I believe you, Charlie. You didn't kill Sally, but you killed me. You both betrayed me. My love. My friendship."

Charlie shook his head. "Why wait all this time? Twenty-five years for God's sake."

"Later for questions," Ryker said, adding an extra couple of drops to the cloth. "There'll be plenty of time for that. We've got a long trip ahead of us. But don't worry – I'll make sure you sleep for the entire journey."

Charlie couldn't let them knock him out. If the lights turned out, something terrible was going to happen. He glanced to his left. Empty field, cloaked in darkness. It was an ocean of grass, neglected by moonlight. How fast could he run in that direction? Could he vault the fence before Hutch grabbed him and pinned him down? Charlie had never been much of an athlete, not back in the day. Not now.

"People will look for me," he said. "Everyone knows where I was tonight."

Ryker smiled. "Exactly. But tomorrow, you'll be far away."

"Please don't do this."

"Charlie, my dear Charlie. Your disappearance is the inevitable conclusion to what's been a very upsetting week for you."

"What the hell are you talking about?"

"You've been acting strange all week," Ryker said. "Haven't you?" There was a look of mock concern on his puffy face. "Darcy's been making a video diary, didn't you know? She mentions you a lot in those clips. Watch the videos. I'll show them to you when we reach our final destination. It soon becomes very clear that she's been concerned about your mental health. Documenting your strange behaviour. It's a very convincing record too. One that explains how Charlie Lewis has been on the verge of a nervous breakdown all week. No one who watches Darcy's vlog will be surprised that you disappeared in the end."

Charlie looked at Darcy. "You set me up."

Darcy was standing beside the van, waiting for Hutch as he pulled Charlie's bag out from underneath the passenger seat. She looked back at Charlie and shrugged, almost apologetically. But Charlie was no longer interested in Darcy. He was looking at the Adidas bag. The one Hutch was taking over to Ryker. It was the last of his things and right now, the most important of his things. Charlie felt a flutter of nerves when he thought about what was inside the bag. He had to get a hold of it somehow. That, or running was his only chance.

"What are you going to do to me?" he asked, turning back to Ryker.

Ryker pressed a finger to his lips. "Shush now Charlie. It's time for sleep, not questions."

"How much did you pay them? To kidnap me. To make videos that made me look crazier than I already am."

"Enough to buy their silence."

Charlie nodded. He watched helplessly as Hutch walked over to the Skoda and offered the Adidas bag to Ryker. "This is the last of his things. No trace of Charlie left in the van now. No more room in boot, so you put bag where you want it, ya?"

Ryker nodded. "Good."

"Be careful," Hutch said. "This bag's damn heavy."

"Uh-huh."

Ryker lowered the chloroform bottle, putting it down at his feet. Then he straightened up and reached over for the bag in Hutch's hand. It happened so fast. His big, awkward body seemed to droop to one side as his right hand swung over to his left side and gripped the handle.

His right hand.

His right hand!

Charlie felt an explosion going off inside him. It was excitement. It was horror. It was...hope? He could barely contain himself. But that was the moment he saw the truth staring him in the face for the first time. His would-be captor was right-handed. Only now did he see it. The *real* truth. It must have been the poor light that deceived his mind. The fear in the moment. The shock of what he thought he was seeing.

How could Charlie have got it so wrong?

This man wasn't Ryker.

26

Charlie felt hollow on the inside. As if something monstrous had swooped down and carved out all of his organs and bones, leaving only the shell behind. Now that he'd spotted the chink in his captor's armour, any faint resemblance to a puffy and bloated version of his old friend was fading fast.

How could he have got it so wrong?

This was *not* Ryker.

Charlie's body was one giant taut muscle waiting to snap. "Who are you?"

The other man's eyes flickered with nervous energy as he turned back to Charlie. He took a step forward and stuck his chin out, like a boxer taunting his opponent in the ring. "Who am I?" he said in a voice that was no longer pretending to be something it wasn't. Now it was raspy and hoarse. It was nasal. "Who am I? Who am I?"

"You're not Ryker," Charlie said. "That's for damn sure."

The man started giggling. Now that there was no longer any need for a mask, his face loosened up. There was a smile. A terrible smile, but it looked real. "Took you long enough. But you saw him, didn't you? Know why? Know why you saw Ryker? You saw him because you wanted to see him. Poor Charlie misses his friend." He laughed again. And there was something in that manic spurt of laughter, in those dead eyes, that took Charlie back thirty years in a split second.

It was an electrifying moment of clarity.

Charlie nodded.

"Fletcher," he said. "Fletcher Darbey."

The man's laughter subsided. He clapped slowly – the sarcastic applause of a contemptuous audience. "Long time no see, eh Charlie?"

Chunky wasn't Ryker. He was Sally's brother, wee Fletch, who wasn't so wee anymore. This was the same man who'd called Charlie in his Glasgow hotel room two nights ago, reaching out, Charlie believed at the time, due to the anniversary. Had Fletcher been taunting him? Playing at Chunky outside the hotel one minute, then running around the corner to make a phone call to Charlie's room?

But why?

The Broken Gods' first roadie had worshipped the band from the sidelines. True, the band hadn't always treated him as an equal but Fletcher never seemed to notice. Or perhaps he did. Perhaps Charlie had missed the resentment due to the fact he'd been so focused on the band getting ahead of the game. What Charlie knew for sure was that Fletcher had worshipped Ryker. It was always Ryker, above all the other band members. Ryker was everything that Fletcher wasn't – talented, charismatic and handsome. People were drawn to Ryker and they followed him. Charlie recalled the way that Fletcher's eyes had lingered on Ryker in rehearsal rooms, venues, and everywhere else for that matter. Like he was studying the man.

It was all starting to come back to Charlie.

Fletcher's devotion to the Gods and particularly to Ryker, had become more obvious and uncomfortable over time. Fletcher, three years younger than both Charlie and Ryker, began to copy Ryker's hairstyles, mannerisms, dress style and even his speech patterns. He'd become quite the mimic. Charlie recalled being more than a little creeped out by his behaviour. It was a long time ago but Charlie remembered coming to the conclusion that it wasn't enough for Fletcher to be around Ryker anymore. He wanted to *be* Ryker. Even Sally felt embarrassed for her little brother, his social awkwardness driving a wedge between the siblings, as well as the band.

Even so, Charlie thought. He couldn't reconcile that wide-eyed boy with the dead-eyed heavy standing before him now. His mimicry skills were still on point. He'd played a fat, ageing Ryker because, despite the whole kidnapping thing, there was still a chance that Charlie would get into a car with Ryker. But never with this guy. Not *this* guy. Fletcher looked at least ten years older than his age. His skin was a ghoulish, marble white. Looked like he'd drop dead if he didn't get back in his coffin before sunrise.

Charlie's head was spinning. "Why are you doing this?"

Fletcher's grin fizzled out. "Do you value loyalty?"

"What are you talking about Fletcher?"

"I was always loyal to the band. Wasn't I?"

"I suppose."

Fletcher stared towards the side of the road, his gaze wandering into the open field beyond the wire fence. "I value loyalty. But in the end, I had to schedule appointments to see my own sister. An appointment for God's sake. Why? I was there at the beginning. Calls not returned. Information not shared. I was the original roadie. Co-manager. I'd been there since the very beginning and you..."

"Fletcher," Charlie said, cutting him off. "You were still around after we made it. I saw you in plenty of dressing rooms."

"Oh that's right," Fletcher said. "Yes, I seem to remember that I had to get a special visitor pass to get in though, didn't I? Not a crew pass or a VIP pass. It was a *visitor's* pass. And for the festivals, it was always just a morning pass or an afternoon pass. God forbid, I'd want to spend the whole day with the band. A band that I helped go from nothing to the top of the world. Ha! Regular old guest list. And once I was allowed in, I remember sitting in those horrible, brightly-lit dressing rooms with all your fancy VIP guests and being ignored by absolutely everyone in the *fucking* room. Was I invisible, Charlie? Am I invisible now?"

Charlie didn't answer.

"No," Fletcher snapped. He bent down and picked up the chloroform bottle at his feet. Then he was soaking the cloth in his hand, spilling the clear liquid all over the road. His head swayed from side to side in a way that made Charlie's blood run cold. He thought of a bull that was about to charge. "No, I'm not invisible. You have to see something in order to push it away, right? You have to know it's there. All of you – even my sister for God's sake. You forgot who stood at the side of the stage holding your towels when no one gave a flying fuck about you and your Broken Gods. You forgot who ran around the stage in between songs, handing you beers, taking your guitars, tuning them, replacing broken strings. I did everything. I sweated for every single one of you and I was always there. Me."

"Why am I here?" Charlie said. "Why have you been standing outside my house, pretending to be one of the...?"

"Lewis Loyals?" Fletcher said. "Those fleas who stand outside your house and hotels? It was a way of blending in, I suppose. I had to see you up close again, Charlie. Get the scent." He wagged a finger back and forth and Charlie could smell the chemicals in the air, wafting off the cloth or perhaps off Fletcher's skin. Smelled like disinfectant. "But those people aren't loyal. They're hanging on to their youth and you're the symbol of it. I actually care about you. About *you*, Charlie. I cared about Ryker too. And he knew it. That's why..."

Charlie's ears pricked up. "What?"

Fletcher's head stopped swaying. "That's why he understood. Ryker understood what *had* to happen in the end. It was because I cared, even if he didn't."

Charlie felt a slow chill running down his spine.

"What are you talking about?"

"I loved him like a brother," Fletcher said, his voice distorted and emotional. "That's what I did. That's what *you* should have done. My sister. All the people who claimed to love him. To be his friend. You didn't have the guts to step in."

Charlie lifted his head. He heard or perhaps imagined the distant hum of an engine. Wishful thinking on his part? But not now, he thought. Don't let it come now. He sensed that he was on the brink of uncovering something terrible, but of vital importance.

"What happened?"

"I loved him like a brother," Fletcher repeated.

"You barely knew him," Charlie said. There was no hint of fear in his voice anymore. "Hardly anyone knew him. You worshipped Ryker like a god but he wasn't a god. That sort of adulation freaked him out. That's why Sally had to start putting distance between you and the band – it was at Ryker's request."

"And yours too?"

"Yes."

"Oh, I knew all that anyway," Fletcher said. "And yet I was the one who saved him. Me. You and my sister would have just stood by and let him become even more of a drug addict than he already was. That's how much you loved him. If I hadn't intervened back then, Ryker Marshall would have ended up just another junkie death story on the news."

He giggled. Lowered the chloroform bottle back onto the road. The cloth was still in his hand.

"We got to spend a lot of time together in the end."

Charlie charged at Fletcher, fuelled by rage. He didn't get far. Hutch grabbed Charlie's arm, securing a tight grip around the right bicep. The big drummer yanked Charlie backwards with such force that he was almost knocked off his feet.

"What did you do?" Charlie yelled.

"Easy Charlie," Hutch said, tightening his grip. It felt like a python was trying to strangle Charlie's arm. "Can't let you hurt him man. We need that second payment, ya? Or all this – it's for nothing."

"What the fuck did you do?" Charlie said. Spit flew from his mouth. "What the fuck did you do to him? Did you kill him?"

Fletcher's mouth fell open. "Kill him? I loved him."

"He didn't just disappear on his own though, did he?" Charlie said. "What happened? He left that hotel in 1997, got in his car and let me guess – you were there. And you followed him. Didn't you?"

Fletcher's face hardened into a cold, emotionless mask.

"It was easy. It was so easy. I followed him for a while in

my car and when he stopped for cigarettes, I intercepted him. We had a brief conversation at the side of the road. I told him that Sally was ill and you know as well as I do Charlie, that he would've done anything for my sister. Anything at all. I told him she was at my place. By then you see, I had my little pet shop up and running in Motherwell. Top floor was the shop floor. And downstairs, well, that was for guests."

Charlie heard Darcy whispering at his back.

"Jesus. This guy? He kidnapped Ryker? Hutch...what the actual fuck are we doing here?"

Fletcher held up the piece of chloroform-soaked cloth in his hand. "That day, April 23rd 1997, was the first time I'd ever used chloroform on someone." He spat out a ferocious bark of laughter. "That was when I learned it took time to work. He put up a good fight when he realised that Sally wasn't there at the shop. My God, I was terrified. He didn't understand that I was trying to help him. How could he? I don't mind admitting this now, but I actually pissed myself while we were fighting. I was *that* scared."

"Jesus," Charlie said.

"But it was done. I locked him inside a cage, quite literally. There he was, I had him with me. And as long as I was in charge, he wouldn't ever take drugs again. And he wouldn't turn his back on me."

Charlie felt numb. "What happened to him?"

Fletcher's smile was grotesque. "I kept him."

"You *kept* him?"

"His lodgings were meagre but I always made sure they were clean. In that department, he had no complaints."

"Lodgings?" Charlie said, almost choking on the words. "You put him in a fucking cage!"

"He was always comfortable," Fletcher said. He was

swaying his head from side to side again. "And in the end, he got off the junk."

Charlie blinked hard. He felt like he was going to puke. He glanced at the Adidas bag, sitting on the road at Fletcher's feet. He needed that axe. Needed it right now.

"Why am I here?" he asked Fletcher.

Fletcher's black eyes rolled back in his head. It was as if Charlie had asked a dumb question. "Ryker lasted a long time. Nineteen years, two months and thirteen days to be precise. That's incredible when you think about it. I mean, at the start he had to go cold turkey to get off the drugs. That was hard to watch. I thought on more than one occasion that he'd die of sheer madness."

Charlie felt like he was about to pass out. "Oh Jesus. You kept him locked up for...?"

"He coped," Fletcher said. "He stopped crying. Stopped begging, thank God. He wouldn't have lasted another nineteen days the way he was putting drugs and drink into his body. I saved him from himself. From the neglect of his so-called friends. I think in the end, he understood how much work I'd put into our little arrangement. He could see that I wanted him to be comfortable. Okay, he was quiet at times but he did eat when prompted."

"Fletcher..."

"Charlie. You'll take his place. It's been a long time since he died but I just can't get used to things the way they are. My home feels so empty. I finish work for the day and when I go downstairs, there's no one there. I've been watching you, Charlie. I know you've got problems. Your wife hates you. Your boys have a new dad who's actually there for them. You've fallen out of love with the music business. I'm offering a comfortable, peaceful life. The press will never hound you again. You'll have a TV with Netflix. Books, I can pick up books for you. An acoustic guitar, I got that for Ryker. In the end, he embraced my hospitality. One thing I'd ask however – please don't make vulgar propositions in return for your release. It really put me off Ryker in the end."

Charlie was aware of Hutch's grip on his arm. It was loosening. Maybe Hutch was trying to process the horror that Charlie would have to put aside until later. A deep-rooted survival instinct kicked in.

He could *not* get in that car.

"And now," Fletcher said, raising the chloroform cloth for all to see. "We really must get going."

Charlie's response was to slam his head backwards with all the force he could muster. He felt the back of his skull bludgeoning the drummer's nose and there was a wet, satisfying crunch. Hutch howled in pain. He staggered backwards and Charlie felt the last of the grip disappear. This was it. His window of opportunity. He took off, running at a ferocious speed to the right-hand side of the road. He hurdled the fence, jumped into the dark field.

He heard the flurry of panicked voices at his back. But Charlie kept running, pumping his arms and legs for all they were worth. He kept his eyes straight ahead as his feet pounded over the grass.

This wasn't over by a long shot.

He knew they'd be coming for him.

27

Charlie ran flat out into a wall of darkness. The most potent terror he'd ever experienced fuelled his legs, his heart, his lungs. The thought of Fletcher's insane plan to put him in a cage for the rest of his life, possibly alongside the decomposing corpse of his best friend, was enough to push Charlie beyond all limits.

Brothers forever.

He trampled the grass underfoot, not seeing what was in front of him. He ran blind. Already, he could hear heavy, plodding feet charging after him.

"Charlie!"

Hutch's voice was gargled and hysterical. Charlie wondered if that stinger of a headbutt he'd delivered had done enough to slow the drummer down. Hutch was a big guy, strong for sure, but he wasn't built for sprinting or distance running. Still, he was a lot younger than Charlie. And he was desperate.

"Charlie, stop running! It's no use man. We find you, ya?"

"Fuck off," Charlie yelled into the night. "You sold me out."

"I need the money brother," Hutch yelled back. "Nothing personal. Got big debts back in Helsinki. Family need this, ya?"

"Feels pretty fucking personal to me!" Charlie cried out. He knew they had a better chance of finding him if he kept shouting and alerting them to his location, but he couldn't stop himself. He went on in clipped bursts of anger. "He kidnapped Ryker. Stole money from Ryker's house. Put him in a cage. He'll put me in a cage for God's sake. He's fucking insane and you're working for him."

Charlie crouched to a squat. He tried to take in his surroundings while keeping his head low. Grass. Lots of grass and open space. The dark outline of hills to his back but they were miles away and it would probably take an hour to reach them on foot. Was there another road in between this field and the hills, perhaps? It was so dark he didn't know what he was walking into. Charlie took a deep lungful of air. He straightened up again and spun around, still a little off-balance. His heart was thumping. He strained his ears to hear over it. He could hear something else – that monotonous hum in the distance again. What was it? Machinery? A factory? Was it a car? *Please God, let it be a car and let it distract them or help me or something.* Or was he just imagining it?

"You don't give a shit about us," Hutch called out. He sounded closer. "You break up band. See us back on street. I've been poor before Charlie, ya? Never going back."

"Fletcher's sister killed herself because of what he did!" Charlie yelled, cupping his hands over his mouth. "She jumped off a bridge because that psycho was keeping her boyfriend as a pet. It's not too late to stop this, Hutch. Whatever he's paying you, I'll triple it. I swear to God man, you won't be poor. I'll help you clear your debts."

"It's too late Charlie. Too late for new deals."

Hutch was running now. Sounded like a combine harvester coming through the grass thinking it was a Ferrari. Damn it, Charlie thought. All he'd done by talking was give his location away. The big man was sprinting hard, his boots thundering off the earth as he covered ground impressively for a man his size. With any luck, Charlie thought, Hutch was too drunk to pinpoint his exact location by sound alone.

"Charlie!"

It was Darcy's voice this time. Sounded like she was behind him. Charlie's heart almost stopped when he heard her. She was close too. Had she been creeping up on him all the time he'd been trying dissuade Hutch?

"He'll put me in a cage for the rest of my life," he whispered.

Charlie couldn't keep running in circles when they were closing in on him like this. Sooner or later, they'd find him, grab him and drag him kicking and screaming back to the road. Back to Fletcher and his chloroform. After that, it was off to Motherwell and eventual insanity in the bottom floor of a pet shop. Darcy, he could handle. Hutch was too big. They could hit him at any time and come from any direction and because it was so dark in the field, Charlie wouldn't even know until they were right on top of him.

There was only one solution. He had to get back to the road. The best-case scenario, he figured, was for him to return to the band's van and drive the hell out of there. After all, he still had the keys in his pocket. It was possible, wasn't it? Darcy and Hutch, being the amateur kidnappers they were, hadn't even thought to take the van keys off Charlie. Going back towards the road felt like running into the lion's den but unless Fletcher had some kind of weapon on him, he was of no immediate threat. Charlie was faster. He was bigger (height-wise anyway). He wouldn't let the sick fuck and his chloroform anywhere near him. With any luck, Fletcher hadn't discovered the axe in Charlie's bag.

Coming up with the plan was one thing. Executing it was something else altogether. Charlie faced the road, which was easy to spot because the Skoda's evil-eye headlights were still on – the only light for miles as far as he could see. How far to the road from here? About fifty metres? A sprint all the way. He could do this. What choice did he have?

He turned once more to the hills at his back. There was nothing for him over there and besides, Darcy was most likely still coming from that direction. It seemed obvious now what Darcy and Hutch were doing. They were trying to trap him in the middle.

It was the road or bust.

"Fuck it."

Charlie set off with a looping U-turn towards the road. He ran hunched over, elbows tucked in at the sides, sacrificing speed so that his head and flailing arms wouldn't pop into Darcy or Hutch's radar. The grass, at its longest, only went up to his shins. Charlie was too scared to drop onto his belly and crawl his way to the road because if someone happened upon him, he'd have no time to jump back to his feet.

There was no easy way to do this.

"Find him! You'll get nothing else if you don't find him!" It was Fletcher's voice, spilling into the field from the road. "You'll get arrested, is that what you want?"

"Charlie!"

Now it was Hutch. Charlie could still hear the drummer's heavy breathing somewhere at his back. Closer than ever now. Charging in fast. It was so close he could feel the hot, panicked breath scraping off the back of his neck. The earth trembled under Charlie's feet. The big man was right there behind him, running like peak Usain Bolt on steroids.

Charlie sidestepped the attempted grab. He felt Hutch's fingers graze the back of his shirt and in that brief moment of contact, Charlie felt an explosion of horror pinballing through his veins. He saw the consequences of being captured. Saw a vision of himself in a cage, crapping into his hands and trying to throw it at Fletcher. He'd be Fletcher's pet for as long as he lived. *What shall we do tonight, Charlie? What shall we watch, Charlie? Shall I read to you, Charlie? Play me a song, Charlie. You must eat, Charlie. You must eat something or I'll take away your snacks, Charlie.*

He'd never see his boys again. They'd be left to wonder what happened to their dad. Just like he'd always wondered about Ryker.

"No!"

Charlie dug deep into his reserves, sprinting towards the wire fence. Towards the road. It was at least a thirty-metre run.

Twenty.

Ten.

"Stop Charlie!"

Hutch sounded exhausted too but he wasn't giving up. What the hell sort of debts did this guy owe back in Finland?

Charlie heard the voice of instinct (which sounded a lot like his mother's voice again) telling him to swerve to the right. Play zigzag in the dark. He didn't know if he had it in him to outrun the drummer, but he was willing for his heart to burst in the attempt. He went for broke, zigzagged right and left. There it was. The wire fence. He hurdled the barrier, his shoe scuffing the top wire. Charlie just managed to stay on his feet. He staggered onto the road like a drunk falling out of a Saturday night pub. *To the van, to the van*. At that exact moment, a wave of blinding light swept around the corner to his right. An engine growled and it sounded like a giant mechanical bear heading straight for him.

Charlie screamed. "Shit!"

He dove for the side of the road, kicking his heels off the surface. Charlie was flying like Superman for a second. Then he landed face-first, rolling several times and coming to a stop at the base of the crumbling wall.

Charlie was pushing himself back to his feet when he heard the scream. It sounded like the howl of a tortured animal. At the same time, he heard the hiss and shriek of screeching tyres. Muffled yells, a blaring horn and a sickening thump.

Hutch collapsed like a ton of bricks in the middle of the road. The van that hit him jerked to a sudden stop, skidding at the edge of the cracked asphalt surface. Panicked voices came from within the front cabin.

Charlie's heart and lungs were on fire. He saw Darcy appear on the other side of the wire fence. She stepped slowly onto the road, one hand clamped over her mouth as she took in the aftermath of the accident.

Charlie pointed at Hutch.

"Happy now?"

Darcy looked at Charlie, her eyes blank. Then she turned back to Hutch who was lying face down in the middle of the road. Arms and legs twisted everywhere. A massive stream of dark blood was leaking from a hole in the side of his head.

"Oh fucking hell."

Darcy looked at Charlie. Her bottom lip trembled uncontrollably. She was on the brink of saying something but then she shook her head. Her face twisted up with horror at the realisation of what had happened. Hutch was dead. There was to be no retirement money. Her eyes bulged. Tears flowed at last. She turned around again, leapt over the fence. Charlie saw her running into the field and then she disappeared in the dark. He wondered how far she'd get before throwing up.

28

Jimmy Watt
YouTube Livestream
The Handshake

Jimmy Watt's second livestream is a high-speed pursuit video. It takes place in his work van and begins in Inverness town centre, eventually leading out into the sticks.

Willie Shearer, 62, is the only one in Jimmy's gang who hasn't been drinking all night. He's behind the wheel, flat cap on his head, wiping rivers of sweat off his face as he takes a series of tight corners at dangerous speeds.

Jimmy sits in the passenger seat, phone in hand, barking out directions every ten seconds. Three other mates, Shug, Eric and Boaby, are in the back of the van sliding from side to side along with Jimmy's work gear, some empty cardboard boxes, an old copy of Mayfair, and a crate of Tennent's Lager.

The pursuit takes them deep into the dark roads of the Scottish Highlands. Jimmy checks his phone. The latest reports about

Charlie Lewis's van, some from Twitter, some from a Dark Stars What's App group, suggest he's somewhere on the back roads travelling in an easterly direction. No one knows for sure if it's the real van or a detour vehicle to confuse fans.

Jimmy's gang have taken more wrong turns than they can count. But they're determined. And as the night gets later and later, they're still on the hunt.

JIMMY WATT: (*narrating as the camera remains on the road*) Hurry up Willie, eh? This is ma last chance mate.

WILLIE SHEARER: Fuck's sake Jimmy! Shut up will ye? Ah'm going as fast as ah can withoot killing us aw man. Any faster and ah'll take off.

The others in the back groan as the van skids its way through yet another sharp corner. Boaby makes a gagging noise like he's about to puke.

JIMMY WATT: See that? Up ahead on the road there. Roond the next bend Willie. Did ye see that?

WILLIE SHEARER: Whit?

JIMMY WATT: Lights. That's a car on the road up there. It must be Charlie – it *must* be Charlie. They've stopped for a piss at the side of the road, eh? Something like that.

WILLIE SHEARER: Ah see it! Maybe it's the detour van though, eh?

JIMMY WATT: (*his voice shooting up an octave*) Whit detour van? There's no detour van, that's a load of shite. Go! Go! They'll get back in the van and piss off in a second if we don't move it. We cannae let that happen. Charlie Lewis! You owe me a handshake brother.

Willie, feeling the pressure, puts his foot down on the accelerator. He knows these roads well but driving at high-speed in the dark is a different ball game. The Watt van rounds a series of corners and the vehicle headlights up ahead get closer. Looks like a set of headlights sitting stationary on the road. Voices can be heard as they close in on the target. A man is shouting.

JIMMY WATT: Yesss!

WILLIE SHEARER: You don't know who that is. Could be anybody.

JIMMY WATT: That's the white van they drove doon Bridge Street the night. Ah'm sure of it. Yesss! Roond the corner Willie, pronto ma boy. Ah'm gonna meet Charlie Lewis. Ah'm getting that handshake, jist like ah telt ye. You were aw laughing at me too. Saying I was daft for even thinking it was gonnae happen.

WILLIE SHEARER: That van's no moving, is it? And what's that – is that another car on the road too? That's the one with the headlights on. The van lights are off.

JIMMY WATT: Never mind that, just get aroond that next c...

Willie tears through the final corner. There's a ferocious shriek of tyres. The Watt van's headlights land on two vehicles on the road (a van and car) facing one another. But there's no time for Jimmy or Willie to take any of that in. As soon as they round the corner, someone sprints into the middle of the road. Then they're gone. Seconds later, someone else runs onto the road. A big man.

WILLIE SHEARER: Christ!

The man pays no attention to Jimmy's van at first. It's as if he's concentrating on something else. He's a big blond man with stocky shoulders. Metallica t-shirt. At last, he sees the van, throws his hands in the air but it's too late to avoid the inevitable collision.

WHACK.

The van shudders.

Willie slams the brakes and the van skids to a stop at the side of the road.

WILLIE SHEARER: (*white-faced, voice trembling*) Oh fuck. We've killed someone! We've just killed someone.

JIMMY WATT: Oh shite.

WILLIE SHEARER: Did ye get that on the video Jimmy? You saw that, eh? The guy ran oot in front of me. He's pissed or mental or something. Ah didnae stand a chance man. There was nothing ah could do.

JIMMY WATT: Get oot. We need to get...

Jimmy stops. Someone is running down the side of the road towards the van. A sweat-soaked figure dressed in a shirt and waistcoat. The man pulls the passenger side door open.

WILLIE SHEARER: (*throws his hands in the air as if to surrender*) Look mate, ah'm sorry. But that guy ran right oot in front of...

JIMMY WATT: (*pointing at the man standing at the door*) Charlie Lewis! It's Charlie Lewis. Charlie, how you doing mate?

Jimmy reaches for his hand. Charlie Lewis ignores Jimmy. He barges forward, pushing Jimmy over and making his way into the window-side passenger seat. His eyes are crazed.

CHARLIE LEWIS: Drive! Get the hell out of here.

WILLIE SHEARER: (*shakes his head*) Ah cannae just drive off mate. We've hit someone. There's a boy on the road there. He might still be...

CHARLIE LEWIS: Drive! There's a fucking psycho trying to put me in a cage for the rest of my life. The guy you hit was helping him.

WILLIE SHEARER: But ah cannae just drive off.

By now, the others have exited the van through the back doors. Willie sees his mates run onto the road and after giving Charlie an apologetic look, he opens the driver's door and joins them. They surround the body of Hutch. Realise that he's already dead.

Jimmy's still filming. Now he's pointing the camera at the sweaty figure of Charlie.

JIMMY WATT: Helluva gig back there Charlie.

Charlie doesn't answer. He's looking through the windscreen, past the crowd that's gathered around Hutch. He's looking towards the other vehicle. A silver Skoda. There's someone sitting inside the car. The driver is motionless.

CHARLIE: Oh shit. I need to get out of here.

Charlie shoves past Jimmy. He manoeuvres his way into the driver's seat. Without another word, he lowers the handbrake and backs up the van on the road.

The engine roars.

JIMMY WATT: Woah big man. Whit's going on? We cannae leave ma mates here in the middle of...

Charlie quickly turns the van around. Willie and the others see the van moving off without them and they start to chase after it. Someone is yelling for Charlie to stop.

Charlie doesn't stop.

JIMMY WATT: (*still filming*) Charlie! Whit's going on mate? Where are we going?

CHARLIE LEWIS: Turn that camera off, will you? Don't you understand what's happening? That lunatic back there kidnapped Ryker twenty-five years ago. He kidnapped Ryker and now he wants me to take his place. I know too much. He can't just let me go. Turn that fucking camera off!

Clip ends.

29

Darcy Doyle's Video Diary
(Sunday, April 23rd)

The road is perhaps fifty metres from Darcy's location. The scene is peppered with headlights, flashing hazard lights and iPhone lights. The small iPhone lights dart back and forth like a platoon of dancing fireflies. A cacophony of panicked male voices can be heard drifting across to the blacked-out field where she's hiding.

Someone yells at someone else to call an ambulance. Someone else wants to call the police.

He's not breathing, another voice yells. He's dead. Must have died instantly.

Darcy retreats further from the chaotic scene and the multitude of lights on the road begin to dim. Her sobbing becomes clear. When she talks, her voice is hoarse.

DARCY: Oh God. Please, someone help me.

She kneels down in the grass. Points the camera at her tear-stained face.

DARCY: Okay, listen up guys. Ah *Jaysus*. Something terrible has happened up here in Inverness. It's Charlie –

he's finally snapped. I've been telling you all week, haven't I? Didn't I bleedin' say there was something wrong with the man? Fucking hell. Well, it's happened. Charlie's totally lost it. He was driving me and Hutch back to Glasgow after the gig and we were barely out of Inverness when he started going the wrong way. He went east instead of south. Me and Hutch, we were scared but we let it play out for a while. You know? Didn't say anything because Charlie had that *loco* look on his face. We drove for miles and ended up on these back roads, totally out in the sticks. And then, Charlie just slammed the brakes. Doesn't speak for about a minute, yeah? Then he turns to us. Tells us for the second time tonight that the band's over. Then he pulled this big feckin' knife on us. Pulled it out of nowhere. There was this mad look in his eye, totally mental like, and I knew he was serious about using it. So we pushed the door open. Ran for our lives.

Darcy's sobbing again.

DARCY: He chased Hutch into this massive field, the one I'm hiding in right now, and they went round in circles for ages. I was screaming for help but there's no one out here. Listen to my voice – I'm hoarse. Charlie was screaming too. Telling us over and over that the band had to end. That we weren't as good as Ryker. Hutch managed to escape for a while. He got out of here and back onto the road. But after jumping the fence, this van came around the corner and...

There's a brief silence.

DARCY: Oh feck. It hit him. Hutch is down and I don't know if he's hurt or dead or what. I think an ambulance is on its way. Police, hopefully. But Charlie must have come back to his senses or something when it happened. He's cracked man. He stole the van that slammed into Hutch. I don't know who it belongs to but Charlie took it and he's gone. I'm hiding out here, waiting for the police. No way I'm coming out until I see those flashing sirens. Charlie's out there. I've seen too much. I know too much. I have no doubt he's looking for me.

Clip ends.

30

Charlie didn't know these country roads but that didn't stop him driving like a maniac with a death wish at seventy miles per hour.

He didn't know the van he was driving either, how it handled on sharp turns and what its limits were. How old was it? How hard could he push it? He'd find out soon enough. Charlie already knew that it wasn't as smooth as the official tour van he'd been driving earlier that night. Not even close. This one lurched on the corners. It stuttered when he put the pedal to the floor but all in all, it didn't feel too different to the old clapped-out transits that Charlie had driven back in the early days of The Broken Gods, back when he'd been the designated driver because he was the only one with a driving licence.

Right now, this van was his best friend. It was the only thing standing in between Charlie and life in a cage.

The Skoda's headlights shimmered in the wing mirror. Fletcher was still hot on Charlie's tail, about two car lengths behind the van and holding steady. Those crystalline headlights had been a constant companion ever since Charlie had stolen/borrowed the old van and fled the scene of his near-kidnapping on that eerie little B-road in God knows where.

Fletcher was no slouch when it came to dangerous driving. So far, Charlie had tried everything to give himself the advantage but the Skoda was clearly the quicker of the two vehicles. And it was sticky on his tail.

I'm being hunted, Charlie thought.

He knew that Sally's brother wouldn't give up the chase. *Couldn't* give up. Fletcher had revealed too much back there. Now it was all out in the open. Charlie knew enough about Ryker's fate and he could still see Fletcher's dead-doll eyes staring at him as he talked about tending to Ryker's needs as if he'd been a pet. Holy shit, Charlie thought. His heart was thumping in his chest. He had to get through this. He had to get back to town. Dying was the second-best option after that. Anything was better than taking Ryker's place in Fletcher's basement. And why was this happening? Because of the lingering resentment that Fletcher had felt towards the band for shutting him out almost thirty years ago? The guy was a nutjob. All that talk about helping Ryker get off drugs and clean up his act was bullshit. But that's how Fletcher the loon justified it to himself. How did he justify kidnapping Charlie? Did the crazy bastard even care anymore?

"Slow doon Charlie, slow doon! These roads are killers mate."

Charlie had almost forgotten about the man in the passenger seat. What did he say his name was? Johnny? No, Jimmy. Jimmy wasn't doing too well. He was clinging to the strap of his seatbelt like he was expecting a tornado to blow through the inside of the van and lift him off his feet. Nonetheless, Jimmy had managed to explain to Charlie (several times) that he was the world's biggest Broken Gods fan. Said he wanted a handshake. That's if they lived through the night.

Jimmy's voice shot up an octave as the tyres screeched around another tight bend.

"JESUS!"

Charlie gripped the wheel tight. His knuckles throbbed. His fingers felt like they were on the brink of cramping up. He'd already seen several bouquets of withered flowers wrapped around telegraph poles to mark the site of a fatal car crash. There were a lot of flowers on show, as well as cuddly toys, love hearts and other tributes. It wasn't hard to believe Jimmy when he said it was reckless to drive fast on these tight, snake-like roads. Charlie could only imagine the number of boy racers who'd died whilst impersonating Formula One drivers. Now they were statistics, warning stories for the next generation.

Charlie didn't want to join them.

"Ah've got a wife and two boys," Jimmy said, his voice trembling. He repeated this several times over. "Ah cannae die like this Charlie."

Charlie glanced at the wing mirror. He gasped when he realised that the Skoda had narrowed the gap to one car length. *I can't outrun it.* Unlike Jimmy, it seemed like Fletcher *was* willing to die on these roads tonight. He would die in a fireball rather than face the prospect of letting Charlie go. If Charlie got away, Fletcher's life was over. The Skoda was tearing down the road. It looked like it was flying several inches above the blackened surface. And Charlie could see the outline of Fletcher in the driver's seat. A cold, stationary figure, not fazed in the slightest by death-wish driving.

Charlie hammered the steering wheel with his fist. "Fuck! Fuck! Fuck! I can't get rid of him."

He contemplated spilling the beans there and then. Telling Jimmy about Ryker's fate. Put it all out there on the table before it was too late. There was a chance that, if they were cornered, Jimmy could get away. Maybe, maybe not. In all likelihood, Fletcher would kill Jimmy too. Make it look like a car crash on these dangerous roads. Set the car on fire. A tragic ending, but not unusual around these parts.

"Please," Charlie said, still hitting the wheel in frustration.

He stared through the grimy windscreen onto an endless stretch of dark road with no end in sight. Sharp bends leapt out of nowhere. Charlie kept the van in the middle of the road on the straights, keeping his eyes peeled for arrow signs, trying to keep up with the constant turns. He wanted to see an empty road in the wing mirror. To know that Fletcher had made a mistake and ended up in a ditch. One mistake, that's all it took to end this pursuit. But it could easily happen to Charlie too. The van could take a bend too fast, spin off road, turn upside down and it would be Charlie and Jimmy stranded in a ditch. Charlie envisioned regaining consciousness as Fletcher dragged him out through the smashed window, bloody and battered. Fletcher leaning over him at the side of the road. The stink of chloroform pressing down on his face as a distorted voice whispered in his ear.

Go to sleep Charlie. We've got a long drive ahead of us.

Charlie needed the bright lights of Inverness. It was still early enough, wasn't it? Was it eleven yet? Eleven thirty? The town centre would still be buzzing after the gig. With any luck, the streets would be full of people and noise and excitement. That's where he'd be safe. Fletcher couldn't touch Charlie in front of all those people. And from there, Charlie could park the van. Run to the Hoot. Find Johnny and tell him everything. Tell him about Darcy and Hutch and how they betrayed him. About how the little shits had been willing to hand him over for a payday.

What would Johnny say? What would the rest of the crew think?

They'd think he'd lost the plot once and for all. The crew, including Johnny, would come to the same conclusion – that Charlie was a lunatic. But still, he'd be safe and what other people thought about his sanity (or lack of it) was a worry for another time.

Charlie glanced back and forth between the road and the wing mirror. Not daring to blink. The Skoda was still there, a four-wheeled suckerfish glued to the back of Jimmy's transit van. Charlie looked through the windscreen. He scanned the horizon for a sea of electric light. Maybe not Inverness, but there had to be a town up ahead. Had to be *something*. Maybe even a police station. Behind the next turn, maybe? Nope. Next one? Would the endless line of treetops smothering the horizon part to reveal the warm glow of civilisation?

Where was it?

He checked the mirror. The Skoda was almost on top of him.

"Where are the lights?" Charlie yelled. He went back to thumping the steering wheel. "Where are the towns? Where are the cities?"

It felt like he was trying to coax Dracula towards the light of the sun.

But what if he was going the wrong way?

The thought sent a cold shiver shooting down Charlie's spine. What if he was going deeper into the sticks and thus into oblivion? It was possible, right? He had no way of knowing for sure where he was going in this godforsaken Highland labyrinth and Jimmy, as scared as he was, wasn't much help. It was too dark. They were going too fast to read the occasional signs that appeared at the side of the road. But what else could they do? There was a monster on their tail and they couldn't slow down.

Charlie's eyes checked off a list of items on the dashboard. The speedometer said they were going just over seventy miles per hour. The engine's arrow was leaning too close to hot. And of course, the fuel gauge was almost at empty.

"Oh shit."

Charlie felt like throwing up but he couldn't lose focus. He wanted to think about Ryker, about what he'd just learned about his friend's fate. Ryker didn't abandon them all. He didn't leave his friends and family. Didn't leave his life, as troubled as it was. He was kidnapped by a maniac. Charlie had so much to take in but he couldn't do it now. He couldn't break down. He couldn't start what was sure to be a long mourning process. That was for another time. Right now, he had to live and tell the world.

He took a sharp right that jumped out of nowhere. Charlie squeezed the brakes just enough to ease the van around the turn without sacrificing too much speed. The van didn't shudder this time. He was getting good at this, at least that's what he told himself. He winced at the shriek of brakes behind him. Charlie glanced in the mirror. Saw the bright lights of the Skoda catching up with him. Fletcher was relentless. He was driving at warp speed now. Driving with more urgency. Had he seen something? What had Charlie missed? Charlie put his foot down as a long straight morphed into a left. Another right and he cried out in relief.

The bright lights of civilisation.

"Yes!"

Was it Inverness? Charlie didn't care what it was. It was *somewhere* and wherever it was, he was driving straight towards it.

"Yes! Yes! Yes!"

Charlie's flagging spirits revived in an instant. He let out a roar from his scratched and tired voice and he actually reached a hand towards the windscreen, reaching for those lights as if he could fit them into his hand. He pushed the pedal to the floor. The van rattled at dangerous speed but Charlie was beyond caring about the longevity of the vehicle. *Just a little further baby.*

Fletcher must have known he was in deep shit. He sped up further, pulling the Skoda to the side and trying to level up with the van. He jerked this way and that way. Charlie could hear Jimmy saying the Lord's prayer in the passenger seat. He gripped the wheel, weaving back and forth to block the Skoda from advancing. What was Fletcher going to do if he did level up? Ram the van off the road? Fuck that, Charlie thought. The van was bigger and if it came down to a game of high-speed, Mad Max-style dodgems then Charlie would make sure the little fucker and his psycho mobile were dead.

Charlie floored the van for a final sprint. "C'mon baby!" He was on a long straight and there were buildings popping up on either side of the road. Warehouses. Retail. Civilisation! Then he saw the flashing blue lights up ahead. Wailing sirens. At first, Charlie thought it was a hallucination and that he was only seeing what he wanted to see. He leaned forward in the seat, his chest pressing tight against the wheel. Charlie wiped the sweat out of his eyes. He expected the lights to be gone when he looked again. They were still there. He heard the screaming *woo-woo-woo* and saw the blue flashing lights getting brighter as the other vehicle tore down the road out of town at a hundred miles per hour.

"Ambulance!" Jimmy yelled. "It's an ambulance."

"It's the police," Charlie said, shaking his head. "It's the police!" He slammed the brakes, yanking the wheel hard to the right. The van spun around, jerking to a clumsy stop in the middle of the road. Charlie punched the hazard lights on, shoved the driver's door open and ran onto the road, waving his arms frantically in the air like he was trying to shake them off at the shoulders. His legs were rubbery. He almost toppled over twice before he gave up on the running.

"STOP!" he called out. "STOP!"

It was a single squad car coming towards him, but it was making the noise of an entire unit. It didn't show any sign of slowing down. The horn blared. For a brief second, Charlie envisioned the car splitting him in half. It was going to go right through him, continuing in the direction from where Charlie and Jimmy had just fled from.

Charlie screamed at the top of his lungs. This was the last that his beleaguered voice had to offer.

"STOP!"

He closed his eyes. Thought about his boys. About the regret of not booking that holiday and showing them how much he loved being around them.

The police car screeched to a sudden halt. Charlie opened his eyes, gasped with relief and his jelly legs were working again. He hurried towards the vehicle. Two police officers, a man and a woman, stepped out of the car.

"What's going on?" the female officer said. She looked pissed off to say the least. "What are you doing on the road?"

Charlie staggered forward, hands in the air. Sweat gushed off his brow. Body and voice trembled uncontrollably. "My name's Charlie Lewis. There's a man...trying to drive me off the road...he wants...kidnap..."

He felt like he'd been tasered. All he could do was jerk his thumb over his shoulder. Hope that the officers understood what he was trying to say.

"Skoda."

He turned around but Fletcher and his car were gone. There was only an empty road leading away from the lights, back into nowhere.

Charlie doubled over, hands pressed to his knees. "He's...he's chasing me. He...kidnapped...Ryker."

"Sir?" the female officer said. She was standing over him now, peering down with concern and suspicion intermingled in one expression. "How much have you had to drink this evening? Are you aware that you've blocked the road with your van? We're en route to an emergency situation outside of town. Someone's been hit by a car. You need to move your van immediately or we'll have to arrest you."

Charlie dropped to his knees.

"Help me."

At this, the male officer barraged Charlie with questions. His colleague walked towards the van where a wide-eyed Jimmy was still waiting in the cabin. Charlie heard the questions coming his way, rattling like hailstones off the inside of his head, but he couldn't answer them. Not now. There was no voice left to speak with. All he could do was stare at the empty road that led out of town. Fletcher was on that road, somewhere.

Charlie closed his eyes. He could see it, even if no one else could.

The back of the Skoda, vanishing into the night.

Three weeks later...

31

Charlie was back in the isolation of his farmhouse in Kintyre.

It was late evening, a little after eight-thirty and he was sitting on the bed. The wind tapped softly on the roof as if it wanted to come inside. The walls groaned and sounded almost human. Loose floorboards creaked. Charlie sat there, basking in the sounds that surrounded the house.

He'd missed this.

God, he'd missed it.

Charlie took a sip of water and put the glass down on the bedside table. He looked at the dozen or so newspaper clippings that he'd brought with him from Glasgow, a cluster of full-pages and foldouts (but Charlie still referred to them as clippings), spread out across the wrinkled sheets in three rows of four. These were all recent cut-outs. He was going to add them to the Kintyre collection he'd built up over the years. A collection about the Gods. About Ryker and Sally. It felt appropriate to finish the story, no matter how grim the ending.

After that, Charlie told himself, no more looking back.

He browsed the latest additions, searching for the first clipping he'd put aside back in Glasgow. This one, a double-page feature, covered the shock announcement of Charlie's resignation from the music industry. He was done. The Dark Stars had called it quits following the sudden death of their drummer, Hutch Heikkinen, on an isolated stretch of road east of Inverness. Details of the incident were sketchy but Hutch, a notoriously heavy drinker, had been on the road (directly at the corner) when a van ploughed through him. The driver of the van and his passengers claimed that the collision was inevitable. Hutch was on the road, just standing there. Like he was waiting to die. There were already rumours of suicide. Of crippling debts in his native Finland that had pushed him to the brink.

Hutch's blood level concentration was recorded at 0.10%.

The same article only briefly mentioned Darcy Doyle, the Irish guitarist who'd been 'so prominent on the Back-To-Basics tour and with The Dark Stars in general'. The author wrote that Darcy had made contradictory statements to police following the accident that killed Hutch. It's believed that she tried to blame Charlie for Hutch's death, but witnesses to the accident said that Charlie wasn't even there at the time. A Back-To-Basics crew member stated that Darcy was bitter after Charlie had disbanded the group earlier that evening. Darcy hadn't been heard from since leaving the police station in Inverness on Monday April 24th. Perhaps, the writer concluded with some glee, someone would spot her on a street corner in London. Busking for pennies.

Or maybe, Charlie thought, Fletcher caught up with you before you could say anything else.

Either way, good riddance.

There was nothing about Charlie's involvement in

Hutch's death, despite Darcy's attempt to put him in the frame. Charlie had conjured up a fanciful story at the police station, one that took him away from the accident scene. He told police that, as he'd driven the van out of Inverness with his bandmates after the gig, a convoy of fans had aggressively pursued him in cars, vans and several motorcycles. After suffering a panic attack at the wheel, Charlie had asked Darcy and Hutch to drop him off at the side of the road. He needed the air. Told his inebriated bandmates to leave him right there in the middle of nowhere.

They said he was crazy. But he was their boss. So they dropped him off and drove away to shake off the convoy.

Charlie's story continued with him walking back to Inverness on dark roads with only the light of a mobile phone to guide the way. Despite being on foot, Charlie felt better under the stars. Under the light of the moon. No one was chasing him now. After walking for about twenty minutes at the side of the road, another van pulled over beside Charlie. A panicked Jimmy Watt was sitting behind the wheel, on his way back to town to report an accident. He and his mates had hit someone with their work van. Jimmy was driving back in case his mates at the scene couldn't get a signal on their phones. He told Charlie that he was still miles from Inverness and that walking was crazy. The roads were lethal, that's what he said. People shouldn't be walking out here. Charlie accepted the offer of a lift. At that point, he didn't know it was Hutch who'd been hit by the van. Seeing that Jimmy was in shock, Charlie offered to take the wheel and drive them back to town. Five minutes after setting off, much to Charlie's horror, yet another crazed fan began pursuing them. This time in a silver Skoda. There was a high-speed pursuit. They eventually lost the stalker when a traumatised Charlie flagged down a police car outside the town centre.

Hell of a night, he'd told the troopers in the station. One hell of a night. Some of the officers had apologised to Charlie. They told him they didn't get many rock stars in their neck of the woods. The locals, they'd said, were prone to getting overexcited.

Jimmy had made a promise to Charlie prior to their arrival at the station. A promise to keep quiet about Charlie's presence at the accident scene. At Charlie's request, Jimmy made a point of asking Willie and the rest of his mates to also avoid any mention of Charlie at the crash scene. Jimmy was pleased to help. Anything for his hero, he'd said. All he wanted in return was a handshake.

He got a hug.

After he got home to Glasgow, Charlie's retirement announcement was met with a wave of scepticism. The fans, his manager, his ex-wife, all the people who couldn't imagine Charlie Lewis doing anything else, they all said the same thing – *you'll be back Charlie*. But Charlie knew better. For now, he'd stay in the farmhouse. Live like a recluse. He had to process what had happened to Ryker and that wasn't going to be easy.

He browsed the clippings on the bed. Picked up the one about the discovery of human remains in a Motherwell pet shop. Police had received an anonymous tip prior to the raid on the property. Someone had called, claiming that the proprietor, Fletcher Darbey, was worth checking out in relation to the disappearance of Ryker Marshall in 1997. Neighbours and customers were interviewed. Some of them labelled Darbey as 'a quiet man'. 'A strange man'. Kept to himself but there was 'definitely something off about him'.

The excavation of Fletcher's basement, already dubbed a

'torture chamber' by the press, was ongoing. Charlie knew what they'd find there. He didn't want to be anywhere near the press when they uncovered what was left of his old friend. He didn't want to see tabloid pictures of someone in white coveralls covering a container with 'human remains' inside. He wasn't ready for that.

Charlie gathered the clippings and put them on the floor. With any luck, he'd deal with them in the morning.

There'd be a funeral in Glasgow. Annie and the rest of the Marshall family would want Charlie to be there for the service. They might even ask him to speak. To sing something. Charlie wasn't sure he could handle it.

It was a decision for another time.

He stretched out on the bed, letting his head sink deep into the pillow. His breathing slowed. Eyelids grew heavy. Charlie was just beginning to drift off to sleep when he heard a faint knock on the door.

At last, he thought.

Charlie didn't feel anything as he pushed himself off the bed and walked to the front door. He might as well have been on his way to collect the post. His gaze never left the wooden door at the end of the hallway as he covered the ground, somewhat mechanically, between the bedroom and the front entrance. The floor creaked under his feet. He stopped at the door. Before turning the handle, he peered through the peephole, which he'd cleaned upon his arrival in Kintyre. There was a second, impatient knock. Charlie stepped back, unlocked the door and pulled it open. A gust of cold air rushed into the farmhouse.

"Took you long enough," Fletcher said.

Charlie smiled. "Took *you* long enough. I've been here five days."

Now it was Fletcher's turn to smile. He was dressed in a

blood red anorak that trailed down to the knees, its large oversized hood covering his head, the outer fabric damp and clinging to his face at the sides. He wore waterproof trousers and hiking boots. His face sported the early stages of a light brown beard, the jagged-looking tips soaked with droplets of water that glistened under the entrance light. Fletcher had been caught in the recent shower by the looks of it. His eyes were bloodshot and he was breathing heavy.

"I had to come," he said. "You know I had to come here."

"Where else would you go?" Charlie asked. "Bit of a trek, isn't it?"

Fletcher nodded. "I'll say. Not much police out here though, is there? Not when you leave Campbeltown behind."

He looked at Charlie, his eyes burning with hatred.

"Speaking of the police, Charlie. So you made an anonymous call, did you? Such a good citizen."

"I am a good citizen," Charlie said. "But I'm glad you got away before they came knocking at your door."

"Oh really? Why's that?"

"It's like you said, Fletcher. You had to come here. And so did I."

Charlie opened the door a few inches further, leaning his way into the freezing cold gap. Even though it was almost summer, he could still feel something of winter in that icy gust of wind that was now circulating around the hallway. "You know, I was afraid you might have fled the country."

He slid his hand along the back of the door. Steered it towards the giant coat hook.

"Hard to flee the country without a passport," Fletcher said. "Didn't have time to go and get it. Even if I had one, it's probably useless. It's hard to escape the prying eyes of the world, especially these days."

"True."

Fletcher took a step back from the doorway. He lifted his head to the starry sky, then glanced around the exterior of the property, taking in the vast stretch of woodland at the back of the farmhouse. He let out a soft whistle of approval.

"Beautiful."

Charlie nodded. "It's home."

"Well," Fletcher said, returning his full attention to Charlie. "I'm here now. Can I...can I see her?"

"No," Charlie said, not missing a beat. "You can't."

Fletcher's laugh was stale and bitter. "So what now, Charlie? You think I'm just going to turn around and walk back across this green hell in the dark? Go to the police station and give myself up? I've got nothing left to lose. Do you understand?"

"Quite frankly," Charlie said, "I don't give a shit what you do."

"Charlie, we're friends."

"We were never friends."

Something in Charlie's tone reignited the fire in Fletcher's eyes, which had cooled for a moment. Maybe it was the indifference that Charlie was offering up. Fletcher had come a long way and so far, he was getting nothing in return. Not fear, not anger. Nothing. Charlie had already braced himself for the inevitable backlash but even that preparation didn't stop his heart skipping a beat as he watched Fletcher pull a short, curved machete out of a makeshift sheath under his anorak.

"I had to come."

Fletcher's face was scrunched in concentration as he observed the exterior of the property for a second time.

"Yes, yes. This will do."

"What are you talking about?" Charlie asked.

"This will be my home," Fletcher said, turning back to Charlie. "I know, I know. We're going to have to make it work, old friend. You and me. Just like it was with Ryker in the home you took away from me."

Fletcher approached the entrance with his stiff walk. There was a look in his eyes that said this was already a done deal.

Charlie's hand was still pressed against the back of the door. He grabbed the handle of the axe and pulled it off the coat hook. Then he squeezed down tight, knowing what he had to do. He'd hung the axe there on the door upon arrival. There was another one tucked under the bed. And one in the living room.

"Why don't you come in?" he said, grinning at Fletcher.

He swung the door open, almost pulling it off the hinges. Raised the axe over his head and charged towards the figure in the doorway. Forget about the machete, he told himself. Strike first, strike hard. He'd been practicing every day with the axe, chopping wood out back, and by now he was used to the heavy weight.

Fletcher saw what was coming. He gasped. "Charlie!"

But Charlie didn't hesitate. He was too far gone for doubt. He swung hard, bringing the blade down with all the speed and power his fifty-year-old arms could generate. Fletcher screamed and it sounded like a child running loose inside the small confines of the farmhouse. Charlie intended to split the bastard's head in two but he missed the target and instead, the axe sliced through the right shoulder. It sank deep into the flesh.

Fletcher screamed again. Charlie panicked. He twisted the blade from side to side, opening up the wound, mangling the flesh further before yanking it back out. There was a wet, squelching noise as the axe came free.

"Bastard!" Charlie yelled.

A river of blood gushed from the ragged hole in Fletcher's anorak. Somehow, Fletcher was still carrying the machete in his right hand. He staggered through the doorway, forcing Charlie to backpedal into the hall at speed. He held the machete aloft. Let out a wild gasping noise as he hacked at thin air, the curved blade searching hungrily for a target.

"We'll make it work!" he cried out in a shrill, terrified voice. "We have to make it work."

Charlie was backing up too fast. As he retreated into the hallway, he tripped over his feet. To his horror, Charlie felt the axe slipping through his fingers. Oh shit, he thought. He fell hard onto his side. Lost the axe at that very moment. Fletcher made a loud cackling noise and rushed at Charlie, his feet making a shuffling noise on the floor. Fletcher raised the machete above his head and brought it down as if to cut Charlie's face in half. Charlie saw it coming. He rolled to the side before the steel blade raked against the wooden floor, just inches from his head. Charlie rolled again, opening up enough space to get back to his feet. He jumped up, staggering onto unsteady legs. Then he went for broke, charging in and rugby-tackling Fletcher before the bastard could reset and take a second swing at him again. Both men crashed onto the floor but Fletcher's back took the worst of the impact. The house trembled in protest as the two men fought wildly on the floor. Charlie punched him in the face. Fletcher screamed in pain, dropped the machete and when he realised it was gone, his eyes bulged in terror. He made a squealing noise. His arm flapped to the side as his fingers scrambled for the handle. Charlie pinned him down, restraining Fletcher's frantic attempts to get reacquainted with the curved blade. He thudded an elbow into Fletcher's forehead. He did it again. Then he reached over and pushed the machete away from Fletcher's grasping fingers. Fletcher saw this and cried out in a high-pitched shriek.

"Charlie...please...don't..."

But Charlie's hands were already wrapped around Fletcher's neck, gargling the words of protest. With all the strength he had left, Charlie squeezed hard. His insides were on fire. This was it, he was doing it. Killing a man. Not knocking him unconscious, killing him. But Charlie couldn't let himself get caught up in doubt. He couldn't think about the man underneath him. Couldn't think about what he was doing right now, playing judge, jury and executioner. Killing a man. A man he'd laughed with a long time ago. Drank with. Grew up with. No more thinking about the man underneath. Charlie had agonised for weeks back in Glasgow, speculating over the atrocities that Ryker had endured during his nineteen years of captivity. It was the stuff of nightmares and would be for years to come. Charlie couldn't save Ryker, not this time. And he couldn't save Sally either.

But he could do this one thing.

This was *something*.

Fletcher's body convulsed for what felt like hours. But Charlie never grew tired. He squeezed harder. Fletcher's legs spasmed, the heel of his boots kicking off the wood like he was trying to hammer two holes in the floor. Charlie heard his name in the dying man's gasps, the word still gargled and wet. His face was covered in hot spit.

Charlie winced, closed his eyes. Felt Fletcher's legs thrashing some more.

Soon enough, the house was quiet again.

32

The Brit Awards
February 19th, 1996.
Earls Court Exhibition Centre, London

The Broken Gods are winning everything tonight. It's a glorious moment for the band and one that's seen them pick up awards for best song, best album and now at the end of the night, they're back up on stage to collect the best band award. This time, they've got everyone up there with them: partners, management, parents, siblings and friends. The stage is spilling over with people.

After a few minutes of pandemonium, Charlie and Ryker take their place side by side at the podium. Along with their two band-mates, Tommy and Bobby, standing behind them, they take in a rapturous standing ovation that threatens to blow the roof off the building.

Charlie tries to speak. He's drowned out by the relentless screaming and is forced to wait another two minutes before he can even begin to make himself heard. The country (and the world) has seen nothing like this since Beatlemania more than thirty years earlier.

CHARLIE: (*to audience*) Thank you, thank you. Please, if we can just...

He has to wait a while longer.

CHARLIE: (*signalling for quiet*) Alright now – that's enough. Thank you, thank you. Shush! Please! Shut the bloody hell up, will you? On behalf of myself and the rest of the band, I'd just like to thank everyone again who we've already thanked tonight. Half of 'em are up here on the stage with us so if that's you – thank you.

RYKER: (*leans into the mic. Points to crowd*) And we'd like to thank you again too. None of this is possible without you, the fans. Give yourselves a round of applause.

The crowd give themselves a cheer.

Ryker glances over his shoulder, signals with a wave of the hand for a blond-haired woman to join him at the podium. Sally looks beautiful, dressed in a retro sixties-style mod dress in the colours of the Union Jack. She's reluctant to engage but comes forward and embraces Ryker. Then she hugs Charlie and the other band members.

RYKER: Without this incredible woman, this band is nothing. Without her, I'm nothing. She was there at the start and if she hadn't believed in us back then, we'd still be stuck in the garage playing for ourselves. Let's hear it for our first manager and the love of my life, Sally Darbey.

Ryker and Sally kiss to a resounding roar of approval from the crowd.

Someone else is working his way towards the podium. A smaller man, dressed in a Ryker-like manner – waistcoat, shirt and matching fedora. Ryker signals to the man with another wave. He reaches over, pulls him towards the podium. The man's eyes light up as he's dragged into the spotlight. He looks up at Ryker and shrieks with laughter. He's totally in awe of the moment.

RYKER: Let's not forget my future brother-in-law, Fletcher Darbey. Wee Fletch. This guy's a legend. He was there at the start too, our first ever roadie, tuning our guitars and carrying our equipment when no one else would. Including us. He deserves this award as much as any of us. Love ya Fletch.

Ryker and Fletcher share a warm embrace. Most people begin to leave the stage while Fletcher stares adoringly at Ryker. Eventually, Ryker walks off stage, one arm wrapped around Sally, the other around Charlie.

Fletcher keeps watching.

33

Charlie had everything he needed.

He had the plastic to wrap the body in. He had the gloves. He had the tape to hold the plastic together. And he'd gone to work immediately, wrapping up Fletcher's body as quickly and as thoroughly as he could. The next matter was transportation. The gravesite was a long walk from the house, especially long since Charlie would be dragging an overweight dead body the full distance. But at least it was ready to go. Charlie had dug the grave in the woods on day one, the same day he'd planted axes all over the house. But being prepared was cold comfort. This was going to be a tough night and that was putting it mildly. There were bloodstains all over the hallway floor. Red spray on the walls. It was the sort of mess that Charlie had been hoping to avoid by keeping the fight outside. If a forensic team was to pay him a visit anytime soon, it was game over, no matter how well he cleaned up tonight and tomorrow.

Nonetheless, Charlie was confident that no one would come looking for Fletcher Darbey. Not in Kintyre. Sure, the police were searching for him in Glasgow but as long as nobody had paid Fletcher any special attention in Campbeltown, it was unlikely that anyone would assume he'd pay a visit to Charlie next.

If only they knew who they were dealing with, Charlie thought.

He stood over the blood-soaked plastic. It didn't look like there was a person wrapped up in there. It didn't look real. This was just a thing now. A thing to be moved, to be dispensed with. Like an old rug that no longer warmed up the room. In the end, it wasn't Charlie who would vanish off the face of the earth. It was Fletcher. Nobody would hear from Fletcher again and although he'd gotten off lightly compared to what Ryker had gone through, Charlie felt some satisfaction that Fletcher was dead. If there was any justice, there'd be a small cage in the hottest corner of Hell. And it would have Fletcher's name on the front.

Charlie bent over and grabbed the closest end of the bag (the legs end) and pulled both sides together, twisting them around to form a crude handle. Using the handle, he dragged the body through the hall and kitchen, making his way towards the back door.

"God!"

Fletcher was a heavy fucker in both life and death. Felt to Charlie like there was a lead doll in the bag.

He opened the back door, steered the body along the winding path and away from the farmhouse. Plastic scraped off the stone slabs. It sounded like paper being torn slowly as a form of torment. There'd once been a row of fencing out back, dating back to the property's farming days in the mid-to-late twentieth century. The fence was long gone. Now there were no boundaries to the property, just a long stretch of lush grass and wildflowers growing alongside the path. The path, which seemed to be disappearing under nature, led to a steep incline that fed into the dense blanket of woodland.

Charlie hauled the body to the end of the path. He lowered it onto one of the concrete slabs and straightened up with a loud groan that made him sound like a much older man. His arms ached. There was a loud click in his back that felt like a warning from his body, telling him to take it easy. But he had to finish the work.

The last of the day's birdsong whistled overhead.

Charlie glanced to the right. Over towards the grassy square, the only semi-cultivated area at the back of the house. A single stone monument stood in the centre.

He found himself approaching the grave. As he walked, he heard wings flapping over his head and another melodious spurt of birdsong.

The headstone was a simple one, unadorned except for the word 'Sally' carved front and centre. The carving was clumsy, almost childlike. Sally had loved this place and its wild, rugged emptiness as much as Charlie and although it took the Darbey family a long time to come around to his suggestion, in the end they'd agreed that Sally would have wanted to be buried here. Away from everything.

Charlie stood by the grave, never knowing what to say to her. He wiped some dirt off the top of the stone. Ran a hand along the smooth surface. Then, as he stood there, he looked uphill to the crude dirt track that led into the woods. From where he was standing, it resembled a set of gaping jaws.

"I know he's your brother Sally. But there's no way I'm putting him beside you."

The temperature outside was dropping fast. Charlie could feel a cold night coming on but he was still warm after the struggle with Fletcher, after wrapping up the body and dragging it outside. He couldn't stop now. He had so much work left to do and he was going to have to work fast to put Fletcher in the ground and cover him up before the real, late night dark came to swallow him up.

Better take a torch, he thought. The iPhone wouldn't be enough.

"Sally." His finger traced over the carving of her name. "I'll talk to Annie, okay? Once they get his body out of there. I mean, once everything's done and he's released to the family. I'll put him beside you, I swear it."

He took his hand off the stone.

Above Charlie's head, the clouds were parting. The stars were out. Moonlight seeped through the gaps, its pale glow running down the western spine of the Kintyre peninsula in sight of the crashing Atlantic waves. Charlie grabbed a torch from the hut. Checked the batteries were working, then clipped it to his belt. He walked back to the path and hauled Fletcher's body up the steep incline, taking it towards the entrance of the woods. Nobody ever went into the woods. This was private property and there was no reason to think that anyone would ever find Fletcher up there.

Charlie would sleep well tonight.

And he was hopeful that once he closed his eyes, Ryker would come to visit.

THE END

OTHER THRILLER/SUSPENSE BOOKS BY MARK GILLESPIE

Lisa Granger did the unthinkable. She committed a shocking act of betrayal that no one would ever believe.

One year later, there's a price to pay.

And the cost is everything...

Make It Up To Me

Three men are kidnapped on the eve of their high school reunion and wake up trapped inside a remote cabin in the Scottish Highlands.

What comes next is the discovery that one of them is a killer.

The Old Boys

The starlet and the starmaker. It's an age-old story in Hollywood. Now that story's about to be rewritten. In blood.

Scream Test

Mike Harvey just broke up with his girlfriend. Now her daddy, the Devil, is coming after him. And Daddy's mad as Hell.

Devil in the Dark Woods

POST APOCALYPTIC/DYSTOPIAN TITLES BY MARK GILLESPIE

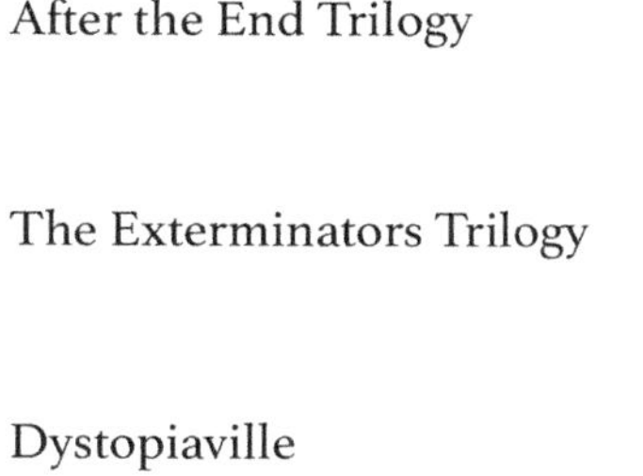

After the End Trilogy

The Exterminators Trilogy

Dystopiaville

The Butch Nolan Trilogy

Mark Gillespie's author website
www.markgillespieauthor.com

Mark Gillespie on Facebook
www.facebook.com/markgillespieswritingstuff

Mark Gillespie on Twitter
www.twitter.com/MarkG_Author

Mark Gillespie on Bookbub
https://www.bookbub.com/profile/mark-gillespie

Printed in Great Britain
by Amazon